CAN'T TOUCH THIS

CAN'T TOUCH THIS

MARLEY GIBSON

CHAPTER ONE

The receptionist looks like she's got one hell of a secret and she's dying to let it out.

I smile at her through the glass-front door as I punch in my security code and push into the foyer. "You okay, Janine?"

"Hey, Vanessa," she says, looking around to see if anyone's watching. "Actually, something's up."

I lift an eyebrow.

The telephone rings and she jumps in her seat. "Big announcement today. Big. Huge. The biggest," Janine whispers. She hits the button on the phone, turns her personality to instant perk and says, "DigitalDirection, how may I direct your call?"

I give her a sidelong glance. Since she's on the phone, I can't probe any further on this alleged huge announcement. So, I turn the corner and head down the hallway through the corporate ant farm to my cube. I pass the hodge-podge of office equipment that sits in the far corner. The printer is inactive. Morning reports aren't churning. Are we still in business? Is this a federal holiday I don't know about?

The air is pungent with the smell of fresh toner. Hmm... at least the office manager's busy doing her job. I walk by the president and vice president's offices. The doors are closed. They're never closed.

Something big must be stewing indeed.

I stop outside my cubicle. I don't hear any lively chatter, more like a dull buzz of muted tête-à-têtes. The normal sound of fingers machine-gunning on keyboards has been silenced.

Just as I sit down, my work buddy, Isabella Perry, appears suddenly, hanging over the side divider of my cube. I slap a hand to my heart as my pulse pounds out of whack. "You scared hell and three dollars out of me, Griz!"

I'd dubbed Isabella "Griz"—short for Grizabella the Glamour Cat—when she'd share her obsessive love of the musical "Cats" with me over cocktails and scoping guys one night at a bar in downtown Boston. She'd seen the kids on "Glee" sing about it and now it's like her theme song or something. However, Griz is a lot like the down and out cat, trying to make a name for herself in the big city, just like me.

"Did you see him?" she asks.

"Him? Who?"

"The babe in the tight pants who was walking down the hallway."

"I just got here. What have I missed?"

Griz screws her nose up. "Nothing yet, but something's up."

"That's what everyone keeps telling me." Geez, I haven't even had my morning coffee and things are percolating here. I love when there's office intrigue in the air. "What's going on? Spill it!"

"I can't tell you more than I know," Griz says and then darts her gaze around the room.

"Which is?"

"Not a lick or a damn."

Frustrated, I mock at strangling her. "Don't make me..."

She raises an eyebrow and grabs a chair from the empty cubicle across from mine, dragging it into my small veal-pen space. "Well, I heard there's some shuffling in the higher ranks around here."

"No way!" Seriously? If the ax is falling, I hope it doesn't chop off my head. I start straightening things on my desk, like neatness will count if someone comes around to fire me. *Get real, Vanessa!*

Griz presses on. "Word is we've lost six clients because the new software version isn't ready. Change is definitely in the air. You can count on it."

In this sad-sack of an economy where so many people are on unemployment and trying to figure out how to pay their mortgages so the banks don't confiscate their homes and cars, losing one client is *not* an option. Clients leaving the company equals lack of profit. Lack of profit means cutting personnel. Cutting personnel means I'm updating my resume and e-mailing it all over town. My heartbeat triples at the thought of being dire, desperate, and downright panicked.

Instead of thinking about the heavy gloom of the nation's economy that surrounds us, I refocus on the cute guy that's been spotted in the hallway. "And this alleged babe you mentioned? What's his deal?"

"Don't know. He's in Jiles' office as we speak," Griz reports proudly.

Jiles Chancey. President and CEO. And pain in my ass. What kind of name is Jiles? I mean, I've heard of Giles— which means *baby goat*. No kidding. I looked it up one day on a name-your-baby website. Anyway, he's got this weird shape to him, like he wasn't turned enough as a sleeping baby, because his head isn't rounded quite right. His close-clipped blond beard hides how he talks out of the side of his mouth in a not-so-trustworthy manner.

He's top dog here at DigitalDirection. When I first started here, I quickly learned that Jiles is a control freak who doesn't take suggestions—especially from women. Especially a junior marketing flunky like me. He nearly snapped my head off the first time I dared to speak during a meeting. Definitely a victim of Little Man Syndrome. Standing a grunt over five-feet-five, he's someone I look down on...particularly when I'm wearing my trademark three inch heels, which put me up around five-eight on a good day.

Griz bounces in place. "Go walk past his office and look in the window. See what you can see."

I wave her off. "I don't think so. What if it's a negotiator they've brought in to do layoffs?" The one thing I can't imagine is losing my job, no matter how much certain people annoy me. I need the money, the stability, and the security. That's why I work my ass off, staying late and doing whatever menial tasks this Marketing Coordinator has to perform day in and day out to keep her health care, stock options, and subsidized MBTA pass when there are thousands of people in this city who don't have any of those things. I can't even begin to think about updating my resume, hitting the online job searches, or pounding the pavement. I love what I do. Great co-workers (a lot of cute ones), a good atmosphere and plenty of after work activities to keep my social calendar full. "Does your boss know anything, Griz?"

"She's not talking'," Griz says sternly in her nasally Midwestern accent.

Originally from the suburbs of Chicago, Isabella moved to Boston six months ago to work on the design team, enhancing our software's graphical interface. She's the cutest thing, too. And I don't mean that in a lesbian way. Since she's still fairly new to Boston, I've taken it upon myself to show her the ropes at work and around town.

"So what do you think?" Griz asks.

"It can't be anything too horrible," I say, fidgeting with the pens in my cup. "DigitalDirection is important. We develop state-of-the-art customer relationship management solutions for all businesses." *Whatever that means.*

"I'm so sick of hearing the CRM buzzword." Griz points her finger into her mouth and pretends to gag in an oh-so-twelve-year-old-girl way. "Besides, you helped write that marketing crap."

I can't help but laugh. I guess my minor in creative writing from American University sure is paying off. But I return to the serious, professional Vanessa Virtue. The Vanessa Virtue who has a stack of bills at home and a student loan teetering on the edge of default. I need this job. I don't want to be forced to throw in the white towel and admit to my parents—particularly my Air Force Colonel father—that I'm not capable of cutting it on my own...even at twenty-five. They've kind of been expecting me to fail and come running home. "Oh you know Vanessa...off chasing her crazy dreams." They can't understand that I'm a grown up now and can live my life on my own without the structure and strictness of the military lifestyle.

I expel the deep breath I've been holding and think about peeking into Jiles' office. The anxiety of what's to come is getting to me. I was thinking positively, but now I'm not so optimistic. Shit always happens in business when you least expect it. My heart is pounding out of control, my hands are sweating, and the tension in the air is palpable. "This could be really bad."

"Calm down," Griz says. "We don't even know what's going on. Lord Almighty, you take things so damn serious, Vanessa."

I snicker nervously at her. Griz is the daughter of a Baptist minister. Very strict, much like my military father. Only

Mr. Perry's general is God. Griz usually chastises herself for taking the Lord's name in vain, something instilled in her by years of churchgoing and sermons of fire and brimstone. I'm a terrible influence, though. She's turned into quite the potty mouth in her months hanging with me after work.

I run my fingers through my wavy hair, messing up the coif I worked so hard on first thing this morning before I left for work. "I should try to find my boss. Or at least check my e-mail." My BlackBerry has been silent all morning, so if someone knows anything, they're not talking—at least not to me—yet.

Griz peers over my shoulder as I stealthily input my password into the network system.

"There's something," she exclaims and points at my inbox.

"Back off, will you? There might be personal message in here." I never get anything but jokes from my marketing teammate, Jack, and an endless stream of SPAM inviting me to find singles in my area, start my career with a new adult undergraduate program, or purchase a new 4G Android online for only fifteen dollars. No thanks. I'm not *that* naive.

"There's an e-mail from Jiles announcing a company meeting at two today." I look at her. "Didn't you get this?"

"I haven't been at my desk. First I've heard of it."

Slightly relieved, I turn back to my friend. We have company meetings all of the time. "Okay. Until then, we need to chill and just get our work done."

Griz stands and fingers her hair behind her ears. "Right. Work. Let's meet up for lunch."

I snort at her one-track mind. I haven't even finished my chai soy latte and she wants a meal. All part of her charm, though. "Noon-thirty?"

"You're on. We'll go to that new place across the street. We can split one of their *huge* sandwiches," she says.

"How are you so skinny when all you do is eat?" I ask incredulously.

"Clean living," she says with a smile.

Frustrated as hell at the beginning of the morning and my friend who seems way too chipper than this day calls for, I lay my head on my desk and softly flail up and down a couple of times.

A quieter voice interrupts. "Vanessa, may I speak to you for a minute?"

I bolt upright at the sight of my very pregnant boss standing where Griz was moments ago.

"Oh. Hi, Aislin," I say as my cheeks heat.

Aislin Honan. Tall, beautiful red hair showing her Irish heritage, and thirty-eight. She's totally the woman I want to be someday. Smart, successful, mature…and married.

I watch as she rubs her distended belly. "Let's go to a conference room."

"Sure thing, Ais."

Aislin's my perfect mentor. Although I studied communications in school, I'd been flying by the seat of my pants with the marketing assignments at my first company out of college. Now I'm learning from Aislin and making sure the textbook knowledge I gained in school applies to real work situations. Instinct's one thing, but actually succeeding and helping the company's bottom line grow is another.

Okay, maybe Griz is right. I am too serious about everything.

I need a boyfriend. Something else in my life besides work. Something other than watching *The Food Network* when I get home, or playing Frontierville on Facebook into the wee hours.

I get no kicks from the online dating sites. The guys are after one thing and one thing only. What happened to getting to know someone or flirting or clicking? It's all about making the move, getting drunk, and falling into bed. I didn't even do that in college (not very well anyway), so why would I want to do it at twenty-five?

Besides, I have to be committed to my position here at The Compass. I want to make a difference. I don't want to do anything to screw up my chances here. Took me three interviews to get in the door here. I want to do a good job, get recognized for it, learn, grow, and support myself. (And keep the company management complaints to myself.)

I follow Aislin into the Great Barrier Reef conference room. All of our conference rooms are named after the Natural Wonders of the World. Since no one wants to sign up for the Iguassu Falls or Bay of Fundy conference rooms because they can't spell them, the HR department has devised a company-wide contest to rename the seven rooms, hoping for something more user-friendly.

My entry: The Seven Dwarfs. (To reflect the size of management.)

Once in the room, Aislin lowers her girth into the chair, which moans accepting her and her unborn child that looks overdue at this point. "I have some news for you, Vanessa."

My pulse accelerates and I silently send up a prayer that my job isn't on the line.

I sit opposite Aislin and lace my fingers together on top of the table in the most professional manner possible. My heart slams against my ribcage in a cocktail of anticipation, trepidation, and a bit of excitement when I see a smile break across her face.

She leans forward, her Irish green eyes bright like she knows a huge secret. "I'd like to congratulate you on your promotion."

I bite my lower lip to squash the desire to shout like I'm at a Patriots' playoffs game. I can't help but beam at her. "A promotion?"

"Yes. You've been doing a great job since we hired you. You're dedicated, trustworthy, creative, and very responsible."

It feels as if my skin is scorched from her amazing words. No one's ever complimented my work like this before. Prior to joining The Compass, I worked thankless hours at one of the big boy financial institutes downtown answering phones, making coffee, and doing other people's shit work that they didn't want to do. To get out of that mundane position, I reworked my resume detailing everything I did for the bubbly marketing chick—who had hair the color of whatever dye was on sale at CVS that week—and landed me the position here at DigitalDirection on Aislin's team. And now…a promotion!

"Since I'll be taking maternity leave in a few weeks, Jiles and I decided to split my responsibilities evenly between you and Jack."

Jack Daniels—not the guy who makes the whiskey—is my marketing teammate and resident webmaster. Jack—short for Johannes—is half Norwegian, half American. He spent most of his life in Norway, so he doesn't *get* that his name is the same as the God of College Alcoholics.

Jack's one of those hurly-burly, muscular Scandinavian speed skater types you see in the Olympics. But I don't flirt with him or have any interest in dating him. Or any of the guys at The Compass, although it's a virtual smorgasbord of hot men in business casual attire.

Company policy: *No Dating.*

It's in the employee handbook in black and white on page twenty-three. Even the mere hint of flirting with a co-worker can land you a starring role in the office e-mail loops and coffee machine gossip. I am focused on my career. No time for a quicky in the copy room with a co-worker.

Aislin continues, "Jack will work on promotions, handle ads, and manage the web design." She passes a piece of paper along the tabletop. "You'll be in charge of tradeshows and events, as well as the marketing budget. Nothing more than a few invoices and reporting to Jiles."

I gulp hard and read the title on the job description. "Marketing Events Manager." Me...a manager.

Aislin talks on about the bump in salary—*thank you!*—and the new responsibilities, but I barely hear her as I am still focused on the word *manager*. Sure, I can get ahead in my student loan payments and maybe buy that awesome Kenneth Cole carrier bag I've had my eye on, but more importantly, I'll get new business cards that I can send to my parents that read, "Vanessa Virtue. Marketing Events Manager."

Aislin clears her throat. "Here's everything you'll need to know about the Atlantic City show."

Taking the bright yellow folder labeled "CRM Strategic Conference," I await further explanation. I'm going to Atlantic City?

"You'll need to ship the tradeshow booth to the Taj Mahal Casino and Hotel," Aislin slides over a small silver key. "Don't lose that. It unlocks the booth and is our only one." I take the tiny key as she continues. "You'll be staying at the Taj Mahal with Ted Spencer, since New Jersey is his territory. He can teach you how to put the tradeshow booth together."

"Excellent," I say. Wait a sec. What do I know about building a booth? Do I need nails and a hammer? Should I not get a manicure beforehand? What are we doing at a casino? Will people be more interested in seeing software demos or gambling?

"So, just the two of us—Ted and me?" Ted is a bit of a corporate dork who wears attitude glasses and sports a closely-cropped goatee. I don't know how much fun a trip with him will be. Wait a minute...it's not about fun. It's about work. Must be a professional at all times no matter how much I want to celebrate right now.

"Well, I shouldn't say anything until the company meeting, but there might be a new person coming with you. More on that later. In the meantime, send Ted an e-mail. He'll need to give you a crash course in demoing the software."

I thumb through the paperwork. "What's the gist of this show?"

"It's all about CRM—customer relationship management, you know. And since our software provides such a huge client services function, we need to make sure we show up our competition."

"You mean SalesTracker?" I'll admit I don't know much about how our software works, but I do know who our competition is. Or SalesWankers as our British transplant sales person, Penelope Dunsbury coined them when she first started working here. They've been around a few years more than DigitalDirection and they're rumored to have just received a huge influx of venture capital and have vowed to put the rest of us out of business. True wankers.

"Exactly," Aislin stands and pushes her chair under the table. "I know you're going to do a great job, Vanessa."

"Thanks for believing in me." I crush the desire to scream for joy. Not professional. Or dance. Not the place. Or at least call Griz and give her the news. More doable.

And how cool is this? I'll be able to travel and meet new people and...

Oh God...

Travel. I gulp hard at the sudden lump of anxiety in my throat.

That means airplanes.

Security checks. Take offs. Landings.

The folder in my hand begins to shake. I think my blood pressure just went into the danger zone. Someone hand me a Zocor...no wait, that's for high cholesterol. I can't think.

Mentally, I shake it off, realizing I don't need to dwell on my insecurity at this moment. Not when all of this good news is still soaking in. I'll deal with it. I always have.

As we leave to return to our cubes, Aislin says, "One more thing. I've requested a company credit card for your travel-related expenses. You're going to be on the road quite a bit."

Nothing's better than traveling on the company's dime. I tamp down the apprehension of facing my biggest fear, forcing it to the pit of my stomach. This will be an adventure. More work experience to add to my resume.

The door to Jiles' office opens and I see the back of the mystery man Griz was talking about. If the front looks anything as nice as the back...*well...wow...*

The rest of him better not be good looking.

It doesn't matter. Company policy...no fraternization or cavorting.

And I'm not going to let anything—not even a cute ass—get in the way of my success.

CHAPTER TWO

Jiles Chancey stands on a raised platform at the front of the Paricutan Volcano room and claps his hands to get everyone's attention, spreading them wide like he's the Messiah about to feed loaves and fishes to all of us.

Jack, who's sitting next to me, must've picked up on my thought because he leans over and says, "Jiles acts like he walks on water."

"I dread dealing with him directly." With Aislin about to take maternity leave, I'm not looking forward to working with Jiles.

"Who does he think he is?" Jack mutters as the room quiets down. "Little Baby Jesus? His initials *are* J.C. What kind of coincidence is that?"

I stifle a laugh by clearing my throat. I also elbow Jack. He's my touchstone here at work and totally knows how to cut to the chase about the bullshit in the office. He and I do our jobs and do them right, but we always find time to make each other laugh about the corporate crap that swirls around on a day-to-day basis.

"That's it...that's going to be our code word for him," Jack says quietly. "Little Baby Jesus."

I muffle my choked laugh. "I can't. It's sacrilegious, Jack." Not like that'll stop us at this point. The name totally fits.

"Okay, we'll just refer to him as 'LBJ' like the former president. But you'll know what it really means."

"Stop it," I hiss.

Aislin looks over at us and places her index finger to her lips. Up ahead, I see the backs of three men that I don't recognize sitting in the front row. Is one of them the "babe" Griz was referring to? Not like it matters, but a girl can look.

Jiles clears his throat; a phlegm-filled noise that makes my back arch. He's wearing a puke green button-down and navy blue pants. His blond hair is mussed from running his fingers through it and his skin matches his shirt.

Aislin said Jiles was catching a lot of crap from the clients over their level of customer satisfaction. Seeing how we've lost some clients to SalesWanker, Jiles apparently has been staying at the office until eleven-ish most nights. I won't cry for Argentina, though, because the guy makes a small fortune and it *is* his responsibility to manage this company. He's anything but a traditional manager. I mean, he might play at all the corporate games, but the only thing that matters to him is that bonus at the end of the year. His professionalism...well...it lacks.

"People, let's get started," Jiles shouts out. "We've got a lot to do here, so let's rock and roll."

The mumbling around the room subsides.

"It's time to get down to brass balls," Jiles says. "Our chief competitor has been beating us on some very important sales, all because of the industry buzz on Twitter and Facebook about their new software version. But it's vaporware. Not like our new improvements. We've got to watch that they don't get the jump in the market over us."

I shift in my seat as I scribble notes with the keywords Jiles mentions, thinking that Jack needs to start massaging our social media outlets a bit more to get our own industry buzz up on the trending topics list.

LBJ continues, "The Board of Directors has given me the authority to run this company any way I see fit. Think of me as the corporate gynecologist. I'm going to spread the company's legs, punch 'em into the stirrups, glove up our fingers and then delve on in and see what's going on up there. Then, if there are any infections, we'll treat them. Warts and all."

My mouth drops open. So does pretty much everyone else's. Every woman in the room cringes over his revolting analogy. Some of the men seem uncomfortable as well.

"Our sales forecast is lower than projected. We're hurting, people. We've got to cut expenditures to get some results-driven actions around here," Jiles says, pacing as he talks out of the side of his mouth. "We *can* and *will* do better."

I'm on the edge of my seat, wondering how this will affect my new position.

Jiles stands behind the podium, hushing people as they murmur over his announcement. Yeah, Little Baby Jesus fits him just fine. He loves the power and control he has over a room of a hundred and twenty people. I hope my new responsibilities don't put me on the Jiles radar as being something that's not good for the bottom line. He blathers on about win-win situations, but I'm more curious about the Three Wise Men with him at the front of the room.

"As of this morning," Jiles says, "we've let a few people go. Head of development, two top programmers and our VP of Client Services. They didn't know what they were doing, so they're gone."

There's more mumbling as this information soaks in. Those were top people he just named. I hold onto my chair in the event that he wants to throw out the marketing manager with the company bath water. But Jiles has bigger fish to fry than me.

"We've hired three new people to help get control of the market and our customers. I'd like everyone to meet them now. Guys...come on up here."

Two men in their mid-to-late forties climb onto the stage and stand next to Jiles. Behind them is what I can only describe as a mouth-watering hunk-and-a-half. Okay, okay, no dating other employees and all of that, but the handbook says nothing about looking and appreciating what I see. And look I do. If my eyes could devour him, he'd be the blue plate special on my lunch menu. But seriously...how can I *not* notice him when nearly every female in the room gasps?

Griz makes eye contact with me from her seat three rows ahead and mouths, "He's hot."

Damn right. Someone call the Boston Fire Department.

Then I mentally berate myself. I shouldn't be gawking at this guy like he's a slab of meat. He's a co-worker for heaven's sake. Correction. He's an ever so yummy co-worker and I can't help but stare. Young, athletic build, and handsome enough to make me lick my lips involuntarily. He's off limits though. Even mentally.

"Down girl," Jack notes with a grin and a nudge.

Oh God, I'm being obvious. "Shut up."

Jiles' introductions bring my attention back to the proceedings. "This is Will Fletcher, our new VP for Business Affairs." He points to the taller of the two older men. "And this, is Will Coglin, VP for Client Services."

Is it just me or do these two guys look exactly alike?

Jiles cracks himself up when he adds, "Will Fletcher and Will Coglin. Because every company needs a couple of good Willies."

The room roars with laughter. I just shake my head. Why are these brown-nosers encouraging him?

"And this is our new Consulting Manager for Client Services, Kyle Nettles," Jiles says, reaching around the Willies to pull the well-dressed hottie forward.

Hmmm...Kyle Nettles, huh? He definitely took his breathtakingly handsome vitamins as a kid. Tall, dark spikey hair and clear, vivid hazel eyes. I can make them out from my vantage point on the eighth row. His teeth are straight and white and there is a tiny dimple in his right cheek when he smiles.

It's been a while since I've been inspired by a dimple. This one has potential written all over it if it weren't for the asinine company rule. But eyeing him, I'm sure many women in the room are considering bucking company policy and are scheduling full flirt sessions with him in calendars.

"Kyle comes to us from T.R. Manning Corporation where he's earned the reputation of being an expert on client focus. We've brought him in to think outside the box and reach out to our existing customer base to provide immediate solutions."

I lean forward and whisper to Aislin, "What does that mean?"

"Damage control," she says.

"Ahhh..." Nothing like unhappy customers to send a company into a tailspin.

The three new guys step down from the stage and retake their seats. Kyle Nettles looks out over the crowd and just like that, our eyes sync up. He smiles. I smile back. The room goes blank and silent all at the same time. I half expect a soundtrack of swelling music to kick in, but that would just be ridiculous. An exhilarating spark starts in the base of my throat, dive-bombs into my stomach, and ends in a tingle in my toes.

Kyle is gazing directly at me with an expression that says he knows something. Information I'm not even privy to. I try to glance away, but I'm frozen in his gaze. Every hair on my arm is at attention. He nods and breaks eye contact, retaking his seat with the other new guys.

What the blue-blazing hell was that? That's certainly not in the handbook.

Jiles' soliloquy brings my focus back to him. "Let me wrap up by saying that as of today, this is a whole new company. I'm not lacking in self-confidence or motivation, let me tell you that straight up. I have no life; this is my life—"

"His wife will be happy to hear that," I mumble to Jack.

"—Part of me wants to say that what happened today— the firings—is deplorable. But it's not. It's like pulling off a Band-Aid and seeing what's underneath. We're going to run fast, people. If you're going to sit back for the ride, this is no place for you. Are you with me?"

What choice do I have after a speech like that? Nasty-ass Band-Aid analogy and all.

The room bursts into applause with everyone chanting, cheering, and patting each other on the back. Jack and I gather our things and join the heard of corporate cattle slowly moving out of the conference room back to the cube farm. I turn when I hear Aislin call out my name.

"There she is," she says to someone. "Vanessa!"

When the person pushes through the crowd, I gasp. Mother of God, the new client services guy is even more gorgeous up close than from a distance. I curse that damn employee manual as I imagine myself having this guy's children and settling into a nice two-story Colonial in Cambridge while our kids go to private school.

"You're Vanessa Virtue?" Kyle Nettles asks, his clear eyes sparkling.

I gulp down my nervousness and try to ease the dryness in my throat. I toss my hair a bit in an attempt to exude much-needed confidence. "That's me. In the flesh."

He extends a strong, capable hand that firmly encompasses mine in warmth. My body tingles at the contact, though I try not to show it. "Great to meet you, Vanessa. Kyle Nettles. So, I hear we're going to Atlantic City together."

I flash him my most charming and confident smile. This promotion just got a hell of a lot more interesting.

CHAPTER THREE

"**I** already told you I'm not interested in an office romance," I nearly shout into the phone to Griz as I flit around my tiny bedroom, packing for my first trip. "I'm not risking my job because of a chiseled ass and a sexy dimple."

It's not like guys are falling at my feet. My handful of recent first dates attests to that. There's nothing wrong with me. I'm just not a Victoria's Secret model. I'm a regular gal who rides the T, dresses sensibly, and doesn't want to sleep around.

"But Vanessa you're traveling with the cute sales guys... and that babe, Kyle Nettles. Get over it and have a wild fling," Griz says over a scraping sound.

"Are you kidding? Have you not read your Compass Employee's Handbook?" I trot over to my desk and pull my HR packet from of the drawer. "Section 7: 'It is strict policy of DigitalDirection that employees will refrain from sexual liaisons with fellow co-workers. Such behavior could result in termination.'"

Griz snickers and the scraping continues. "That's only mumbo-jumbo corporate crap."

I'm horrified at her blasé attitude. "It's the rules!"

"You could break them for that hottie Kyle. He's worth it."

"*What* is that god-awful sound in the background?"

20

"I've got the PedEgg on my feet," she admits.

I sigh out of frustration. Not just from my friend's... oddness, from everything. The promo, the new duties, the impending travel, and Kyle. My body is alive and buzzing from my brief contact with him, but I can't entertain the idea of a fling. No way, no how. "It's not worth it. And what... become the star of the office gossip mill and get called into HR? No thank you. You weren't around for Reagan Vanbiesbrouck and Donovan Hughes' big affair. Cost the company, big time!"

She giggles across the phone line. "Are they the ones who got caught in the server room going at it like a couple of rabbits in heat?"

Shaking my head like she can see me, I explain. "It was during a customer training session. They were on a break and decided to go for a quickie. But they knocked the server off-line with their...umm..."

"Love-making," Griz says so innocently.

"I don't know if you'd call what they were doing making love. He was married and she was engaged."

I hear Griz click her tongue. "That's not exactly the company's business."

"It is when they're doing it on company time. When they disconnected the server, the computers went black and the IT guys discovered them. One of them took a pic and uploaded it to his Twitter. The customers in the office were horrified and dropped us because of it. They even heard about it at SalesTracker. They refer to us as DigitalDickingAround."

She laughs. "Okay, you have to admit that's a bit clever."

"No it's not," I say, tripping over clothes on the floor. Why doesn't Griz get this? We're not in college anymore. This isn't an internship to help you get a good grade. This is real life. Paying your own bills. Making it on your own.

"Is that why they made the 'no touchy' rule at the office?"

"Yeah, and I'm not going to buck it. Reagan and Donovan were a *scandal.* He got fired and she got put on notice."

"Why didn't she get fired?" Griz asks.

"She was pulling in more new business than anyone else. Still is, only working out of an apartment in Portland, Oregon where she ran off to. Money talks. Bullshit walks, you know."

"Ahhh...the good old bottom line."

She's not listening to me. "Well, no one could stop talking about it, trust me."

"Who cares what people think or talk about? An affair with the Hazel-Eyed Hunk would be awesome," she presses.

"It's unrealistic. You're talking plain old Vanessa Virtue. You know this about me. I'm the girl who's had one *serious* boyfriend in her entire life." Besides, even if I were willing to forego the company edict, no one that looks like the Hazel-Eyed Hunk will give me the time of day. He'd go for someone named Brandi or Ashlee or some girl who looks like the models on magazines covers. That brief exchange after the company meeting two weeks ago was him merely being nice. Every time I've seen him since he's been trailing Jiles and the Willies like a puppy dog. Already a corporate suck up. God, I hate people like that.

"Like I believe that you've only had one boyfriend," Griz says.

"You think I'm kidding. His name was Alan Partridge. We went out for three months during my junior year in college. When I wouldn't let him into my pants, which apparently was his only quest, he broke it off."

"What a jerk. You should have broken *it* off."

Okay, I snicker at that as I fold up a pair of black slacks. "Good one."

Griz presses me, though. "So you don't like sex?" she asks seriously. I'm tempted to hit the disconnect button on the cordless.

"Of course I like sex!" I blurt out. "I'm not a prude, but having sex in the back of his Audi wasn't my idea of true romance."

"Why have you never told me any of this before?"

"It's embarrassing. I'm not one to talk about my sex life." Or lack thereof. "Anyway, men don't fall at my feet, tell me how gorgeous I am or try to nudge their way into my bed. Doesn't happen." I'll never be one to make people turn their head or fall over their feet. My parents insist I'm pretty, but they're supposed to say that. My friends call me cute, yet as much as I stare in the mirror, all I see is an ordinary gal. Not too thin, not pudgy...clear eyes and straight hair. Like I said...ordinary.

"I know what you mean," Griz says. "The guys I've dated always end up disappointing me. Or they're bad in bed." She stops and lowers her voice to a horrified whisper. "Oh my God...you're not a *virgin* are you?"

I almost fall into my open suitcase. "I've had sex, Griz, but I've never had anyone who moved the earth for me. I don't feel like wasting time with someone who doesn't have *potential.*"

"I guess that makes sense. There's nothing wrong with being picky."

"I don't necessarily need a man in my life," I say. "I don't feel inadequate or incomplete. But I do dream about that perfect guy. He'll be kind, sensitive, caring, and put me ahead of everything."

"Well, honey, don't we all wish for that? You think someone like that actually exists?"

"He has to," I say quietly.

After a moment, she says, "You'll find it."

"But, Griz, I haven't had that many dates recently."

"You just need some self-confidence. A little flirting will help boost you up."

Maybe she's right. I have to stop seeing myself as some sort of inferior person unworthy of success in work relationships. "Maybe I'll meet someone at one of these tradeshows." The company handbook doesn't say anything against that.

"Vanessa's gonna get lucky on the road," Griz sings out with a laugh.

"But not with Kyle or anyone from The Compass!"

"Whatever. It's gonna happen."

"Care to make a wager on it?" Since I know myself and my track record with guys, especially wicked cute ones, I know this is a sucker's bet. This'll be an easy win for me.

"Ahh, she's a betting woman," Griz says triumphantly.

"Not really. I just know me and what will and won't happen." There I go again, being negative.

She harrumphs. "A hundred bucks says you'll get lucky on a trip."

Why not? I have nothing to lose. If miracle upon miracle something does happen, I'll be out a Benjamin, but hey, it'll mean I'm getting some well-needed loving. "You're on."

"Text me from Atlantic City."

"Will do." I hang up and toss my BlackBerry onto the pile of pillows. What clothes aren't already in the dryer are spread out over the bed. I have no idea how to dress for this excursion to Atlantic City. Business casual? Professional? Sultry? No, no, no. I have to get Griz's romantic interlude prediction out of my head. This is about representing The Compass.

Where *are* my black boots? I can never find anything in this mess of a room. The closet space is infinitesimal so

I end up piling things on the chair and the floor. The unused Bowflex in the corner is a good place to hang my pants, skirts, shirts, and tights. Maybe my boots are back there?

My apartment is your typical Boston area rental situation—crappy landlord, fun roommates, and a first-rate location near the T. It's the middle floor of a three-family house in Cambridge, near Porter Square. Three bedrooms, one bathroom, shared with a gay guy, a budding nursing student, and me. We're all terrible primps.

The apartment is a conglomerated mess of surplus milk crates from my college days, plaid rugs and blankets from one roommate's aunt in Nova Scotia and a Victorian couch my other roommate inherited it from her cousin in The Azores. An eclectic mix of styles. Shitty chic.

"Here's that black shirt you were looking for," William says, tossing it at me. "I wore it the other day."

William McEwan is twenty-five, like me, simply adorable, and is the typical fabulously clichéd gay best friend. It is Boston, after all. I met him at a bar literally crying into his beer about a relationship gone bad. He needed a place to crash, so my other roommate, Mia Pimental, agreed he could stay. Mia's awesome whenever she's around, which is never. So, William and I have sort of become a "couple" ever since. He's the Will to my Grace, and he lands much more action than I could ever think of getting.

I look at him standing in the doorway, a waif of a man. "It sucks that you can wear my clothes. I thought I'd lost this shirt in the murky underbelly of my room."

William cautiously enters and climbs over the gaping maw of my empty suitcase to plop a stack of clothes on my bed. "I just took these out of the dryer," he says.

"You're the best, Wills."

"And I accidentally dried this." He holds up one of my lace mesh underwire bras. "I wasn't supposed to, was I?"

I shake my head, take the flimsy material, and pop him on the behind with it as he runs from me. He squeals like a little girl and I hear Mia pound on the wall to her room. "Shhh," I say. "Mia's studying."

William stands outside my door—out of harm's way—and fingers one of the two diamond studs he wears in his right ear. "I've got to get to work soon, so if you need help, ask now." He works at Harvard University during the day and bartends at night at The Gray Gander (he calls it the Gay Gander) downtown.

"Wanna pack all this up for me?" I ask.

"Not on your life. This room reminds me of the trash compactor scene in 'Star Wars.' I'm afraid something will pull me under."

I throw a pillow at him. "You're a dick."

"No, I'm not, but I do love them."

I roll my eyes and then gather up another load of clothes and go down the back stairs to our storage area in the basement where we have a washer and dryer. The basement looks like the one from the "The Blair Witch Project"—creepy as hell!—and I always expect to see someone with a video camera in the corner screaming bloody murder. I hate going down there after dark. I try to focus on kittens, bunnies, and puppies as I switch on the overhead light and pull the knob to start the water flowing into the washer.

Furry creatures hop and scamper out of my mind and a clear visual of Kyle Nettles morphs into plain view. He looked so incredible walking down the hall at work yesterday in his Tommy Hilfiger slacks and a black button-down. Images of those strong, masculine arms wrapped around me instigate tingly sensations in my stomach and below. What am I thinking? He's a colleague. A manager. Someone I have to *travel* with. Besides, no matter how amazingly handsome he is, he's Jiles' corporate lapdog and I loathe suck ups. I can't be entertaining fantasies of...

There's a scurrying sound in the back corner and my heart starts hammering away.

Shit! What was that?

I choke on my scream when I hear a shuffle behind me followed by a creepy Hannibal Lecter-type, "Hello, Vanessa."

It's our landlord, Dan Paulsen, a fifty-year-old work-from-home accountant with obsessive-compulsive disorder. He lurches toward me holding a garden hose in his hand.

"Holy mother of God! You scared the hell out of me!"

"Such language, Vanessa."

"Sorry." The guy took three years off my life. What did he expect? "Is there something I can help you with, Mr. Paulsen?"

"Just looking for this." He holds up the hose in an ominous I-could-choke-you posture.

At nine o'clock at night?

I jam my clothes into the washer, slam the lid, and take off for the stairs without a word.

"William!" I scream when I get back upstairs. "Never, ever again am I going back down there."

"Mr. Paulsen?"

I nod profusely.

William snorts. "I don't even want to know."

"I'll never go into the basement again."

William wraps his arm around me and escorts me back to my room. "You won't have to. I'll do your laundry from here on."

The pounding of my heart returns to normal and I set back to the task at hand. The hell with creepy Mr. Paulsen.

It's all about my career now. Impressing the boss. And impressing Kyle. Why did Griz put such thoughts into my head? I'm not losing my job for flirting with the new guy! I need to do a bang up job and prove they promoted the right girl.

Although flying makes me want to wretch into an inflight paper bag, this Marketing Coordinator is ready for wheel's up.

Chapter Four

Ted Spencer and I share a cab from our Cambridge office to the airport. Bumper-to-bumper traffic hampers our commute on I-93 south to the Callahan tunnel. And I'm stuck with someone who can't stop complaining about every single thing.

"This traffic is *retahded*," Ted says in a thick New England accent, not even looking up from his Android. "We should have left earlier."

"We left in plenty of time," I say. "Traffic's traffic."

"I hate this town," he mutters.

The cabbie just looks in the mirror and glares at us.

Ted's typically an okay guy, but because he's so into himself, it's hard to like him. Poor guy's got more hair on his face than on the top of his head. As the sales manager for The Compass, he's one of those dying-to-be-a-millionaire types. Always scuttling of to his cell phone to check online stock prices. He's quite pretentious, but then I'd expect no less from a guy with an eight-by-ten glossy of himself teeing off at some famous golf course on his cubicle wall.

Twenty-eight minutes later, we pile out of the cab at Logan Airport. We get our boarding passes at the kiosk and check our bags. Then, we slip over to the Samuel Adams Pub to meet Kyle, who was smart enough to take the T instead of a cab.

When I first see him in his blue dress shirt and baggy jeans, I feel like my tongue almost lolls out of my head and licks him up one side and down the other like a dog that has been without love and affection for years. I need to stop gawking at him like this. It will get me nowhere and I don't need to be distracted while I'm representing the company. As if my nerves aren't already an unsettled mess at the thought of engine failure at 35,000 feet, twisted steel, and babies crying.

"Hey guys," Kyle says when he sees us. "I got us some seats."

"Great," Ted says. "I need a beer."

Maybe I can get away with one glass of wine.

As Jerry the Bartender hands over an eight-ounce glass of white wine he calls a "lahhhge Chah-duhnay," Ted and Kyle chat as if I'm not there discussing a client issue they've been working on together. I try to sip the wine, but the thought of the impending flight makes me take much bigger gulps that I usually would. I signal for another glass of wine while the guys keep talking about the quality assurance we need to do for the customer. I'm just hoping the ground crew here at Logan did *their* quality assurance on the airplane I'm about to get on.

"You okay, Vanessa?" Kyle asks. He grins at me and then tips his beer in my direction.

"Yeah, yeah, I'm fine."

He nods and gives me a sidelong glance that somehow tempers my frazzled nerves. As the wine settles into me, I grow calm knowing Kyle will be on the flight with me.

Ted slurps the last of his beer and slams the glass down on the bar much to the chagrin of good old Jerry the Bartender. I down the last sip of my Chardonnay and signal for the tab.

"No, this is on me, Ted says as his hand moves for the bill. "We'll turn in the receipt and get reimbursed after some creative accounting."

I specifically remember the employee handbook reads there will be "No monetary compensation for alcohol-related expenses while traveling on company business." Is Ted bucking the rules? How come guys can do that and get away with it?

I pick up my things and follow my co-workers through the scrutinous security check, trying not to think of the thousands of germs on the airport floor that I just had to walk on in my bare feet. Ted is randomly selected for a thorough search, so Kyle and I go on ahead to the gate. The plane is boarding as soon as we get there and we quickly move to our seats. I take my place by the window and let out a long, pent-up sigh as I look out over the wing.

"Looks like we're sitting together," Kyle stretches out in the aisle seat of row twenty-seven. I notice that his hands are large and tanned as they rest on his thigh. Not that I should be looking or making a mental comparison to other parts of his body.

That's when the skivvies kick back in.

The small compartment.

The close quarters.

The airtight door that will soon seal me into this flying coffin.

I'm on an airplane.

Oh God.

My hands begin to shake and sweat at the same time.

I try some deep breathing exercises to try and calm my nerves for the impending flight. The plane is abuzz with activity and energy of people making last minute phone calls, checking their texts and e-mails, or just playing a game.

Why do I feel such sudden doom?

A loud slam brings me upright in the seat and knocks me into reality. My tingling nerves wipe out thoughts of anything other than faulty landing gear and malfunctioning flaps.

Should I warn Kyle that I might hurl my morning biscuit once this 737 starts rumbling down the runway? I try to think of normal, everyday things like how much is in my 401(k) or if I paid the cable bill, to calm my frazzled nerves. I snag the *Skymall* magazine from the back of the seat just to have something to do with my hands.

Kyle interrupts my inner musings. "Sorry we haven't had a chance to talk more since the company meeting. Jiles kind of swept me away these past two weeks to teach me the ropes. But, I've heard a lot of good things about you from Aislin."

The products in the magazine fade into obscurity as I notice Kyle's stunning eyes. We're talking traffic stopping beautiful. Crystal clear. I focus on his ultra-white teeth and that Hollywood smile of his. The creased dimple on his face gives him an air of rakishness that hints to a rogue side to him.

"That's okay. Things are crazy at the office these days," I say. Then, I breathe out and extend my hand to him professionally across the vacant middle seat. "I'm Vanessa Virtue. Welcome to DigitalDirection. You'll make a great part of our team," I manage to get out through my sure-to-be-soon panic attack.

He takes my hand and shakes it slightly, yet playfully. I relax into the seat and luxuriate in the warmth of our skin touching. Damn, he's cute. Why couldn't I have met him in a club when I was out with Griz? Why does he have to be a not-for-consumption co-worker? No way am I jeopardizing my job due to a set of sexy eyes. I certainly don't want the high schoolers in the research room to add me to their list of people they backstab and crucify weekly.

"I've been meaning to ask you to lunch," he says, removing his hand. I slump a little when he pulls away.

Did he just say lunch? "Oh yeah?" I try to wrap my mind around his words while the wine numbs my senses a bit too much. Is he asking me out? This can't be happening. Hasn't he read the handbook? "I simply adore lunch," I hear myself say.

"We can talk just as easily now," he says.

I angle my body in the seat toward his, as much as I can with the seatbelt on, and keep my mouth shut for fear of saying something in appropriate. Talking to Kyle will distract me from my fear of this flight. I'll concentrate on the smooth texture of his face, letting it calm me.

He withdraws a battered legal pad from his leather carry-on. "It's essential as we move forward, that we set up a customer plan of action. Tradeshows are a great way to reach out to our client base and let them know we're the leader in the marketplace."

Disappointment hits me like a Tae Kwon Do chop. Kyle Nettles has Corporatitis. Too bad.

I shake my head. What exactly do I mean by "too bad?" Obviously he *has* read the handbook and is keeping things strictly business. Like I should.

Over the loud speaker, we hear, "Flight attendants cross check and prepare the cabin for takeoff."

Lights flicker. Doors swoosh shut. The air conditioning stalls.

I can't breathe.

I'm trapped.

There's no way out.

I need that air.

Shit! Now the plane's moving. Why didn't I mention to Aislin that I have an unhealthy fear of flying? Why won't the wine kick in more?

I squeeze my eyes tightly.

Oh please, oh please, oh please...

Breathe. Breathe. Breathe.

"Are you okay, Vanessa?" Kyle asks with concern.

My chest is heaving like I've been underwater too long and I've just broken the surface for some precious air. I dart my gaze to him, then look away, ashamed. "Umm... Yeah, sorry, the taking off part freaks me out a little." I swallow hard and look him square in the eyes. "I have pteromerhanophobia."

He smirks a little. "Is that contagious?"

I take a swipe at him, but return my palms to grip the armrest. "Don't be a jerk. It's not funny. Pteromerhanophobia is the fear of flying. I've been tested for it."

"I thought fear of flying was called aviophobia."

I shake my head. "My dad says it's pteromerhanophobia. And he should know. He used to be an Air Force pilot. Even took me up in an F-16 once when I was a teenager to help me get over it."

"That sounds amazing," he says. "What happened?"

"I puked in the flight mask."

Kyle politely covers his snort and laughter with his fisted hand to his mouth.

Why am I telling him such a gruesome and embarrassing memory? And why hasn't the pilot turned the air conditioner back on? I'm turning into a huge ball of sweat and my heart's going to come bursting out of my clothing at any moment.

The plane bounces along on the tarmac and my blood pressure accelerates. I don't know if I can do this. It would be extremely embarrassing for me to ask them to turn the plane back.

Kyle reaches over and soothes my hand with his. "Hey, Vanessa. It's okay. You'll be all right."

"I don't think—"

"Don't think," he says softly. "Gaze out at the horizon and just breathe."

His voice is soothing and kind and I find myself doing as he says. Somehow, my fingers have laced through his larger ones, gripping to him like a lifeline. I'm too terrified to be embarrassed, so I continue to cling. He doesn't make any effort to separate himself from me, only telling me to breathe and focus. I peer out the window at Boston Harbor as it rushes by on my right and then suddenly, we lift off the ground and bank up over the ocean below. Once we're airborne, I stare out the window in horror as the flaps groan and moan like they haven't been serviced in years. Of course they slip back into place and all is well as we bank into a cloud. Kyle is eyeballing me and I don't know whether to be self-conscious or grateful for his concern.

"You're doing just fine," he says to encourage me.

The plane climbs higher with all sorts of bumps, grinds, and noises going on. Kyle explains each one, letting me know we're okay and this is all normal. "When they announce that you can use your electronics, you'll know it was a good take-off and we're set to relax."

The words jar me momentarily. Then before I know it, we level out, the seatbelt light is extinguished, and the flight attendants are taking drink orders.

I glance down and see my hand still pretzeled with his. Reluctantly, I let go, unable to meet his gaze that I feel on my skin.

"See," Kyle says softly and very close to me. "You did it."

I breathe for what feels like the first time since I sat in my seat. "Thanks. So far, so good."

"Can I get you something? Some water?" he asks. "A barf bag?"

I laugh and loosen my death grip on the armrest to push my hair out of my face. "I need more wine."

"Definitely."

He signals the flight attendant to bring me a Chardonnay.

"Make it two," I say.

Kyle scoffs, ever the businessman. "Oh, I don't want one."

"No, they're both for me."

He laughs and hands over his credit card to the flight attendant in exchange for the small bottles. He opens one and pours it into the plastic airline cup for me. "A little medication for you."

"Thanks, you're really nice, Kyle." What a relief to have a thoughtful person with me as I defy death in this flying cylinder that continues to bounce along in the choppy air pockets.

Kyle runs his hands through his hair. "I used to have a little fear of flying when I first started traveling for work."

And he even admits it...cool. "What did you do to combat it?"

He laughs. "I kept getting on airplanes. Sooner or later, you get used to being up here."

"I'll try to remember that." I drink the cold wine down in nearly one gulp. I can see Kyle watching and I hope he won't report me to Jiles. "Oh that Vanessa, what a lush."

"So, let me distract you. We can talk about the customer service plan," Kyle says, trying to avert my bout of panic. The wine tingles inside me and I think I'll be all right. Maybe even a little buzzed.

I smooth my hands down the sides of my pants, quelling the tension that's built up from balling my fists. Work. I'll focus on work and not think about how high up I am in the air.

As Kyle flips through the pages of his iPad, flicking his finger against the screen, I admire his finely designed body, from firm arms—apparent because of the fitted blue shirt—and broad shoulders that taper to his waist and a nice butt. Okay, so I looked at his gorgeous ass earlier when he stashed his bag in the overhead bin.

His legs look solid, like tree trunks encased in denim. He must work out religiously to have such a sculpted body. I stare at the top of his head as he talks about a ten-city client tour. I need to stop lusting after him. This is not a good thing. It won't get me anywhere. We're co-workers. There are rules. Besides, guys like Kyle have tall, skinny blondes waiting somewhere for them with lips pursed for kissing and bodies tight for all-night sex. And here I sit downing Chardonnay like a bar fly.

Besides, although he's been my Dr. Freud so far, helping me combat my phobia, he's still corporate through and through. He reeks of his newfound position. While I appreciate a hard worker and trying to succeed, I much prefer someone who bucks the system and doesn't merely follow the leader. Especially when that leader is Little Baby Jesus and his brigade of Willies. I don't have the guts to break the rules—not yet anyhow.

So, I sigh wistfully, tune out the corporate prattling, and open up my second Chardonnay, hoping this flight ends soon.

CHAPTER FIVE

When we touch down in Philly, I'm completely buzzed, although I do my best to try and hide it. So much for being the consummate professional. I'm mortified with myself.

It's a bit of a haul in our rental van that Ted drives over the Walt Whitman Bridge and down the Expressway to Atlantic City, where the CRM Strategic Conference is being held at the Taj Mahal. When we check in the hotel, I find that my room looks like a bordello, with red curtains, a purple bedspread, and outlandish fluffy green chairs. I look up, thinking there will be a disco ball hanging from the ceiling. Thank heavens, there's not one.

I meet the guys back downstairs at the vendor check-in area and get all the paperwork for our space. I thumb through the registration packet that holds my badge, the itinerary, and drink tickets. I announce, "There's a reception tonight with an open bar and another party down the Boardwalk later." Lovely, just what I need, more alcohol.

"It'll be a great jumping off place to experience the tradeshow world and network with our customers," Kyle says to me. "Now that you're past the flying part."

Maybe there's some medication I can take so I'm not so anxious in the air. I certainly can't get blitzed like this every time since I won't always have Kyle along to assuage my fears. And while we're at it, let's get some medication for Kyle's constant obsession with business-chatter.

When Ted asks for the booth key, I realize I'd left it on my desk in Cambridge, like an idiot!

"Don't worry. I know how to pick the lock." The gleam in his eye tells me he's done that a time or two. See, now Ted's got the right idea. Although he's not in the least bit attractive to me or anyone I'd ever go for, he is more of a corporate raider than a follower with his expense fudging and lock picking. For that, I'll give him props.

Thanks to his instructions, we throw the portable booth up in a heartbeat. (It's small enough that we don't have to use union help.) The pieces slide together easily, no need for tools. The whole "build the booth" concept makes a lot more sense to me now as I adhere the Velcro graphic panels in place. Ted shows me how to set up the pop-up tradeshow booth, which is a lot easier than I imagined. The panels are decorated with rich graphics and screenshots of our DigitalDirection software. Very flashy and impressive. We hook up the TV monitors we've rented and then Ted gives us a crash course on the software. My brain is overloaded with the bells, whistles, and features. Kyle concentrates on everything Ted says and takes copious notes. I do my best to follow along so I'll be able to show attendees what our product is all about.

Kyle must notice that I'm starting to fade because he offers to finishes the last computer station. "There you go. All set. Anything else I can do?"

Okay, so he's helpful. With muscles like that, he should be. I resist the urge to reach out and see if they're actually as solid as they look. "I think I need a nap before tonight's reception. All that wine's getting the best of me."

Ted wraps his arm around my shoulder. Kyle seems taken aback by the show of affection. Before today, I'd spoken to Ted maybe six times, now all of a sudden he's my best bud?

"I hope you brought your drinking shoes, girly girl. 'Cause we got lots of partying to do. Starting in three hours," Ted says, looking at his Rolex.

This isn't the reason I'm in town. I have to represent the company. It's my job to embody DigitalDirection. I'm an icon for the corporation. Maybe partying is simply an aspect of the business I've yet to see being stuck in an office all these years.

I look at Kyle, who's grinning from ear to ear. That delectable dimple pops out and makes my stomach flip flop in a delicious pang. He apparently understands the party circuit of tradeshows.

All right, I won't worry what people back in Boston think and will simply hang with my co-workers. As long as we do our job and come back with a ton of leads, that's the main thing.

The festivities open up with a gigantic reception in a grand ballroom of the Taj Mahal. Attendees are dressed appropriately in khakis and company golf shirts. I opted for a knee-length black skirt with strappy sandals and a scoop neck black top. I'm clearly overdressed. Ted's in his standard casual Friday outfit and I've yet to see Kyle. I'm sure he'll look good no matter what.

Buffet tables overflow with boiled shrimp, mini crab cakes, cheeses, fruit, eggrolls and chicken fingers. Two open bars (sponsored by a social networking company) are at either end of the room and people line up double-fisting free drinks.

"Fill up on food and we'll use our bar bills later tonight as meal receipts," Ted informs me.

"Ah, I'm starting to understand how this works."

At the serving platter of chicken fingers, I pile a couple of the greasy treats onto my plate. Sure enough, I drop a dollop of honey mustard sauce on my left boob.

"Perfect," I mutter under my breath. *Way to go, Grace.*

"Can I help with that?" a deep, husky voice asks.

I look up—and I mean *up*—to see a blond, blue-eyed man staring down at me.

"I've got it, thanks." I dab my paper napkin into my Tanqueray and tonic and wipe at the spot.

"Yeah, but it's not as fun that way," he teases while staring at my cleaning action.

I can't decide whether to be offended or flattered.

He must pick up on my trepidation on judging the situation, and then adds, "You know, what happens at the tradeshows, stays at the tradeshows. One of the best perks to being in sales, don't you think?" He tacks a wink onto the end of the sentence for good measure.

I take inventory: Caribbean blue eyes, long, lean chin, strong jaw, broad shoulders leading to a trim waist and legs that go on forever. He must be over six-feet. And older than me. At least in his mid-thirties. I wipe the corner of my mouth unconsciously as he gazes at me.

Be charming. Be cool. Above all, be professional.

"Boy, you don't waste any time." No way this guy would pick me out of the crowd without a reason. "The show doesn't start for"—looking at my watch—"twelve hours and you're already in sleazy salesman mode?"

He laughs, a bubbly, rolling type, because he knows I've bested him. Extending his large hand, he says, "Rory Ellery. I'm with SalesTracker."

I stifle a snicker as I reach for his hand. Ah-ha! The competition. Not what I expected. They sure grow them nice and handsome at SalesTracker.

But here's *my* chance to play the corporate games.

My brain sizzles with a brilliant idea.

I'll play him for information and score big at work.

Reaching out, I give him my hand and shake firmly. I'm bound and determined to win. Look out SalesTracker, here comes Vanessa Virtue!

CHAPTER SIX

My fingers tingle at the contact with Rory Ellery's firm, warm grip. "I'm Vanessa Virtue. I work for DigitalDirection."

As I wait for his reaction, I wonder if I can find out anything that might help us get the edge back from SalesTracker.

But he's all charm and casualness. "Nice to meet you, Vanessa. So you came out from Boston?" He piles a couple of eggrolls onto his plate and then steps out of the way so another man can reach the bounty.

"Yeah. We're your competition, you know." I'm slightly offended that he doesn't acknowledge this. I want him to know I'm here to play, but he doesn't flinch. Instead he smiles.

Deadly blue eyes lock on mine and I feel a slight tremor in my tummy. "Well, Vanessa, I don't consider DigitalDirection to be my competition. It's more like *you're* in competition with us." He's quite sure of himself. "Who wants to talk work anyway when there's a beautiful woman in front of me?"

Okay...I know I'm blushing. Think fast. Be clever. The guy is just playing the corporate bullshit games. "Oh, well," I say, trying to sound mature. "I'm in marketing, so I'm not into all that sales competition stuff."

"Then I guess we can be friends," he says, winking. He jumbles his thick blond hair and then asks if I want to meet his colleague. *Colleague.* What a step up. When I was a flunky at my last job, my only associate was the telephone.

Rory places his hand on my elbow (very Stage Four of intimacy) and guides me through the crowd super gentleman-like. He introduces me to Gene Cappucci, a fellow salesman for SalesTracker, based out of Seattle, Washington. Gene is Italian through and through, beefy with thick charcoal-colored hair and a bushy black mustache.

"Well, aren't you a cutie," Gene says to me.

I bite my tongue from telling him he's not. He's old enough to be my dad.

"We're headed over to EG Venture Capital's swing party in a bit," Rory says. "You wanna come along?"

"I'm here with folks from my company. Can they come, too?" There. Safe. Bring along the guys.

"Who's with you? Ted Spencer?" Gene asks. "I can't tell you how many times I beat him out for a new customer."

"Ted's here with me," I point to where he stands, holding two cocktails. "And our new client services manager is here, too." I glance over to see Kyle in a heated conversation with a leggy blonde, but I don't point him out. My confidence sinks momentarily when I see the woman laugh at something Kyle says and then touch his shirtsleeve. I find myself glaring.

Rory reaches into his pocket and counts out three tickets. "Here you go. EG's a client of mine. Hope you show up."

"Sounds like fun."

Excellent. The adventure has begun. Rory Ellery will see the charms of Vanessa Virtue and tell her all of his trade secrets. God that even sounds ludicrous in my own head. It's an excellent plan, though. Besides, what harm is there in a little tradeshow flirting? Nothing in The Compass handbook about that. I mean, look at Kyle over there.

Rory starts to head off, but then stops and turns toward me.

"And Vanessa..." he trails off.

"Yes?"

"Save a dance for me."

Later, as we're sitting at the bar of the Hard Rock Café, I keep looking for the "work" part of what we're doing here in Atlantic City. Ted's busy flirting with our waitress and Kyle chomps away at a cheeseburger (obviously didn't get enough of the free food earlier while talking to the blonde woman.) He's been quiet and reserved so far, making voice notes on his Android. I think he's concentrating on meeting the clients and potential customers.

Ted, on the other hand, is puffing away on one cigarette after the next. He nearly falls off his barstool in an attempt to put his arm around me. I think he needs to brush up on the company handbook. I'm not remotely interested in him.

Now, Rory Ellery... he's a different story.

Thoughts of our brief encounter are in full view and I'm itching to see him again. His parting words resonate in my head and slight giddiness fills my senses at the thought of someone so intriguing being interested in me. Mischievously, I want to explore this more as there's no harm in a little frat-ernization with the competition.

When I stave Ted off with my hands pressed flat to his chest, he says, "Don't worry, 'Nessa. What hasssppens on the road stays on the road."

Kyle slides over to gently move Ted away. "Come on, man. You've had a lot to drink."

I thank Kyle with my eyes and he smiles back.

Ted grabs for the empty pack of cigarettes. "I'm fine."

"Why don't we check out the EG swing party?" I suggest, waving the complimentary passes in the air.

Kyle's face lights up. "Where'd you get those? Jiles wants me to talk to their president. This is the perfect opportunity."

I shrug noncommittally and just say, "Some guy gave them to me."

Score one for me! I can distract Rory while Kyle makes the move on his client. DigitalDirection will rule the day. Okay, maybe I've had too much wine. I'm getting into the corporate competitiveness way too much. But then, that's why I'm here.

We stumble out into the warm summer night; Ted and Kyle flank me. We walk past families pushing their kids in strollers and guys in wetsuits heading out for some night surfing. The aromatic scents of coffee beans, cotton candy, and pizza fill the air as we walk the three blocks, past Merv Griffin's Resorts hotel, to the club where the party is taking place.

Before we walk in, I tug on Kyle's sleeve. Since he's totally Mr. Business, perhaps I can help out. "Hey, Kyle. You want a moment with the president of EG?"

Interest sparks his striking eyes. "Absolutely."

"Why don't I run interference with the SalesTracker people? I already met them at the cocktail party."

"That would be excellent." He fist-bumps me like we're on the basketball court. Then Ted looks at us and puts his hand up in the air. Kyle laughs and smacks his hand, too. "Let's go."

As soon as we walk in, my eyes lock with Rory's and he gives me the thumbs up. My pulse races and I dare my feet not to do the same, chiding myself to not be over anxious.

When I reach the bar where he stands, Rory hands me a lowball full of sparkling tawny liquid.

"I've been watching the door and waiting for you," he says.

Smooth, very smooth. "You didn't have to buy me a drink," I yell over the music.

"I didn't. It's an open bar." He dazzles me with his smile and I notice he has a small brown mole about two inches under his left eye. I don't know if that's necessarily considered to be a beauty mark, but it is to me.

Behind me, Ted slips up to the bar between two older women and orders a drink. Kyle is back in the corner with a smartly dressed older man that I surmise is the president of EG. Kyle certainly didn't waste any time.

I take a huge sip of the drink Rory handed me, thinking it's Ginger Ale. The liquid chars my throat and I start coughing and hacking. Rory pats me on the back and laughs as the strobe lights reflect in his blue eyes.

"First Kamikaze you've ever had?"

"I thought it was something softer," I say, swallowing hard. "I've mostly been drinking wine all evening." I'm not counting the G&T I carried around for half an hour.

Rory leans in close to my ear. "You're such a lady."

I don't know how to react, so I glance back toward Kyle who's shaking hands with the very moneyed-looking man and swapping business cards with him.

"Do you know the big cheese over there?" Rory asked, swigging back his beer.

I don't want to point out Kyle as a co-worker of mine, so I focus instead on the older gentleman he's talking to. "The man looks rich."

"Yeah, he's got more money than God. And he's a royal pain in the ass."

I gaze into Rory's eyes, giving him all my attention as he serves me with a cocky smile. "Who is he?"

Rory chuckles. "This is his party."

"Oh," is all I can get out when his arm slides onto the back of my chair. Earlier, I'd pegged him as a sleazy salesman, but I was totally wrong about him. Sure, he pours on the charm when clients are around—as most successful sales people do—however, it seems that I'm the center of Rory's attention right now. And I like it. I focus on his mouth for what seems like six years. Full, firm lips that curl up on the edge when he smiles as if I'm the only woman in the world right now. When he leans in to order more drinks, I can't help but appreciate his long legs in tan Dockers. His teal golf shirt stretches over his broad chest; the short sleeves demo his tanned arms. He turns back to me, ignoring the party around us and leaning in to whisper, "You're the hottest-looking woman at this lousy event."

My cheeks flare from the compliment as other parts of my body begin to react, as well. Rory's lit a fire deep within me that both alarms and invigorates me. To break the tension in our mutual gazes, I turn to look about the room.

Kyle's eyes meet mine and suddenly my breath hitches. I feel like I'm being unfaithful to him. No, not him. Unfaithful to my company. It's part of the plan, I remind myself. I'm the distraction Kyle needs in order to get in good with Rory's customers.

My co-worker smiles, nods, and returns to his conversation. It's all about business.

Not with Rory, though. He's here to have a good time and apparently, I'm part of his plans. He pulls me to the dance floor where a Big Bad Voodoo Daddy tune blasts from the DJ's booth. The more I sip the Kamikaze the smoother it seems to go down. Perhaps I'm anesthetized to the effects of the pungent liquor. I'm astounded by the amount of alcohol I've consumed throughout the course of the day. (Good thing I built up a tolerance at all those college frat parties.)

Rory's co-worker, Gene, the Italian Stallion, asks me to dance. As a slow song starts, Gene gathers me to him. I push away, allowing room for the Holy Ghost.

"You know who you remind me of?" Gene asks.

"Vanessa Virtue from DigitalDirection," I tart off.

"No, you remind me of my first wife."

"What wife are you on now?"

He holds up three fingers and laughs. I don't care for him to think I'm interested in applying for the job of number four.

When the song ends, Rory has a fresh drink for me. I merely hold on to it with no intention of drinking any. My surroundings are starting to appear very aquarium-ish as it is.

Ted appears on my left. "Have you seen my cigarettes?"

"Not my responsibility," I say cheekily.

Ted sneers in our competition's direction. Then, he tugs my arm and excuses us for a minute. "What are you doing with that jerk, Vanessa?" he asks sharply.

"Nothing. Just hanging out," I say in my defense.

"He's a piece of shit. Watch yourself, kid."

Irritation boils within me. It's degrading to be called "kid."

"I can take care of myself, Ted. Thanks, though." We have to work together, no use getting into a pissing contest with a skunk. A drunk one at that.

Glancing around, he changes the subject. "I really need a cigarette. Help me out." He looks around the room and spots a man at the bar, puffing away. "There, see him?"

"Yeah... so?"

"Go bum one off him for me."

Shaking my head, I say, "No way, Ted. I don't even smoke." I want to dance. With Rory. Sure, I'd set out to pump him for information. I just never expected to be so charmed by him.

"Puh-leeeeze, Vanessa!" Ted circles my wrist with his hand.

"Why don't you go ask him for one?" This is ridiculous.

"Men love to help cute chicks. He'll give you one. Come on!"

I slip away from his Kung Fu grip and make my way to the brass and oak bar, maneuvering between the smoking man and the woman. "May I bum a cigarette?"

The man holds up empty hands, so the woman fishes a cancer stick out of her handbag. It's one of those "female" cigarettes—slender and long. Ted is going to kill me, but he asked for it. "Thanks."

"Here. Take this nasty thing." I shove the feminine product at Ted. "Don't ever ask me to do that again. And don't call me 'kid' either, okay?"

"This is a Capri! I can't smoke a Capri in public. I'll look gay." He glances around as if he's done something wrong.

"Sorry. It was all they had. It's that or nothing, Ted."

"Come on, Vanessa. Let's dance," Rory interrupts. He pulls me by the hand and secures me against him. Even though I'm a lot shorter, I fit quite snugly. This feels good. Too good. Better than anything the dating sites set up for me in Boston. I shouldn't be enjoying myself this much. I'm only supposed to be hanging with Rory to get info. Not for him to make my toes curl inside my shoes.

As we turn on the dance floor, I look back to see Ted smoking the ridiculously long cigarette like a teenager not wanting to be caught by his parents, hiding it behind his back between drags.

I couldn't have planned that any better.

CHAPTER SEVEN

After dancing for two hours, we all stumble back to the Taj Mahal where the guys want to hit the casino floor. I have enough financial problems with my credit card debt and student loan payments without throwing away good money on gambling, so I decide to stand back and watch.

"I owe you one, Vanessa," Kyle says in a whisper as we round the corner into the casino. I catch a trace of his spicy cologne. The scent, mixed with his soft words against my neck, makes me tingle all over. Or maybe it's the alcohol in me.

"For what?"

"For distracting Ellery." He continues, "I had a great talk with EG's president. They're interested in a software change and are willing to look at The Director." The Director is our CRM software package. Kyle squeezes my arm. "Keep up the good work."

I feel bad that Rory might lose a customer because of me, but that's how business works. Kyle seems pleased, so maybe I've scored brownie points with him... and the company.

Rory waves at me from the craps table and I swallow hard, secretly wishing Kyle were paying this much attention to me. I seriously need to stop thinking about him in sexual terms. But I'm not sure flirting with the competition is any better, although there's nothing in Section seven about that.

Rory scores big on the dice. Red and black Twenty-five dollar chips pile up in front of him and he winks at me. I'm tipsy from all the wine and cocktails and I lean over too far on the table. The dealer pokes me back with the dice retrieving stick.

"Back off the table, lady."

How completely humiliating. Rory seizes the opportunity to wrap his arm around my waist, steadying me. I check my watch and can't believe it's after two in the morning. I look toward the blackjack table. Ted and Kyle are gone. Have they blown me off?

I should go to bed. My work is done here for now. The show starts in a few hours and I'm going to look like crap if I don't get some sleep. Besides, it doesn't appear that I'm going to get any company scoop from Rory tonight despite the questions I've been asking here and there. Ironically, he's been more focused on entertaining me. Maybe I can get him to give me a demo of SalesTracker tomorrow so I can see what they're up to.

He holds the dice out in front of me and his eyes crinkle into the brightest of smiles. "Be my good luck charm, Vanessa."

"What do you mean?"

"Blow on them."

Oh, I've seen this on television before. But usually it's some busty blonde at the end of the table that brings the gambler good luck. I purse my lips and blow a steady stream over the red and white dice. Rory's eyes focus on my lips and I swear it seems like he wants to kiss me. My insides tighten and I step back as he jiggles his fist and then hurls the dice.

"Lucky Seven. You're a winner!"

Rory sweeps me off my feet and swings me around. I guess this means he won. Look at me being a good luck charm. He sets me back to the ground, our bodies sliding together. The mellifluous sensation cascades throughout my body and I'm thinking Rory might be a heck of a lot more fun than just a source of information.

But it's late; I'm inebriated and need to get to bed. Alone. Rory's gorgeous and a nice guy, but I don't want the SalesTracker people to think I'm an easy lay.

"I, umm, guess I'll head up to bed now."

"Yeah, it is kind of late. Let me cash in and I'll walk you to your room."

I follow him to the cage where he collects his payoff. Not bad for a couple of hours of shooting dice.

Standing in front of the elevator, I notice our reflection. We look pretty good together if I do say so myself. I see him lean down toward me. "Wanna take me to my room?" he whispers.

"Rory, I..." I look up and see my blush reflected in the elevator door.

"Actually, Gene and I are sharing, so..." His eyes cut deep into mine and he doesn't have to utter another word. I've apparently turned off the "sensible thinking" button as we step into the elevator.

Quite frankly, I don't remember asking him to my room or saying he could come in. Next thing I know, though, we're standing at the end of the bed with my arms wrapped around his neck and his tongue down my throat. I haven't been kissed like this in a long time, if ever. There's nothing like a first kiss when strange lips blend together for the first time. Yet, there's a heat and desperation to this one. His hands are everywhere, circling my waist, and moving up my sides to touch my breasts. Waves of concern crash around me. Part of me wants to give in and let the floodgate of sexual tension rush forward at this handsome man. However, the sensible girl that I am—the one who doesn't want to get a reputation as someone who's "easy—breaks loose from his searing kiss. He pulls my bottom lip gently through his teeth, playfully nipping at me, before letting go.

"I shouldn't be doing this," I breathe, trying somehow to get ahold of the situation. "I don't even know if you're married or engaged or—"

He holds up his left hand and laughs. "Do you see a ring?"

Actually, I don't. So I mentally open the door to the floodgate and go for it.

We fall back onto the bed. No more thinking. Only action. A need to touch and be touched. My hands work up under his company shirt, dragging along his firm, hardened chest. Man, this feels amazing. It's been a *really* long time since I've felt special, wanted, and sexy. My ears ring and my head spins madly. I don't know what's going on, but I don't want to stop. All I know is my actions are completely insane, wanton, and delightful.

Rory's tongue sweeps inside my mouth, circling and diving for more. My fingers plunder through his thick hair, pulling him closer. I'm aware of his noticeable erection on my right thigh and wonder if I should take this any further—or let him? I'm not kidding when I say it's been a *really* long time since I've been this... well, this intimate.

"Do you... you know... *have* something?" I ask between kisses.

"Like a condom?" he responds.

"Yeah," I manage to say in a wisp of a breath.

"No, I'm not a playboy." His laugh is warm on my throat as he nibbles at the top of my collarbone. "Do you?"

"No! Certainly not. I didn't plan on anything like this." I squirm away. I have to take control of my senses and this situation. I don't care how attractive he is, I only met him a few hours ago. And, I'm not the one-night stand type.

He sighs. "Then don't worry about it. We'll cuddle."

And with that, he rolls over and gathers me next to him. His body presses into my rear and I fear such close contact won't do anything to subdue his desire.

Last thing I remember is his hand closing over my breast. Then I fall into a deep sleep.

Okay. I pass out.

When my wake up call comes at seven, Rory is gone, but there's a note.

"You're beautiful when you're sleeping. R."

Okay, he's forgiven for not being here. Besides, since he's sharing with Gene, I'm sure he wanted to get back before too many questions got asked.

I sit up and run my fingers through my messy hair, massaging the dull wine and Kamikaze ache. I rub my eyes hard and look over at the other bed where my briefcase and laptop sit. The blue glow from the monitors reflects on the shiny purple bedspread. I don't remember leaving my computer on, but then again, a lot of last night is a virtual blur.

However, as I power the machine down and snap the cover closed, I can't help but recognize the niggling sensation in the back of my head that wonders if Rory messed with it. No. He wouldn't. But then again, if he had, I would have heard him and awakened.

I rub my head again and laugh in spite of myself and my overactive imagination. I've obviously watched one too many TV crime shows. The shower's calling, and I've got work to do.

❧ ❧ ❧

Our booth is overrun with people lining up for demos of The Director software. We're almost out of brochures and I've gathered tons of business cards. People love the free Slinkies and stress balls I brought as giveaways.

Kyle is the perfect picture of professionalism. He showed up five minutes early, freshly showered, wearing a suit and tie. I know he had a lot to drink last night, but he doesn't seem bothered at all. Ted, on the other hand, is the worse for wear. His eyes are bloodshot and he has a clear case of the shakes.

I could use about eight more Tylenols and another twelve hours of sleep, but it's show time. I only have myself to blame for the circles under my eyes that my concealer doesn't cover.

"You look great, Vanessa. What's with the glow?" Kyle compliments. His words set my heart racing like some foolish schoolgirl and I smooth my hands over my white blouse and black mini skirt that has always flattered my rather ordinary figure.

"Glow? I'm not glowing."

He tilts his head and smiles. "You look different today, that's all. Must be the light in here."

Maybe Kyle senses my early morning activities with the competition. I bite my lip and hope he doesn't know anything about my romping around the hotel room with Rory.

I change the subject. "Your meeting go well last night?"

"Couldn't have done it without you." Kyle flashes a bright smile and goes back to work as soon as more attendees filter into the booth. Okay, so now I really am glowing. It's because I'm appreciated.

Around noon, Ted and I leave Kyle to slip out for lunch at the California Pizza Kitchen. We order one with roasted chicken and extra cheese to split. I wash it down with a large

Dr. Pepper—my college hangover cure-all. I almost puke when I see Ted's remedy: chocolate milk and root beer together.

Our table by the window overlooks the Boardwalk. As I struggle with a long string of dangling cheese, I hear a tap on the glass and look up to see Rory's smiling face. My heart skips a beat finally seeing him after what happened. What should I say? How should I act? How will he behave? I know Ted doesn't like—or trust—Rory because he's our competition, so I don't say anything about my brief tryst last night.

Rory stops by our table. He has two men with him who are engrossed in their cell phones.

"Slow going in your booth, huh, Spencer?"

"No, Ellery," Ted says with a slight chocolate milk mustache on his upper lip. "I've got an excellent colleague who's taking care of things. Enough time for me to grab a meal."

"Yeah, but I've got prospects with me and all you've got is your marketing girl," he says with a teasing wink.

"Who are you calling a girl?" I speak up.

"I'm just messin' with you," Rory laughs. "Enjoy your lunch, you two."

Ted misses the affectionate pinch Rory gives my arm before walking off. I don't know how to handle this. I mean, I like Rory. He's sexy and a hell of kisser, but I don't know where I stand with him. Don't know where I want to stand. Wasn't I merely on a fishing expedition? Seems like I caught a live one.

After a long day on the tradeshow floor swamped with prospects and interest in The Director, we finally pull our booth down and pack it up. I struggle to be ladylike in my skirt as

I reach overhead for graphic pieces and roll them up into their tubes. I hear a whistle, but ignore it. Men don't usually whistle at me.

But it *is* for me.

Stepping down from the chair I'm standing on, I say, "Hey, Rory. How'd the show go for you?" I want so much to sidle up to him and nab another taste of his lips—I'll admit it, I'm into him—but Kyle is standing there disconnecting his laptop cables.

"It's been hectic," he says, looking around. "The show go well for you? How many leads did you get?"

I haven't actually counted them yet so I say, "Five hundred."

He nodded. "Impressive. So, can I get your card? You know...in case we're doing other shows at the same time?"

This is the business equivalent of asking for my phone number, so I dig out my purse and nab an ivory business card.

Rory glances at his watch. "My flight leaves in two hours."

"Are you headed straight back to Seattle?" I ask, not knowing what else to say at this point.

Kyle glances over at me and lifts his eyebrow.

"Yeah, gotta get to work on these leads," Rory, the ever-dedicated salesman, says.

I press the cardstock into the palm of his hand. He takes it and then grasps onto my hand for a couple of seconds. No words are exchanged, but I understand the look in his eyes.

He likes me. He likes me a lot.

"It's been a pleasure, Ms. Virtue. I hope to see you again soon. *Real* soon."

I drop my eyes briefly, coyly, and then say, "I'd like that."

"I'll be in touch." Before he strolls out of the ballroom, he turns back. "Count on it."

CHAPTER EIGHT

"**O**h my God! What *happened* to you? Were you in a car wreck?" I ask Griz on Monday morning.

"I wish it were something that normal," she notes. I brace the office door open as she hobbles in on crutches. There's a Band-Aid on her right cheek and her wrist is in an Ace bandage. I follow her through the office to her desk.

Helping her ease into her seat, I ask, "Is this story as good as the one about when you parked in a handicapped zone, your wheel got booted, and you tried to drive away with it?"

Poor Griz has the worst luck of anyone I've ever met, always getting into ridiculous situations.

"Almost, but more painful." She tries to get comfortable in her standard issue Compass chair. "I was walking to the Green Line train when this *wicked* cute guy jogged past. He wasn't wearing a shirt and oh, you should've seen the pecs on him. I turned to watch him and I fell off the curb and twisted my ankle real bad."

I wince. Only Isabella Perry would gawk at some guy and fall on *her face*?

"Tell me you didn't land on your—" I say, covering my mouth with my hands. "Oh Griz! You poor thing."

"How else do you think I got this?" She points to her cheek. "I put my hand out, my wrist buckled and I landed—wham! Lord, you should have heard me scream. And here's the worst part..."

I sit on the edge of her desk and rub her shoulder.

"...he didn't even stop to help me."

"Who? The guy with the great pec?"

"Yeah. He saw me fall and kept going."

What a jerk. "Oh, Griz, only you," I say.

"There you are, Vanessa," Jack interrupts. "Come on, we're having bagels and coffee for Aislin in the Bobby Orr room." The renaming of the conference rooms has gone from bad to worse. Now, instead of having meetings in Natural Wonders we're having them inside men...rooms named for famous Boston athletes: Bobby Orr, Ted Williams, Larry Bird and four others I've never heard of. Guess they didn't like my seven dwarfs idea.

"Be right there," I say, eyeballing Griz.

"I still have to hear about your trip and whether you and that hunky Kyle got it on," Griz says in a stage whisper.

Why does she keep doing this to me? I know I've had your stereotypical bad date syndrome in the past, but she's not doing anything to help by pushing me at a work guy. "Would you be quiet?" I say shushing her. Down the hall, Jack signals for me to hurry.

"We're not done, Vanessa," Griz calls out after me.

"I'm sure we're not," I mutter.

I step into the room full of sales and client service people there to send Aislin off into motherhood. There are presents lining one table and piles of fresh bagels and cream cheese down the middle of another. There's also a sheet cake with a picture of a stork on it. Aislin, about to burst at the seams, starts to cry over the gesture.

I covet a slice of cake, but move back into the corner of the room so Jack can give a quick speech. "We're going to miss her, but Vanessa and I can hold down the marketing fort while she's gone," he says.

"Think you can handle it all?" Ted asks me. There's a blob of pink icing in the threads of his goatee and I find it hard not to focus on it.

"Hey, it's my opportunity to prove my worth, right?" I say.

"Jiles likes team players."

"Well, that's who I am." I'm going to be one of the company's best.

Aislin sits in front of me and scoops a bite of cake into her mouth, then says, "You've talked to Kyle Nettles about his client services plan, right?"

"We talked a little bit about it on the plane," I say. "He's a nice guy. Wicked cute, too." I lick cream cheese off my fingers and hope Aislin didn't catch the last bit.

Did I really say that out loud? I have to watch myself.

"Did I hear my name?"

I smell him before I see him. A tangy, citrus scent that mixes lightly in the air. Panic zips through me as I wait to see if he heard what I said. It doesn't look like he did, so I let out a relieved sigh. It's true, though. I bet the girls back in research already have the skinny on everything Kyle-related. I'm still afraid he's just a Jiles Wannabe. Plus, he's for looking, not touching. A no-fly zone, so to speak. Good thing for company rules, otherwise, I'd be obsessed with this guy. But I'm Vanessa Virtue, marketing professional. I'm focused.

I swallow hard and say, "Aislin and I were talking about your customer service plan."

Kyle nods his head and presses into worker-bee mode. I notice he's wearing the same color scheme as Jiles and the Willies and wonder if they called each other this morning to see what the others were wearing. Is he really this much of a suck up or is it just dumb luck?

He explains. "We want to do this ten city tour with client round-table discussions to address concerns they have. We're trying to be pro-active and start a dialogue. I can't worry about booking the room, making sure there's water on the tables, what's for lunch...so, that's where Vanessa comes in."

Aislin nods. "Right up your alley."

I'm still blinking hard over the term "start a dialogue." Do they teach you to talk like this in business school? No wonder our American economy is in such a challenge when companies and clients can't just *talk* to each other. They have to "start a dialogue."

Jack feigns interest in the business-talk as he flips through the "Curious George" book I gave Aislin for the baby. "Oh, this is the one where George eats the puzzle piece and goes to the hospital," he exclaims.

"I had a crush on The Man in the Yellow Hat when I was a kid," Aislin adds.

"Me too," I admit.

Kyle snickers. "You like tall men, don't you?"

Taken aback, I ask, "What do you mean by that?" Kyle can't possibly know that Rory sent the night in my room. Not unless he'd been parked outside my room, which I doubt he did. I decide to cover the awkward moment with a laugh.

Jack looks at me like I'm nuts. "You're both sick, lusting after a cartoon character. Course, Jessica Rabbit was *hot.*"

Kyle nods in agreement.

"Now who's sick?" I retort to the two of them. Next thing I know, it'll be Veronica from the Archie cartoon or the pretty one from Scooby Doo.

"Back to the plan, please," Aislin says, very mother-like.

I don't miss a beat. "I'll coordinate the meetings. Kyle will charm the socks off our customers, Jiles and the Board will be happy, and we'll all get big bonuses at the end of the year, right, Ais?"

"It works on paper. It's all in the execution and I know that Jiles will be happy to see you and Kyle working so closely to get this done for our clients," she says with a smile.

I'm going to dread reporting to Little Baby Jesus. (Damn Jack for having me call Jiles that.) Then there's the marketing budgeting stuff. I'm so not a numbers person—my SAT math score was testament to that—and I don't relish the thought of sitting in Jiles' office while he plays with his beard as we go over facts and figures.

"You'll do fine, Vanessa," Kyle says and pats my back. "If you ever need me to run interference, just let me know."

There's a warm fuzzy feeling on my skin where Kyle touches me. It's as if I'm back in high school and the cutest guy on campus is paying attention to me. I've got to get a grip. I sigh and will my heart to stop racing like a stock car while I entertain visions of Kyle on the back of a white horse.

Jesus! I've obviously had too much sugar this morning.

I'm in the middle of preparing this killer spreadsheet to report the daily sales leads to Jiles, when my Microsoft Outlook notification pops up.

From Jack: "Who said 'I am the way, the truth and what's always right?'"

I reply: "What does LBJ want from you?"

Jack: "Everything. And He wanted it ten minutes ago. He's in a foul mood. Must not be getting it at home."

My response: "I don't want to imagine Him in the throes of ecstasy, thank you."

Jack: "No, you'd rather picture Kyle Nettles in the throes...with you."

Where did that come from? God, is my attraction *that* obvious?

Me: "I don't think so, Jack."

Jack and I only sit two cubes away from each other, but it doesn't stop the never-ending flow of e-mails. And, crap, he's picked up on my unconscious lusting of Kyle. Not good. Can't let that happen anymore. Don't need Nancy Mendelssohn from HR marching over with the employee manual and a "warning." I need to concentrate. I have to come up with creative ways of doing tradeshows to get leads for little or no money. I have to prove my worth to everyone at DigitalDirection. From Jiles on down. This job is my life-source. My oasis of independence.

Outlook dings again and I silently curse Jack.

It's not Jack, though. It's from: *rory_ellery@salestracker. com.*

My eyebrow lifts in anticipation. My heart strums hard in my chest and I reach my hand out toward my mouse. I high-light the e-mail entitled "*Hey you,*" double-click and read:

"*Vanessa: I can't stop thinking about you. When can I see you again? Are you doing the InfoTech show in San Francisco in two months? Or maybe you'll be in Miami in two weeks? Let me know. R.*"

I read it a second time, and a third. His words on the screen reach out to me as if spoken from his mouth. He can't stop thinking about *me?* But that's not what was supposed to happen. Wasn't I merely flirting with him to get information on SalesTracker? There was nothing information-gathering about rolling around with him on the bed in my room.

I remember the feel of his soft lips on mine and my knees go weak. Okay, I'm sitting down, but they still go weak. I swallow hard and look at the e-mail details again. San Francisco, huh? And Miami? I see Aislin has these shows "penciled" in to the calendar, but I haven't filled out the paperwork or initiated payment yet. I've always wanted to visit the city by the bay, as well as South Beach. And, seeing where things could lead with Rory will squash these ridiculous—forbidden—thoughts of Kyle.

Maybe I should get Griz's advice. Of course, I haven't even told her about Rory yet. My roommate, William, is the only one who knows anything and that's only because and he seduced it out of me by baking homemade double-chocolate brownies when I got home from my trip. I've got to think.

I spend the next hour researching the burgeoning InfoTech Show and the smaller event in Miami online. They're exactly the sort of events we need: good target audiences and a bundle of likely sales leads. Perfect. I price direct flights on American through Bing Travel and get some killer fares. Excellent. In Miami, the event is at the famed Eden Roc Resort Hotel, so I book the rooms. Then, for the SF show, I find a room at the Sir Frances Drake in Union Square. Even better. Reagan Vanbiesbrouck, our top sales woman, is scheduled to be in Fort Lauderdale, so she can do the Miami show. She also has a trip planned to San Jose, according to her calendar. And Ted's got clients in San Francisco. This'll work.

I think about spending time with Rory in a couple of awesome cities. I hesitate a moment and bite down on my lip, reminding myself that I was only using Rory to get information about his company. Suddenly that plan doesn't seem sound. I honestly like him and he's made it clear that he's interested in me. It's better than any online prospect from the dating sites. Rory's his own man. He's cocky, charming, and doesn't march to corporate rules. He bucks the system, unlike someone else I know.

I really need to stop making comparisons between Rory and Kyle. Kyle's a colleague, plain and simple. End of discussion.

I dash off an e-mail to Aislin asking if these are the kind of opportunities I should be looking for. Two minutes later, she's outside my cube with a Twix bar, beaming from ear to ear.

"Vanessa, you are amazing. Both shows are perfect," she nods her auburn head. "From now on, these decisions are yours."

Pride beams off of me as I turn back to my work. I contact the directors of each show, secure booth space, and confirm my flights. Only after everything is in place—three hours after getting his message—do I respond to Rory's e-mail.

I write:

"Hi Rory, I've been thinking about you, too. I'll be in Miami at The Eden Roc. And then in San Francisco. Staying at the Sir Frances Drake. See you then. Vanessa"

I hit send and imagine my message zipping along the fiber optic cables of the information super highway out to Seattle. I gnaw on my index finger as I contemplate just how forward I'm being. Then I harrumph when I remember that his tongue has been in my mouth. I deserve to be forthright.

Ten minutes later I get: *"Can't wait to show you South Beach. It's a hell of a town. And what do you know, I'm staying at the Sir Frances in San Francisco, too. Can I wait that long to see you? R."*

Now I have two weeks to figure out what the hell I'm doing.

CHAPTER NINE

I fill Griz in on Rory over drinks at Cuchi Cuchi, a lounge and tapas place in Kendall Square in Cambridge near our office. You can always find a crowd of happening people there to peer at as you guzzle Godiva chocolate martinis and break down the remains of the business day. I sip the blood orange martini that's before me and order up the tuna tartar coronets that look like they're in tiny ice cream cones.

Setting her crutches against the bar, Griz pulls herself up onto the stool next to me. "So you and this Rory guy do it?"

"My God, Griz, what grade are you in? And no, we didn't *do it*. It's called having sex. Making love. Fu—"

She waves her hand at me. "Don't say the 'f' word. I hate it. It makes me cringe and you'll never—ever—hear me say it."

"I've heard you say it plenty," I snap.

The bartender pauses in front of us and Griz orders a strawberry basil martini. As he turns to make her drink she says to me, "I probably should have just ordered a glass of wine. I've got a ton of work to do when I get home."

I draw my finger around the rim of my glass. "William brought home some wine in a box from the bar that no one else would drink. I'll bring it to you. I wouldn't be seen dead drinking wine from a box."

She reaches to check her cell phone and then laughs. "You know, I had some of that at my uncle's funeral and it wasn't that bad."

I scowl in confusion. "Wait a minute. You drank at your uncle's funeral?"

"No, afterwards. It was like a family reunion. And believe me, my family's religious, but they know how to put away the alcohol." She reaches across the bar for my hand. "Who cares about dead people and boxed wine, tell me about this Cory guy."

"*Rory.*" The bartender sets her cocktail in front of her. We clink stemware and sip as I fill her in on Atlantic City and today's e-mails.

"Here I am thinking I'm going use him to get SalesTracker inside information, but Griz, he actually likes me."

"Of course he does. What's not to like? Do you like him?"

I pause and think. "I really do. I had an amazing time with him." Certainly hadn't factored that into my equation.

She plays with the edge of the menu. "You know, it was good you didn't have sex. That would've been too slutty. Wait until the third date."

The cold cocktail trickles into my empty stomach, which gurgles with a mixture of nerves and hunger pains. "It's hard to 'date' when I'm in Boston and he's in Seattle. We only see each other on business trips. How does that factor into the third date sex rule?"

She counts on her fingers. "Atlantic City is one. Miami is two. San Francisco will be three." She wiggles her eyebrows at me and I understand exactly what she means to happen in San Fran.

"Can I get an order of the potato croquettes?" she asks our bartender.

Food doesn't matter at this moment. I need to think. Hard. Until my head hurts and I know exactly what I'm doing.

I gulp at the martini again. "I'm attracted to Rory, but I don't know much about him other than he's SalesTracker's top guy. Which is weird because he's not all engrossed in the business world twenty-four seven." Not like most of the golf club swinging crowd at DigitalDirection. Not like Kyle. "Besides, he's our competition." I stare off for a minute as a vivid image or Rory colors my memory.

"So what?" Griz spouts and then she gasps. "Oh wait, you're already gone on this guy."

"I am not."

"You most certainly are."

"It's true that Rory's more mature than guys we meet here." And even though he's successful in his job, he doesn't appear to be the type to suck up to the boss or think only in terms of bottom lines or customer satisfaction. Again, like Kyle, although I don't know why he always factors into the equation.

"You haven't been dating a lot, so you're over-analyzing everything," my friend tells me.

Like I need to be reminded of this.

"I don't know, Griz. Being with Rory felt good and it was fun." No, I don't need a guy for validation, but it's nice to know someone wants to be with me. What girl doesn't want that?

Griz clears her throat. "If I may be so bold, when was the last time you had sex?"

I sip my drink then hang my head. "A long time."

"You're twenty-five. You're not a vestal virgin. You're an adult. You're out on your own—as you always say. If you want him, go for it. Who's gonna judge you?"

Everyone at work, if it gets out. Although, I don't have to put it in the company newsletter, do I? *Vanessa Virtue Does the Competition.* "I'm more of a relationship gal," I say, trying to justify. "Or I'd like to be. I don't know if I'm up for a road fling."

I'm confused by my own I backpedaling? I've never been the type to just hook up here and there. I need a connection. I don't know why I can't just grow up and do what everyone else does. Brush aside the hesitation. Rory is gorgeous and sexy. I'm healthy and have wants and desires. Griz is right. Maybe the reluctance is because I can't get Kyle Nettles, corporate boy extraordinaire, out of my brain.

Griz shakes her head at me. "What did I predict?"

"I don't owe you a penny yet. Nothing's happened."

"Whatever. In this day and age, honey, take what you can get. Make it happen. Don't let the opportunity pass you by. You never know when another one will show up." She picks up her glass. "I have so many friends who are married to their high school or college sweetheart because they never had the guts to take chances. My college roommate slept with one guy in four years at Notre Dame and married him. Two years into the marriage, she found out he had seven online identifications, secret e-mails, and was having affairs morning, noon, and night. She settled," Griz says. "You don't have to."

"I know I don't. I'm not looking to settle. I'm looking to *mean* something to someone. Not be just a fling."

Griz laughs. "Most all relationships start out with the sexual energy building into a combustible force. Flings happen, but they can also develop and grow into something more."

"Like your friend's husband?"

"Bad example," she says, taking another sip of the red concoction in front of her.

"But those people you described aren't like you and me," I say. "We take the bull by the horns."

"We don't go around our elbows to get to our asses," she adds with a laugh.

I nearly choke on my drink. "You've got to stop. I'm serious."

She turns to face me, her brows knitted together. "So am I. If you want something, go after it, Vanessa. The hell with everyone else. Because you know what? You'll wake up one day at thirty-five and wonder why you wasted these years following the rules or being picky or wondering what people think. You've got this free passport to travel and meet new-guys. Don't worry about the consequences. Just live."

I collapse back into my bar seat as if I've just been beaten senseless. Perhaps I've just had some sense metaphorically beaten into me. "Excellent speech, Ms. Perry."

She draws her martini glass to her lips. "I thought so, too."

The bartender sets our tapas in front of us. "Here you go, ladies. Enjoy."

"Looks amazing. I'm starving," Griz says and then dives into her potato appetizer.

Maybe she's right. What am I saving myself for? I moved to Boston to be my own person, free from parental rules and regulations, able to make my own decisions. I need to shut the hell up and do what I say I want to do. It's the twenty-first century, for Christ's sake. Women aren't expected to behave like June Cleaver, or even their own mothers, for that matter. We are single and independent. I'll go with the flow and see what happens with Rory.

Griz quickly wipes her mouth with her napkin. "And speaking of appetizing, look at what just walked in." She points toward the door.

I crane my head to see who she's waving to. My stomach does one of those crazy roller coast zooms, but I take control and clench my fists. "Is this some sort of set-up?"

"I don't know what you're talking about," she says innocently.

Two familiar guys walk right through the crowd making their way to the bar.

Griz raises her eyebrow. "Look at the potential."

"Are you crazy, Griz? Someone might see us with them."

She brushes me off. "We're just having drinks, not doing it in the server room."

"Hey there, Isabella," says Rick Churchman. "Hope we didn't keep you waiting long."

Rick works for Kyle on the client services team. I know Griz thinks he's hot, but I had no idea she'd been ballsy enough to ask him out like this.

"Hey, Vanessa."

Behind Rick is said boss...and those amazing hazel eyes I've been trying to get out of my thoughts.

"Hey, Kyle. What are you doing here?" I ask.

"I was invited," he says with a smile.

Great, now we're really treading into dangerous waters. A lot of DigitalDirection staffers hang out here, so I look around for anyone who might make this out to be more than it is. Looks like we're good since I don't recognize any other familiar faces.

"Hey guys," Griz says in a sexy way. "Why don't we get a table?"

"That's okay, we're—" I say as I stay rooted to my bar stool.

"Great idea," Kyle says.

"I can move your food and check," the bartender tells us, making everything oh, so convenient.

As Griz gets her crutches, I grab my purse and clench my teeth at her. "Is this some sort of date?"

"No, but I did tell Rick we'd be here and that they should stop by."

"I don't believe you." I take my purse and brush past her.

She grabs my arm. "Where are you going?"

"To the bathroom."

She seethes. "Like hell you are." She pushes me forward and I have no choice but to follow the guys to the table where my drink now sits.

Rick sits next to Griz and Kyle slides in next to me. Taking a breath to calm my nerves and my irritation, I make a mental checklist. Hair: good. Makeup: simple. Stomach: suck in.

Griz stares me down as if to remind me of our previous conversation, and I do my best to just chill out. I try to play it cool, acting like it isn't a forced get-together. I don't trust Griz as far as I can throw her. Rick's up to no good, too. I can't believe that Kyle, Corporate Lapdog, agreed to this.

"Do you mind?" Kyle asks, pointing to my tuna coronets. "I haven't eaten all day. Jiles had me on one conference call after the next."

I push the plate in front of him. "Oh sure. Please help yourself."

"We'll order more." Kyle pops the raw tuna into his mouth.

"I need a beer," Rick says as he stretches out in his seat.

Rick Churchman is an athletic sort with a blond crew cut and a nice smile. To break the ice, I say, "So, Rick, you're going with me to the tradeshow in Las Vegas next month, right?"

"He's only going for the gambling," Griz says, touching him on the arm.

I furrow my brows at her gross PDA, worried that DigitalDirection spies might be aloft to take notes and report back to HR.

"Vegas, baby!" Rick says in a deep voice.

My father was stationed at Nellis Air Force Base, outside of Vegas, when I was ten years old. Most of my friends' parents worked as bartenders, waitresses or dealers. It's going to be weird going back there after all these years.

"Kyle, are you going on that trip too?" Griz asks before she sips her drink.

Kyle moves his arm behind me on my chair to turn in Griz's direction. This feels too much like a date and I'm sure it looks that way, as well. I try not to react as he says, "I don't think so. I'm supposed to meet up with clients in Reno. But you guys should have a lot of fun, huh, Vanessa?"

I can feel the heat from his body as we sit in close contact. He's so near that if I turn my head in his direction, I might bump my nose against his cheek. Anyone who walks by our table will think we're on a double date. We're so going to get busted like Reagan and Donovan did, only without the public sex part. Kyle's totally gorgeous, but I still can't get involved with a co-worker. Besides, I've already gotten Rory's attention and I should be thinking about him, not the beefcake next to me.

"Drinks, guys?" the waiter asks.

Rick orders a Sam Adams and Kyle looks at my glass. "I'll have what she's having."

I can't help but smile. He gives me a warm grin back. There's something about this guy—those sparkling eyes and oh, God... that damn dimple, make my insides weep.

Rick stops the waiter before he runs off. "Let's have the duck crepes, more potato croquettes, and the fried artichoke hearts."

Kyle points at my tuna. "And another one of these."

Apparently, he and Kyle are here to stay for a while.

The waiter scribbles the order and hurries off. I shift my gaze nervously toward Kyle and wonder if he's as uncomfortable with this apparent arrangement as I am. Griz and Rick have their heads bent together and I have to question how long they've had this planned. Apparently I need to read Section Seven to her again.

"This is kind of awkward, huh?" I say to Kyle.

He leans over and speaks in a low tone. "How so?"

My pulse speeds up and I try not to stumble on my words. "Oh, you know, the company handbook that says no dating or stuff like that."

Kyle sort of smirks. "This isn't a date." Then he adds, "Although I do think Rick has a thing for Isabella."

My heart falls to my feet as his words shoot me down. Gulping hard, I manage to say, "I see. That's nice of you to suffer through being his wing man."

"Oh, I'm not encouraging this," he shrugs. "Don't need to piss off Jiles or the Willies with an office romance gone bad."

I'm about to ask why he assumes Rick and Griz will go bad when I hear, "Vanessa! I didn't know you were coming here tonight."

My roommate, William, pushes through the crowd to our table. He snatches a chair from an empty table and scootches next to me—smashing me over into Kyle—and plants a kiss on my cheek. Kyle moves his arm off the back of the seat and flips his cell phone over and over in his palm. I'm now sandwiched next to Kyle with the warmth of his body touching me in pulse points at the shoulder, hip, and knees.

"So, I want to hear what happened with your friend from Oz?" William asks.

"Oz? Like *Wizard of*?" Isabella asks.

Rick and Kyle swap inquisitive looks while I glare at both of my friends.

William nods. "Exactly. Seattle. The Emerald City." He reaches over and drains my cocktail.

"Who is this guy?" Kyle asks. "Your boyfriend?"

"Good lord, no! He's my roommate," I say defensively.

William won't shut up, though. "So, what about it, Double Vee?"

I cringe because I don't want people from the office to know about Rory. "*Wills*," I say emphatically. "I work with these guys. This is Rick Churchman and Kyle Nettles."

He bites his lip noticeably and panic flashes in his eyes.

Griz finally catches on. "Ohhhh, he means..." she trails off. "You told him before you told me?" I kick her good leg under the table.

"Ouch!"

"What are you guys talking about?" Rick asks. "I feel like I need a decoder or something."

I'm afraid to meet Kyle's stare for fear I'll have to explain. After all, he may have picked up that the vibe between Rory and me was more than simple corporate interference. I don't want Kyle to know anything. Not that I'm ashamed of what happened with Rory, but I'm still unsure of this weird sensation I get whenever Kyle's around, too. Besides, it's *my* business.

William recognizes his faux pas and escapes to the little boy's room. I'll skin him alive later. For now, I've got to change the subject.

Unknowingly, Griz does it for me. "You know, William looks like Ewan McGregor in that old movie 'Reality Bites.'"

"Ewan McGregor wasn't in 'Reality Bites,'" Rick corrects her. "You're thinking of Ethan Hawke."

"That guy who never washes his hair? Who's married to Jodie Foster?"

I shake my head. "Geez, Griz, don't you watch TMZ? Ethan Hawke used to be married to Uma Thurman. Not Jodie Foster. She's a lesbian."

"Uma's a lesbian? The kick-ass chick from 'Kill Bill?'"

I grab two handfuls of my hair and let out a yelp. "No! Uma was married to Ethan. Neither is gay. Jodie's allegedly gay."

"But she's got kids."

"Lesbians can have children."

Rick looks confuzzled. "I don't get it. Who's gay?"

"How are you keeping up with this?" Kyle asks with a laugh.

Griz's train of thought is oftentimes impossible to follow. Instead of trying, I reach over and take her cocktail away and drink it since William helped himself to mine.

She levels her eyes on me and snags back her cocktail. "Your hormones are out of whack, Double Vee." She might not know anything about pop culture, but she can read me like a book.

Kyle returns his arm behind me and laughs. His dreamy eyes lock on mine. "You guys are too much. A real comedy team. Lucy and Ethel. Laverne and Shirley."

"Nothing current?" I ask with a laugh.

He chuckles. "Give me more time to watch you two in action."

As I stare at him, I blink hard. If I have to focus on these eyes much longer, I fear I'll be handing over a hundred bucks to Griz in the very near future.

CHAPTER TEN

The minute I step outside of Miami International Airport, the searing heat washes across my face. I quickly hail a cab and the next thing I know, I'm zooming across the causeway headed for South Beach.

Finally.

After two long weeks of Griz torturing me about how she and Rick are tempting the gods of the office with their subversive dating and me trying to keep my churning lusts for Kyle Nettles under control and play by the company rules, I've arrived in Miami Beach for the next tradeshow.

The place where I'll see Rory Ellery.

The Eden Roc Resort takes my breath away as I step out of the taxi and into the marbled lobby. I could get used to this, I think, as a dutiful attendant grabs my bags and escorts me to the counter. The plush hotel sits on prime real estate facing Miami Beach and the Atlantic Ocean. The tangy salt aroma in the air makes me lick my lips as I stand in line for my room.

I set my purse on the Italian marble and mahogany reception desk and announce proudly, "Vanessa Virtue with DigitalDirection. I have a reservation."

I take in the grand circular lobby that welcomes guests with a spacious bar area, already filled to capacity at two in the afternoon. A staircase leads from the marble-encased lobby up to the resorts' spa center. Once I'm checked in and have my key, the bellhop escorts me to the bank of elevators and up to my room. It's the perfect location to be with Rory. Tropical. Elegant. Sexy and balmy.

Perfect… until I open the door of my room.

It's a smoking room. I am not even considering having a romantic tryst in this bar-funk smelling space.

I glare at the bellhop. "I don't mean to be difficult, but I requested a queen non-smoking. I can't stay here. I'm allergic." I fake sneeze for emphasis.

He leaves to use a house phone while I fume. He probably thinks I'm a total bitch, but I want what I specifically reserved. I've been looking forward to this trip for two weeks. I even went to the tanning bed in anticipation of the great weather and getting outside to enjoy it. No tan lines. None of that spray-tan shit for me. I'll worry about wrinkling when I hit my forties.

Five minutes later, the bellhop retrieves my bags and ushers me down the hall. "This should be more to your liking, Ms. Virtue," he says. "I'm sorry for the mix-up."

We step into an end room overlooking the ocean. Much better.

"Thank you so much."

I tip the guy for his troubles and then write down the amount so I'll know how much to put on my expenses when I get home. I set about unpacking and think of Rory's most recent e-mail. He said he couldn't tell me how much he was looking forward to seeing me. We're in the same city and the same hotel. Hopefully, I can woo him back to my spider's web.

I can't help but laugh at myself. I'm not sure exactly what I'm looking for this weekend. I'm not really after a quick roll in the hay. Well, okay. Yes. Maybe. I don't know.

Men confuse me with their flirting, their sexy eyes eyes, endearing smiles, and the way they look at you. No wonder we're such easy targets for a charmer. Or a dimple.

I watch my reflection in the mirror and smooth the wrinkles from my new outfit. Before my trip, William and I went shipping to find me the perfect little black cocktail dress. We found it at JC Penney's of all places. I can't believe what a stylish outfit I bought for only twenty-nine bucks. It will be perfect for the cocktail party scheduled at Forest Lynch's art gallery on posh Lincoln Road tonight.

I open up the double glass doors to the balcony and breathe in the ocean and the sunshine. If I'd known how amazing Miami was, I'd have stayed a week. With Rory. We'd make it to that coveted third date yet. Man, Griz is going to win that bet from me yet. I close my eyes and envision Rory's long legs, magical eyes, and pale hair tangled up on the rich tropical fabric bedcover. There's something about the tropical climate that's made my body come alive.

I hang some of my clothes in the walk-in closet—that's nearly bigger than my entire bedroom at home—and then check out the bathroom. The rich Italian marble from the lobby repeats itself and the peach wall coloring gives it an overall beachy aura.

I'd love to invite Rory back up here, but then this is technically only our second date. Technically there shouldn't be sex this time and we should wait until the tradeshow in San Francisco. Stupid, antiquated dating rules. In any event, I *did* get a bikini wax in anticipation. And boy, did that hurt like hell.

Reagan Vanbiesbrouck, one of our top sales people, is supposed to be coming in from the Left Coast to help me with this show. We're scheduled to meet up in the lobby bar any minute. I hustle downstairs, but I don't see her as

I step off the elevator. The bar area is dotted with smartly dressed men and women, sipping complicated cocktails and designer appetizers.

The registration table for the conference is off to the right from the front desk, so since Reagan isn't here yet, I decide to go ahead and check in.

"May I register?" I ask.

"Sure thing, sugar. You an attendee or an exhibitor?" A buxom brunette named Tawnya greets me.

"Exhibitor. Vanessa Virtue from DigitalDirection."

"Of course. Here you go," she says, handing over a nametag, registration packet, and ticket for tonight's cocktail party. "There's someone from your company already here. You can go ahead and set up in the ballroom. Your materials have been delivered there."

"Thanks," I say, wondering why Reagan would take it upon herself to set up the booth without me.

Trying not to trip on the smooth marble floor in my strappy sandals, I make my way to the ballroom. It's crammed with booths and table top exhibits. Many vendors are unpacking boxes or searching around for power sources and Internet connections.

I see a pair of legs sticking out from under the skirted table in our cordoned-off area. They don't exactly match Reagan's trim figure.

"Excuse me. What are you doing? May I help you?" I ask the stranger.

Obviously startled, the person jumps and I hear the crack of skull against the base of the table.

"Son of a bitch!"

I nearly gasp when Kyle Nettles crawls out rubbing his head. My hand covers my mouth. "You're not supposed to be here, Kyle."

"Nice to see you, too, Vanessa," he says, wincing at the pain.

"I'm sorry, I didn't mean—"

"It's okay. Change of plans. Reagan got called to Oregon, so I'm here to help out."

I swallow noticeably and try to get hold of my freaked out pulse as I look at Kyle in his pressed black pants and fitted yellow Polo shirt. He looks like he's been to the tanning booth, too.

"I, um, well, no one told me."

He continues to rub at his cranium that must be pounding from that whack on the table. "I was up in Tampa when Reagan called to tell me she wasn't going to make it. I figured you couldn't do a show, even one this small, all on your own." He stops and looks over to the booth while I process all of this information. "Say, I've been trying to get into this, but it's locked. Is there a key somewhere?"

"Yeah, I've got it." I dig through my purse and hope that I stashed the key in there. "What? You think we'd ship the booth without some sort of protection?"

A silly grin breaks out over Kyle's face. "Why don't you just wrap a condom around it?"

My stunned laughter bursts forth. Kyle Nettles, Mr. Corporate Boy, made a joke. I'm impressed. I whip out the small silver key and unlock the plastic tubing that holds the makings of our display. In no time flat, Kyle and I have the thing built and our brochures properly exhibited along the table's edge.

Kyle runs his hands through his hair, making it stand on end. I try not to stare at the movement and remember that I'm here to see Rory. It's going to be awkward trying to spend time with Rory with Kyle here, as well. Course, knowing Mr. Corporate Boy, he'll be knee-deep in prospect meetings the whole two days we're here.

I look around the room and spot the familiar teal and blue SalesTracker display across the expansive ballroom. No Rory, though.

Kyle's cell rings and he excuses himself. I take the opportunity to slip into the foyer to locate a house phone.

"Rory Ellery's room, please," I say when the operator answers. My heart races as the line buzzes. After four rings, it goes to the guest voice mail. That means he's checked in, but just not in the room.

Kyle's still on his cell phone when I return. "You know, we can still catch some sun before the formalities begin," he says. "Yo, Vanessa. Did you hear me?"

"Are you talking to me?"

He snickers. "Yeah, who else? What do you say we hit the beach?"

I'm sure there's something in the Employee Handbook that would totally discourage our hanging out for some rays in the middle of the day. However, if Jiles' boy Kyle suggests it, maybe it's not a bad thing. Besides, it's only four and we've done as much work as we can at this point. The cocktail party doesn't start until eight, so there's plenty of time to hang on the beach before I get dolled up to see Rory.

Fifteen minutes later, I meet Kyle on the sand with the ocean's cerulean water sparkling in the Florida sunshine. But the beautiful site of nature is nothing compared to Kyle in his navy swim trunks that mold to his trim waist. Thank God I have sunglasses on and he can't see me staring at his model-perfect chest and flat stomach. Seeing him shirtless like this is only going to generate even more wild fantasies about this unattainable man. He's *way* out of my league. I take the chaise lounge next to him, wondering if I should take off my wrap-around skirt that covers my royal blue tankini.

I try to relax sitting here, but all Kyle does is talk about work. Bottom lines and spreadsheets, leads, and client services. I admire that he's so dedicated to the company, but I'd like to get to know more about him. Where he went to school, how many kids are in his family, what's his favorite ethnic food, how does he take his coffee in the morning. I shake my head hard over the last thought and pick back up on him talking about "quality assurance follow-up" on something or other. I'm a hard worker, but there's a time and a place for everything.

"Why are you so business-focused," I ask and then bite my lip for my forwardness.

"It's my job," he says.

"Sure, it's a job, but it's not your life."

He stares ahead. "Work defines us. It's who we are. We spend more time at the office than at home or with our family. A job worth doing is worth doing well."

I admire a strong work ethic. I also know that unless you're an owner or a major stockholder, you're just a working stiff. And it scared holy hell out of me that with the flick of one person's wishful wrist, I can be gone >>poof<< in a matter of seconds through layoffs or reduction in force.

"My dad worked his ass off for twenty-five years for a company," Kyle says. "His customers loved and respected him. He won awards, garnered accolades, and retired a happy man who made a difference in people's lives. I'm just trying to do what the old man did."

I smile and cut my co-worker a tad bit of slack. Still, we're on the beach and I want to relax.

"Kyle, Kyle…"

He squints over his sunglasses. "What?"

I put my finger to my lips and say, "Shhhh. Let's not talk about work anymore. Let's just enjoy the beauty of nature that's before us."

"Oh. Right. Sorry." He leans back and keeps quiet.

The Eden Roc cabana boys interrupt every now and then, tending to our every need. For a modest fee, cute little Marco brings cushions for the beach chairs and offers to get us drinks. Kyle passes, as do I. Don't want him to report back to Jiles that I'm a lush in the middle of the afternoon.

Unable to talk business non-stop, it seems that Kyle's fallen into a deep sleep. His breathing deepens and he doesn't move. Like his old man, Kyle works his own ass off, so I can see why he's exhausted. However, this gives me the perfect opportunity to inventory his rock-hard muscles that tighten with each of his breaths. He's under a lot of strain and stress in his position at DigitalDirection. Expectations are high in the company, so I do I understand his non-stop business talk and focus. I soften as I scan my eyes up to his face. His parents much be very proud of him and what he's achieved so far. I'm sure his dad brags about him to the neighbors and his fellow retirees.

There's more to Kyle Nettles than just his classic good looks. I hope to learn more as we get to know each other more. For now, I can't help but admire the physical as he sleeps in the sunshine. His chest is sculpted as if it were chiseled by the master artist Rodin and set in his garden in Paris for all to see. My hand lifts to explore the small dusting of dark hair that swirls between his pecs. My pulse accelerates as I gaze upon this magnificent specimen of a man, damning my treacherous thoughts of throwing myself on him right here, right now. I'm out of control. I'm in need of major cooling off.

I spin away from Sleeping Beauty and hoist myself off the chaise. The wrap gets tossed onto the ground and I break into a finish line type run through the sizzling sand. The churning waves pull at me as I rush into the refreshing and cooling waters of the Atlantic. Exactly what I needed to put out the flames of desire threatening to consume me and ruin my career at DigitalDirection.

Damn these men and the control they have over us women. Like the moon tugging at the tides. As I plunge deeper into the ocean, I let the salty waves consume all thoughts of Kyle Nettles. He's off limits. End of story.

Tonight, my focus returns to where it should be: Rory Ellery.

CHAPTER ELEVEN

Dressed to kill in my JC Penney couture, I wait for Kyle in the lobby of the Eden Roc. I scan the myriad faces at the bar for Rory, however, he's nowhere to be seen.

I pluck at the tiny spaghetti straps of my new dress that molds to my bust and midriff and tapers over my hips, ending just above my knee with a nice long slit in the back. I'll admit, I feel kind of sexy as the fabric brushes the back of my bare—freshly shaved and nicely tanned—legs.

I'm pleased with my appearance and hope Rory will take notice. I took William's advice when he fussed at me that I need to "quit hiding beneath your hair." So, I swept it up into a messy ponytail leaving wispy tendrils curling around my face just like all of the models in the fashion magazines.

My cubic zirconia earrings and necklace set shimmer like real diamonds against my tanned skin. I look so much healthier now since I've gotten some sun, no longer the pasty-white New Englander.

"Well, aren't you a sight?" I hear from behind me.

My heart rate triples as I turn hoping it's Rory, but it's actually Kyle standing there. He's wearing a thin, white dress shirt with the sleeves rolled to his elbow, accentuating his afternoon tan. His pressed khaki pants flatter his physique and I have to blink hard to keep myself from staring too much at him. Stop. Regroup. Concentrate. Rory. Must think about Rory.

It's hard to think of anyone else with Kyle standing here. "You look great," I say in a cool, nonchalant manner. "Ready to knock the female attendees on their arses?"

Kyle smiles. "Now you know this trip is all about business, not pleasure, Vanessa."

I half-heartedly grin back, knowing he's right, yet knowing I'll push the envelope if Rory actually is around.

Suddenly, conference attendees are herded like cattle into three awaiting air-conditioned buses to transport us down Collins Avenue to Lincoln Road. I glance around at everyone on the bus but don't see him. I glimpse plenty of Ralph Lauren, Tommy Hilfiger, even Versace, but no Rory Ellery.

"Where can he be?" I mumble as I sit down and look out the window.

Kyle takes a seat next to me. "Who's *he?*"

Crap! I didn't mean to say that out loud. I've got to improve upon the inner monologue problem. "He? Oh, I meant *you.* I was, um, saving you a seat."

"Oh, okay. Thanks."

We ride in silence since I'm so afraid of saying the wrong thing in front of Kyle. Which is weird because I've never had a problem talking to people before in my life.

The bus drops us off one block from the Forest Lynch Gallery, made famous when Oprah bought a painting from the artist's collection. Lincoln Road is considered to be the cultural center of South Beach. Once-struggling artists now find their work treasured, adored, and sold on this pedestrian mall. Small cafés, restaurants, and most every upscale designer chain store you can imagine dot the sidewalks, which stretches from the Atlantic Ocean almost to Biscayne

Bay. I breathe in the warm night air and soak in the atmosphere of the cool breeze, the chatter from nearby diners, and the music pounding of Trance music from the CD store across the way.

As our group walks toward the gallery, Kyle touches my elbow and says to me, "You look great tonight, Vanessa. Today's tanning session makes you glow."

This is the second time he's accused me of glowing. I smile though at his sincere compliment. "Thanks, Kyle. I had fun at the beach with you today."

He winks, not in a cheesy way, and says, "We'll have to make it a regular thing on our trips."

Before I have a chance to let this comment really soak in, he opens the glass door for me and we enter the white-walled gallery with the rest of the group. Kyle wastes no time excusing himself, high-tailing it to the bar where he quickly strikes up a conversation with a swanky-looking older woman from the bus. Nearly a hundred people crowd the gallery, which is filled with works of art and paintings by Forest Lynch. I don't know the first thing about art and can't tell if the stuff is inspirational or schlock.

Upon closer inspection, I have to go with the latter.

"Would you like some?" A waiter offers a tray full of hors d'oeuvres. I snag a couple of Phyllo pastries stuffed with mushrooms. Next, I take an offered glass of champagne with a small raspberry floating in the animated amber liquid. As I sip and nibble, I scrutinize the so-called art.

To my left, encased in glass, are four silver toasters welded together and painted in neon colors. Each sport several "FL" initials. Ah, the artist. Looking around the room, I notice everything is decorated with his initials. After perusing one room filled with yard sale welding projects, I make my way into a second corridor full of portraits. Okay, this is better. Real art supplies like oil paints and nylon brushes were used to create these pieces.

But as I look around the starch white room, I notice every portrait on the wall is basically the same thing: a lone pig. Only it's a different color in each portrait. It's some kind of warped, wanna-be Andy Warhol Impressionistic crap.

"Do people actually buy this?" I ask out loud before realizing it came out. A woman in Chanel looks down her nose at me and keeps walking. Best to keep my mouth shut.

I finish my glass of champagne and snag a fresh one from a passing server. Another waiter offers me a chicken pastry purse. After tasting the delectable treat, I take three more. Might as well enjoy myself. There's a small buffet table in the back of the pig display room, so I help myself to crudités, blocks of cheese, and strawberries the size of your fist. The second glass of champagne doesn't last long either, and I quickly delve into a third. Good thing I have a high tolerance for alcohol.

I stand and stare at one pig portrait in particular that makes me think of Arnold from the "Green Acres" re-runs on cable. Behind Arnold stands another pig. I wonder what Foster Lynch was trying to say with this portrait, if anything, or if he just has a thing for the porcine persuasion.

"Shouldn't you be networking, Vanessa?" Kyle asks as he nudges me with his shoulder.

Laughing, I say, "Actually, I'm trying to interpret this painting of an animal with short legs, cloven hooves, bristly hair, and a cartilaginous snout."

The woman from the bar is standing there next to Kyle. I feel a bit ridiculous for going of on the painting within her hearing range. She seems unfazed.

Instead, she shakes his hand and says, "It was great meeting you, Kyle, and let me know if you're coming out to Salt Lake any time for a customer visit. I'll show you a good time."

I bet she will.

She winks and swishes away.

Kyle doesn't get it, though, not even while watching her slink away from him. He's oblivious to all the women staring at him.

"A client?" I ask, already knowing the answer.

"Yep. And a satisfied one at that," he notes.

I snicker. "I'm sure she is."

"That'll make Jiles happy. Sar-Com Products were threatening to go to SalesTracker just last week, so I may have saved that account by telling her what she wanted to hear. A little good will goes a long way." He smiles and then takes a sip from his beer.

"I'm glad I'm not in customer service."

"Why's that?"

"Because, you have to lie." I try sipping my champagne without swallowing the raspberry.

Kyle's lips flatten. "Oh, come off it, Vanessa, I don't lie. I just try to make customers happy."

"By lying."

"By listening to and meeting the customer's needs."

"It's lying," I say, knowing I'm pushing his buttons. Maybe it's the champagne talking.

"I wouldn't say anything, Ms. Marketing," he contends. "Marketing's all about getting people interested in something they probably don't even need. You reel them in, sales chews them up and spits them out, and the client services has to clean up the mess. That's the thing that gets me about DigitalDirection. It's all about money. The hell with the customer. Screw the relationship, get the deal signed, and get the check in the bank."

He's genuinely passionate about his job and truly making clients happy. Just like his father before him. Maybe I should cut the guy some slack for being Corporate Boy.

"I guess I have a lot to learn about business," I concede.

"I mean, look at this painter," he continues. "What's he selling that people actually need? Spray paint on a two-dollar canvas and an ego the size of the Florida panhandle. His initials are even the same as the state. Talk about narcissistic. But it's his expression. It's his vision and it means something to him and to the people who buy his products," he says, fervently, and then points at the two pigs in front of us. "What do you think this says?"

That he's craving a good pork loin or a side of bacon.

"I don't really get it." I point at the other portraits, "Pink piggy, green piggy, blue piggy? Where's Miss Piggy? And look at this one." I stand back to scrutinize the picture of Arnold and friend. I place my hand on my chin and cock my head to one side. "I think I'll call this one 'Piggy Sniffing Other Piggy's Butt.'"

Kyle nearly chokes on his beer from laughing so hard.

"Actually," a stern voice interrupts, "the portrait represents human insecurities and the need for companionship—thus spreading a message of universal friendship."

My mouth drops as I turn to see none other than the artist, Forest Lynch, standing right behind us. It has to be him. He's wearing "FL" on his left breast pocket.

Immediately, Kyle switches into professional mode, extending his hand, "Mr. Lynch, I'm Kyle Nettles from Boston. It's an honor to meet you. May I get you a drink?"

Forest Lynch eyeballs me, but then goes along quietly with Kyle, who heroically rescues me from mortified embarrassment. I totally need to learn to keep my mouth shut.

I glance back at the picture, though. If Forest Lynch's portraits signify human insecurities and the need for companionships, then I exemplify it in my twenty-nine dollar dress and free champagne buzz. Annoyance roils through my veins at the thought of how irresponsible it was for me to drag my company to an event in Miami. All so I could see a guy I spent a couple of hours with in Atlantic City. A guy I've e-mailed a bit with in the meantime. I want to smack my palm to my forehead at my naiveté.

Rory Ellery obviously has better things to do. I'm not one of them.

I gobble down the small Brie and raspberry filled tart on my plate and sip on my glass of champagne, as posers and pretenders flit about around me swapping business cards and cell phone numbers. I don't think this is exactly the idea Jiles Chancy had when he said he wanted us to think up creative and innovative ways of getting leads.

Rory Ellery is the only lead I have and it's a cold one at best. Hot leads have two of three elements to them: ready, willing, and able. In Atlantic City, I was willing and able, but not ready. Now, I'm ready and willing, but I can't be able when there's no one to be able with.

I sigh and take a deep gulp from my champagne, moving the raspberry out of the way with my tongue. That's when I hear the sexy voice in my ear.

"What's a nice girl from Boston doing in a place like this?"

When I look up into blue eyes, I swallow the raspberry.

CHAPTER TWELVE

"How did you sneak up on me like that?" I ask in a breathy manner.

"I was watching you," Rory says. "Waiting for the right time."

My heartbeat trills away under my discount dress and I can't stop the smile from spreading across my face, warming my entire body.

"Let's get out of here," he whispers seductively to me.

Rory is dressed to kill in a light green dress shirt with a white ribbed T-shirt underneath and black dress pants. His skin is deeply bronzed and his blond hair seems lighter than it was a few weeks ago, which is odd considering Seattle is such a rain-soaked city.

Of course, I don't want Kyle to see me with our competition, so I walk over to where he's standing with Forest Lynch, who I think has a definite crush on Kyle.

"Kyle, I'm going to call it a night."

He seems concerned. "Umm, okay," he says, moving his hand to my elbow. "I guess I should make sure you get to the hotel."

My wave off his polite gesture. "I'm good to take a cab. It's not far. I'll see you in the morning at the booth, okay?"

"For you, Kyle," Forest Lynch says, sliding a shot-glass full of black liquid to my co-worker.

"What's that?" he asks.

"Jaegermeister."

Oh God, maybe I *won't* see Kyle tomorrow.

"Call for the cab now, Nettles," I tease and then saunter off. I swear I feel Kyle's gaze on me, but I don't dare turn back and look. Besides, Rory's waiting.

Outside the gallery on the pedestrian mall, Rory is leaning against a palm tree as the night breeze tussles his hair. He takes me by the arm, drawing me closer to him. My skin melts at his touch and it has nothing to do with the humid August evening.

"Come here, you." His face lowers toward me; his mouthing hovering over my lips.

I gasp and close my eyes when his mouth touches mine. His hands slide down my back and his tongue pushes forward seeking pleasure. He tastes nutty, like he's been drinking a fine scotch. I wonder if he can taste the champagne on me. My tongue matches his ferocity as my fingers crawl to the back of his neck and plunge through his hair. So soft. So silky. So sexy. He pulls back and looks at me inquisitively. His finger slips under my chin and his thumb caresses back and forth. "How old are you, Vanessa?"

"Twenty-five."

He seems taken aback. "I see."

"Why? How old are you?"

He couldn't be more than three or four years older than me. But I'm not ready to hear...

"Thirty-eight," he says very matter of fact. My eyes surely bulge out from the shock of his admission. He merely laughs and adds, "I'm a whole generation older than you."

"And then some."

I steady myself, wondering for the kajillionth time what exactly it is that I'm doing. He's *twelve* years older? More than likely, he's forgotten more than I've experienced. As the war rages in my head, the current battle ends when I let him kiss me again. I suppose he has no problem with my age, so I should just chillax and enjoy the moment.

After our romantic sunset kiss underneath the Florida palm, we walk hand-in-hand down to Collins Avenue. The colorful, neon-lit hotels lining the street are packed with people having dinner or drinks. Cars jam the road; music of all genres blares from all around. I start to relax and hear Griz in my head telling me to go with the flow.

"So where have you been all day?" I ask.

"I spent the afternoon deep-sea fishing trip with Zeke, a client of mine," Rory says.

"Catch anything?"

"A buzz, mostly. We drank more than we fished. I'm still a bit hammered from all the beer, waves, and sun."

"Bad boy." I realize part of what attracts me to him is his devil-be-damned attitude. He has confidence in everything he does. Perhaps it'll rub off on me.

"You should see my chest. I'm pretty sunburned 'cause I didn't wear any sunscreen," he says, squeezing my hand.

Hmmm, I'd definitely like to see his chest, and the rest of him for that matter.

We walk a while and then reach Ocean Drive, wandering by the rambunctious atmosphere of the Clevelander Hotel, and then make our way a few more blocks to Mango's, a hot—and I mean sweaty—hip dance club with scantily clad waitresses in leopard attire. It is South Beach, after all. America's Riviera. The line to get into Mango's literally wraps around the corner and Rory doesn't want to wait. We continue along to the next block, down to the famed News Café that stays open twenty-four-seven.

Taking a bistro table in the corner by the sidewalk, Rory orders two Mojitos for us. When the tall drink arrives, I sip deeply, loving the mixture of rum and mint. Our conversation is light and teasing. Not like the dates I've had at home consisting of work carping and arguments on the local Boston sports scene and who the guy has picked for his fantasy sports teams.

Rory sets his drink down and runs his finger up my bare arm. "So tell me all about working for DigitalDirection. Any good industry gossip you care to share?"

I can't concentrate with him touching me like this. "I don't get into all of that," I say. "I just go in and do my job."

"I hear Jiles Chancey is a real pain in the ass to work for," Rory says, taking a swig of his cocktail.

"No, Jiles is great." I totally lie. Bitching and moaning to William when I get home from work is one thing; however, there's no way I'm going to bad mouth the president of my company to the competitor. That's tantamount to professional suicide.

"I do love living in Boston. It's a lot of fun and there are always things to do. Seattle must be a great city, too."

He nods and then asks another question about The Director, our software. "When is the new version coming out?"

"I don't know. I'm still learning the version we've got," I say with a laugh.

I take the high ground and twist the conversation toward him. "Are you from Seattle originally?"

He laughs and claps his hands. I think he's had a bit too much to drink this evening due to the red blotches on his cheeks. "You know, where are any of us really from? America, Earth. It's all so labeled. Yeah, I live in Seattle. I work in Seattle, but am I *from* there? I like to think I'm from wherever I am at the moment. Like, I'm from Miami today."

I frown at his explanation. He *is* drunk.

He gives me a sad puppy look and then leans in closer. "Okay, I was born in Illinois, I went to college in Indiana and lived there a few years, then I wound up in Arizona, then California, followed by a short stint in Oregon, and then I wandered up to Seattle."

"You either have a military background or you're running from something." I laugh as I sip the sugary rum and mint drink.

Rory doesn't laugh. At all.

"I, I have a military background," I say, clarifying my bad joke. "My dad's in the Air Force."

"Oh, okay. I got it." Now he laughs a little.

"So, why Seattle?"

"I was on my way up to Alaska and I got sidetracked in Seattle. I met the owner of SalesTracker and he talked me into coming to work for them two years ago."

I love his voice. The cadence of it oftentimes distracts me from what he's actually saying. It's raspy and lifts slightly when he says certain words. There's no trace of any accent—Midwestern or Pacific. He's like a newscaster.

When we finish our drinks, I can tell Rory is feeling the effects of all he's consumed throughout the day because he isn't talking as much. I decide I'm going to slow down on the potent potables. I want my wits about me and I don't want to pass out this time. That is if we make it back to the hotel soon.

We leave the News Café and Rory hails a cab, pulling me into the backseat with him. I nearly land on his lap, but he doesn't seem to mind. Nor do I. His mouth attacks mine right after he says "Mansion" to the cabbie.

Our lips meld together in a fiery heat that matches the atmosphere of Miami Beach. His hands smooth up my

stomach and his hand finds my breast, molding and form-
ing it in his palm. The touch is exhilarating and sparks a fire
throughout me. I moan into his mouth and adjust my head
to provide his tongue deeper access. Such grown up, mature
kissing. Not the normal sloppy miss-your-mouth-on-the-first-
try from a twenty-something. I trace the inside of his mouth,
his teeth, everything, with my roving tongue, and drag my
fingers along his chest. When I do, he winces.

"Shit! Sunburn." He moves his hand down to my
knee.

"Where are we going?" I ask and place small kisses at the
base of his ear. He tastes slightly of salt and deodorant soap.

"Mansion. It's one of the hippest nightclubs in SoBe."
His hand slips under the hem of my dress.

"Are you trying to impress me?" I toss a wicked glance
his way. I can't believe I'm sitting in this—basically—stranger's lap, in a cab, with his hand stroking my thigh.

"Impress you? I don't know. I'd like to *press* you, though,"
he says, inching his hand toward my private parts. This is
decadent.

"You're insatiable," I laugh against his lips.

"Why don't you satiate me?" He captures my mouth
again.

The cabbie cranks up the CD to blast an old N'Sync
song remixed. It's even more bizarre when the driver starts
singing at the top of his lungs. "I don't want to be a fool for
you. Just another player in your game for two. You may hate
me but it ain't no lie, baby, bye, bye, bye..."

Rory and I break apart, laughing heartily.

"What?" the cabbie asks. He looks at us in the rearview
mirror. "So just because I like listening to N'Sync doesn't
make me a fag, does it?"

I collapse on the seat and Rory answers, "Not necessarily."

"You look like an angel back there, sweetie," the cabbie says, "but you're acting like the devil." He has a thick New York City accent and wears mirrored sunglasses although it's nighttime. "You've got sexy eyes."

"Me or him?" I ask. Rory chokes on his chuckle.

"You, sweetie."

"Thanks," I say, not really knowing how else to react.

The cab inches along on the busy street. "So how long have you two been together?" the man asks.

"We barely know each other." Rory scratches his chin and looks at me. "What's your name again?"

"How dare you, Rory!" I smack at him and lift my eyebrows in shock. I catch the driver peering at me again.

"Ohhhh you're nasty. Nasty, baby," he jeers. "I've been with the same woman for fifteen years now. Lillian, love of my life. And I don't kiss her like that."

I blush from head to toe underneath my fresh sunburn. I don't dare look Rory in the eye.

The cabbie won't let up as he turns from Collins Avenue up the side street and onto Washington. "Maybe I should take a lesson from you two. See, Lillian's a forty-six-year-old Irish feminist who's going through menopause. I hit the Triple Crown!" He pronounces it "men-o-pawwwwwws."

"Are you from New York?" I ask, trying desperately to change the subject. Rory's hand persistently ventures up my dress, teasing me wickedly and I'm about to burst into flames. The cabbie continues to distract me.

"Ha! How could ya tell? Am I obvious?" he asks. "I have a house in Greenwich Village and a condo here. They say Miami Beach is New York's sixth borough. Manhattan in the tropics." The car comes to an abrupt halt. "Here we are, folks," the cabbie says. "You take care of yourself, my little angel."

As Rory pays him, I straighten my dress and climb out of the cab. Beautiful people are queued up inside the red velvet rope area in front of the club. Women are scantily clad, wearing revealing and see-through clothing and skirts cut up to their "see you next Tuesday." Men are buff, tanned, and muscular and look like they've come straight from a modeling session or a TV set.

I pull back on his hand. "Rory, I don't know about this."

"Come on, Vanessa. I have VIP passes."

And with that, we slip right by the bouncer, check in with a dyed-blonde chesty hostess, and are swept into the glitter, swank and pulsation of Mansion. Pink, yellow and white lights flood the room as dancers move everywhere. Servers are wearing fashionable short dresses with stiletto heels as they slither through the tight crowd. As far as the rest of the clientele's wardrobe, the phrase "anything goes" applied. Stylish, chic, and proud of their bodies.

We push our way through the people and Rory holds my hand tightly. A woman in a see-through shirt and a blue sequin thong brushes dangerously by him and says, "Well, hey there, sugar." I glare at her, but Rory laughs.

I don't want to be a prude, but I'm surrounded by nothing but tits and ass and it's completely distracting. I tug at Rory's hand to get his attention. He smiles down at me and suddenly I feel like I don't have anything to worry about. He's here *with* me.

On the dance floor, we groove to the techno-industrial music blasting all around. Rory waves his hands in the air and dances like a true white boy to the groove. I've never heard such electronica, so I jive the best I can. A bouffant brunette in a hint of a hot pink bathing suit comes around carrying a tray of shots in what appear to be test tubes. She knocks Rory on the arm and points to her ample bosoms heaving out over the tray and asks if he wanted any.

He buys two. Shots, that is.

The first one is served to him between said ta-tas. She places the vial in her cleavage and levers herself up onto a stool above him. Slowly, she leans down toward his perched open mouth until the frothy liquid empties. He laughs, licks his lips and then winks at me. I feel like an ass. I'm standing here in my formal black dress, feeling overdressed and neglected.

As people applaud and Miss Test Tube continues through the crowd, I'm on the verge of tears. The alcohol has gone straight to my head and it's clouding my judgment.

Perhaps he's simply being "a guy"—and a drunken one at that—but I'm not letting him get away with it.

The music transitions to a slower song and Rory pulls me to his chest, his stalwart hands wrapping around my back.

"Rory..."

"Mmmm..."

I smack him lightly on the back of his head to get him to open his eyes. I look up into the crystal blue depths and say with brutal honestly, "I can't compete with that."

"With what?"

My head indicates the emaciated chick up on the bar. "That. Her."

Rory seems confused. "Why would you want to compete with that?"

"Because that's all you've been staring at since we walked in."

He shakes his head and grips me tighter. "Shit, Vanessa. I'm sorry. I didn't realize it. It's all the Bud and scotch I've had to drink."

"In any case, I'm not like those girls."

"Aw, come on, Vanessa. There's more to you than that."

I lift my brow, intrigued. "How so?"

His finger traces down my face and gives me chills like nothing else. "You've got looks *and* a brain."

Well, okay. That's smooth. Enough so for me to wrap my hands behind his neck and play a part in a luscious tongue battle in the middle of the dance floor. He is, after all, kissing *me* and not any of the bimbos he's drunkenly ogled.

When we break apart, I tell Rory it's time to go. Back to the hotel. There is a tradeshow and seminar in the morning and I would like some quiet time with him away from the crowds, the drinking, and the dancing. I don't understand why we wasted so much time walking around and coming to this club when we could have been back at the hotel hours ago.

We get a cab up to the Eden Roc and then stumble together through the lobby and onto the elevator. As soon as I press the button for my floor, he's upon me. Kissing, feeling, groping. I return his ardor with the same fire-laden passion. Alcohol only enhances his sexual appetite. When the elevator opens on my floor, I walk backwards down the hall, tugging him along.

Inside my room, I kick off my two-inch high-heeled sandals and pull him in with me. He swoops me into his arms and plops me down on the bed, pressing me into the mattress with his weight. His lips and tongue are on my neck and he trails kisses over my chest and down in between my breasts.

This isn't the third date. I shouldn't let this happen. But he feels so good. And he makes *me* feel so good.

He pulls me up to get to the back zipper of my dress and I cooperate, giving him the access he needs. He eases the black straps off my shoulders and takes in the sight of my strapless demi bra, smoothing his hands over the shiny fabric before returning his mouth to my cleavage. My pulse threatens to break free from my flesh.

"Oh, wait! I've got to put in for a wake-up call," I say, not knowing where in the world that came from. Maybe I'm not ready for this. Perhaps I merely talk a good game inside my head.

I roll away from Rory and reach for the phone on the bedside table. I nearly scream when his wet tongue works its way down my spinal column. I almost forget why I have the receiver in my hands as his deft fingers unlatch my bra and his lips return to the expanse of my back.

Maybe this isn't a good idea. Maybe it is. I can't make up my mind.

Finishing up my quick phone call, I turn back to him. Moonlight from the open windows illuminates us in the dark room, adding a silvery mystique to our foreplay.

I think I need a breather before anything else happens. Just a minute to collect my thoughts. "Rory, I'll be right back." Scooting off the bed, I head into the bathroom.

"Hurry," he calls out from the other side of the door.

Taking a deep breath, I brush my teeth, check my makeup, pick up the bathroom phone to call Griz, put it back down, drink some water, take three Tylenol—to stave off a headache—brush my hair, and then finally decide to return to the room.

In the darkness, I hear Rory's deep breathing. He's sound asleep. I don't know whether to be relieved or offended.

"Rory? Rory, wake up." I shake him slightly, but nothing happens. I try again to wake him up, but he mumbles, "Come here, sweetie." He reaches around my waist and pulls me close to him like a teddy bear. I lay still and listen as his breathing slows again.

My heart hammers in my chest echoing the techno beat from the club. I don't understand guys at all. But then again, most females don't. I'm not sure what Rory wants from me. Maybe he's not even interested in having sex. I have heard of guys like that. Or perhaps he's actually courting me. He might even believe in the no sex until the third date rule, too. If so, that's kind of sweet.

Which means in San Francisco, I'm in for a hell of a ride.

When my wake up call comes the next morning, I'm alone.

My room looks like a tornado hit it. Bedcovers, clothes, and shoes are everywhere. My computer case is in the middle of the floor with a sandal on top of it. Man, I'm a slob on the road. So much so that I don't even remember causing such a hurricane. Course, that's how my room is at home, so why would here be different.

I just hate that Rory's gone. He left another note, though.

"Didn't want to wake you when you looked so peaceful. R."

I stand under the pulsating shower to try and revive myself. Then, I dress in my company shirt and khaki skirt and meet up with Kyle who's already working the crowd.

"Early night last night?" he asks, as if he really knows I was out until all hours of the morning."

"Something like that."

"Are you feeling okay?"

"I'm fine. Ready to get to work," I say cheerfully.

Across the room, I see Rory amongst a group of men, gesturing with his hands and tossing his head back in a fake salesman laugh—not the same laugh he used with me last night. Although he's busy throughout the tradeshow, we play eye tag every now and then over people's heads. It's our own special connection.

I hand out brochures, snag business cards, and bring Kyle whatever information he needs as he's demoing the software. We're inundated with questions about our software, The Director.

As the conference day ends, Rory steps over to our booth with a prospect. I hear him say, "Well, I'm headed out, so call and let me know how you want to proceed after you take a look at my competition." He shakes the guy's hand and pats him on the back.

"Rory?"

"Hey, Vanessa," he says.

"Are you leaving?"

"Yeah, oh, shit, didn't I tell you? I was only down last night and today. I've got to head up to Jacksonville for a meeting and then back to Seattle."

"But what about... I thought... I mean, last night..." I trip over every word, unable to complete a thought.

He leans down and whispers, "Last night was great. You're amazing."

I frown. But nothing happened.

He winks and gives me a small hug. "I'll e-mail you when I get back to the office. Can't wait until the next trip."

And then he hustles off.

Kyle looks warily at me, but returns to the demo he's doing. I really don't need him to question me or what's going on here. I need to focus on this tradeshow and doing my job.

Rory and I will have our time in San Francisco. That will be date number three. The pay off pitch. The sex date.

So, San Francisco it is.

I hear Griz in my head saying, "go with the flow and see what happens."

Thing is, Vanessa Virtue doesn't get too many opportunities.

I don't want to fuck this up.

CHAPTER THIRTEEN

A week later, I'm missing Rory like crazy.
In my valiant effort not to come across like a total, wannabe desperate woman who's totally infatuated with a tall, blond hunk, I, of course, screw it up.

Or so I think.

People who go out for an all-nighter with Griz at The Last Drop in Allston should *not* be allowed to come home, somehow click on her phone, and send a sappy, typo-laden text message to said tall, blond hunk.

I cringe when I re-read the previous night's correspondence:

Hye Rory...I midd u so mych. I hsd sych a grat time in Maimi and cant wait to cc u again. Ihave this stuipd trip to Vegas, but then itts c and me in SanFran. I'll be thnking abot c hope u thnk abot me. Hugs, Double Vee.

My face flames fiery red as I think and overthink what I did. Even when I get to the airport to catch my flight to Vegas. The memory of my foolishness makes my stomach churn. Not even the smell of the fresh tureen of New England clam chowder at Au Bon Pain will satiate this nauseating feeling of utter shame. Then, as I'm on the plane and instructed to turn my phone off, I get a series of texts:

Double Vee...that's cute.

But then, you're cute.

Drinking a little too much last night?
Don't you know you're not supposed to send texts at 2 a.m.?
Have fun in Las Vegas. Bet on 22 black for me.
See ya soon in San Fran
P.S. I midd u, too, and you're all I can thnk of, too. ☺

I smack my palm to my head and groan, laughing at my college-like behavior. I'm way too old to be doing brainless things like that. It's all Griz's fault.

I re-read the messages. Rory did say he misses me and is thinking about me. And that I'm cute. That's a gut-punch moment right there. I'll just focus on that.

My temples pound and my stomach lurches at the thought of another takeoff and landing. Maybe the residual alcohol in my system will act as a tranquilizer and help ease my fear of plummeting to the earth in charred bits. I try to breathe in deeply and calm myself, just like Kyle instructed me to do. It's just an airplane ride. A long, six hour flight across the entire friggin' country and over the Grand Canyon.

Unknowingly, my fingers curl around the arm rest, gripping it like it's the only lifeline I have. I think about Rory, his eyes, his smile and the fact that he likes me, even though I showed my ass off. Laughing in spite of myself, I start to relax a bit and concentrate on doing at good job at this tradeshow. That's what matters the most. Everything else is gravy.

Then I remember that Rick and Kyle (who rescheduled his Reno trip so he could be at the show) are on this trip with me.

I'll just have to make sure I behave in Las Vegas to avoid any further embarrassments.

⚜ ⚜ ⚜

Apparently I don't have to be drunk to make a complete and utter ass of myself.

When my plane lands at the Las Vegas airport, I make a beeline toward the ladies room. My stomach is in turmoil from last night's overindulgence with Griz and the massive amount of unruly turbulence that had me shunting and heavy breathing the whole way out here. I totally have to get some medication for my fear of flying. I make it into the bathroom stall just before I revisit my pretzels, peanuts, and Diet Coke from the plane ride.

When I'm done, I emerge slowly and then splash water on my face. I dig into the black hole that is my purse and revel in the fact that I have a travel-size bottle of Scope amongst the many items. Then, I head to the baggage claim area where I'm meeting up with the boys. They flew Southwest from Dallas because they were at a client site. Ted was supposed to come, but he had to go to Vermont for his uncle's funeral. I heard he also had to deal with something involving inheriting an ostrich farm. Or maybe I just imagined that.

As if my bathroom pyrotechnics aren't enough, I then humiliate myself in front of my co-workers. My very cute, hazel-eyed co-worker whom I'm not supposed to find attractive. If I ever wondered if Kyle Nettles wanted to punt the whole company handbook and ask me out, it's settled when I show him my true graceful ways.

I'm supposed to meet Kyle and Rick Churchman at the baggage carousel. So, I go over to the America West claim area first to lug off my big bag and the tradeshow booth. It takes forever for the luggage to come down the steep conveyer belt and I grow impatient, panning around for the guys. Ten minutes later, tired of waiting and trying to find a place to take a load off, I sit gingerly on the edge of the baggage conveyer. I hear someone call my name and look up to see Kyle and Rick walking toward me. I pull my hands up off my knees and wave. Just then, the bells and lights go off signaling the bags are on their way out. The first piece out is the goddamned tradeshow booth.

And it has me in its sights.

"Watch out, Vanessa!" Kyle shouts.

The container speeds down the steep incline to the bottom of the rack where I sit. Before I can move fast enough or react, the large vinyl case thwacks me in the back sending me sprawling out on the floor of the airport like fresh road kill.

Kyle drops his computer bag and instantly runs to my side. Rick stands there looking slightly amused. I should be reeling in utter humiliation, but then I start laughing hysterically. All three of us crack up as Kyle helps me to my feet. Thank heavens I'm not wearing a skirt. Otherwise, I would have flashed the whole airport.

"I'm so embarrassed," I say, wiping my hands on my shorts. "I hate that fucking booth."

I gaze up into Kyle's soft hazel eyes, awaiting his reaction. He smiles and chuckles. "You okay, Vanessa?"

My heart gives one of those aches, like when you see a cute baby in a television commercial. "Yeah. Thanks, Kyle."

"How'd you like your trip, Grace?" Rick kids.

Ignoring him, I struggle to catch up with the booth as it spins away on the conveyer belt.

"I'll get it," Kyle offers. Okay, so Corporate Boy is a true gentleman. When he stretches out to hoist the bulky booth from the conveyer, I can't help but admire his muscular arms and trim physique. Not what The Handbook would encourage. I really need to snap out of my sexually frustrated funk and concentrate on work. That's why I'm here.

The large computer tradeshow is being held at the Las Vegas Convention Center, so we booked ourselves on the older part of the strip: Circus Circus. Apparently, so did everyone else. The place is packed. Two buses of Baptists from Macon, Georgia—doesn't the Bible say gambling is a sin?—and the geriatric set from central Michigan are all checking in at the same time as us. Talk about kicking it back old school. I had expected glitz, glamour, and the full swank of Las Vegas, not an older, dreary casino filled with old ladies spending their children's inheritance and their own Social Security checks. The place isn't anything like the Travel Channel special I'd seen on it.

After finally checking into our rooms, we head over to the convention center. We get our booth set up in no time and then Kyle, ever the business-minded employee, wants to make the rounds with the other vendors. The SalesTracker booth is far down at the other end of the hall and I see Kyle talking to Gene Cappucci, the Italian Stallion divorcee extraordinaire, whom we'd met in Atlantic City.

Too bad Rory's not here in Sin City. I bet we could get to some real sinning.

For now, I'm stuck with Vegas Boy (Rick) and Mr. Serious (Kyle) and a hangover that won't let go.

"How about FatBurgers?" Rick asks.

Just what I need. A heaping helping of grease. "Show me the way."

Later that night Kyle, Rick and I have an overpriced dinner at Emeril Lagasse's restaurant at Venice and then make our way to several casinos. Kyle tells us he'd rather be back in his room working on the customer service plan, although Rick's trying to get him to loosen up.

I have to say, I admire Kyle's drive. I need to be more like that. I want so much to make a splash at work and prove to them that I'm a great worker—which I am—it's just sometimes I look at this whole corporate world as bullshit games adults play with each other. It's all about money and profit and the bottom line. We're on the road, though, and it's not like we're slacking on our duties. We're simply having fun, that's all. Maybe I should let Kyle in on this revelation.

I touch him on the arm as we're on the tram between The Luxor and Excalibur on our way to New York, New York. "Hey, Kyle, are you okay?"

He looks at me with a start. "Yeah. Sorry. Just thinking about the meeting with RLMP Associates tomorrow. They've agreed to be a beta tester for the new version of The Director."

"You know," I say. "It's okay to relax and have a good time when we're off the clock like this. No one's going to accuse you of being a bad client services manager."

His dimple appears when his smile widens. "Sorry. All I think about is work. You're right, Vanessa. I should just have a good time being here with you."

My hand moves to my chest over his pointed complimentary words.

Kyle must pick up on my interpretation, because he corrects himself. "With you and Rick, I mean." He looks over at our co-worker who's peering out of the window like a kid at Disney for the first time. "He's crazy. He's ready to spend everything he's got on the craps table."

Studying Kyle, I try to see inside the guy standing in front of me. I don't know much about him other than his strong work ethic and his amazing looks. I wish I knew more about the person underneath the corporate persona. I wish that Kyle wasn't such a Jiles wannabe. Then again, maybe I'm judging him too harshly.

Kyle smiles at me. "All right. I won't harp on business tonight. I'll have fun. Will that make you happy?" His eyes sparkle as they meet mine.

"It'll be good for you," I say and knock his arm with my elbow.

"We're here," Rick exclaims. The tram doors slide open and we walk across the street to New York, New York.

Next thing I know, the boys are so zeroed in on gambling, it's almost like I'm not even there. Like I'm a vapor.

"Hey Nettles, let's do Jell-O shots," Rick says, after he wins over a hundred bucks on roulette. "Ummm, you too, Virtue."

Kyle's focused on blackjack and blackjack only. Approaching it methodically and seriously, just like he does his work. "I've got to concentrate. Under no circumstances are you to bother me," he instructs.

Not knowing what to do, I follow Rick to the roulette table. The guy can't lose. Poker chips rain in for him like droplets from a hurricane. After spending an hour trailing him—and his winnings—around, we go to find Kyle.

"Come on, man. You've lost enough for one night. Let's go have some fun," Rick says, breaking the "don't disrupt" rule and clapping his boss on the back.

The redness in Kyle's face spells out his displeasure. "I'm not doing well at all."

Rick holds up his booty. "Let's go ride on the roller coaster."

"I don't think so," Kyle says. "Maybe I should just go back to our hotel and go to bed. We've got a busy day tomorrow and I told Jiles I'd call."

I sigh at him. "Kyle, what did we talk about?"

He scrunches up his mouth and then smiles at me. "Let's go."

We wait in line for fifteen minutes and then when it's our turn, Rick climbs into the front car, followed by a twelve-year-old girl who insists they hold their hands up in the air the whole ride. That leaves me paired up with Kyle. The coaster gets going and I'm jammed up against him. He's solid muscle from shoulder to thigh and I try not to get excited by the close contact.

Rory... must think of Rory. Rory, who can't wait to be with me in San Francisco. Rory, the first guy in a long time who made me feel worthy and special.

As we climb vertically up the first steep hill, Kyle still looks upset. "Don't worry about losing money, you can make it up before we leave tomorrow. Rick wants to hit more casinos."

"Rick can have at it," Kyle says sternly.

"Oh, come on. You didn't have any fun?" I let out a whelp as the roller coaster takes a steep dive, pressing me against Kyle even more so.

"I was distracted," he yells out. The cars zoom up and around another curve. Everyone's screaming, except Kyle. Up ahead, Rick's waving his arms over his head like a lunatic.

The coaster keeps roaring forward into a full loop. I squeal hard, trying to keep my eyes open. Kyle actually lets out a yell as we bottom out and move into the next loop. I scream out as we take another sharp curve. I practically slide into Kyle's lap, which is a little too comfortable. Section seven of the employee handbook says nothing about roller coaster rides.

I steal a glance at my seatmate and he's actually smiling. The sideways loop has me flattened against him and he actually wraps his arm around me. We laugh and scream together and wave when the coaster slows at the appropriate moment to flash and snap a picture of the riders. One more dark tunnel and swoooooosh literally into a part of the casino before we stop where we started. Everyone cheers and talks about how awesome the ride was.

I climb out of the car and say, "By what?"

"What, what?" Kyle asks.

"You said you were distracted and that's why you lost money. What distracted you?"

"Oh," Kyle says, coming back into our pre-coaster conversation. "There was a man sitting next to me smoking a cigar and yelling across the table flirting with this fifty-five year old woman. She was disgusting and he was married. They left together."

"That's classless,"

"Completely. Don't get married if you're going to get away from home and act like that."

I cock my head and listen to him as he rants about good old family values. My heart thunders at his words and I'm once again reminded of the image I had of marrying him and having his children. Good to know he wouldn't cheat on me.

"I just think a guy should respect his family more. And women, too," Kyle adds.

I want to wrap my arms around him and squeeze hard. It's not every day you see a guy with some morals when it comes to women and relationships and family and responsibility. I like this side of Mr. Corporate Boy.

After we're through at New York, New York, followed by a visit to Caesar's and Paris, we finally decided it's time to call it a night. Or a morning, rather. As we're waiting for a cab back to the hotel, I note, "I can't get over the number of families out perusing the streets at this hour. What are these people thinking?" I rail. "There's no way in hell I'd ever bring my kids to Las Freakin' Vegas."

"You need to learn to have an opinion, Vanessa," Rick teases.

Kyle's smile lifts. "You want a family someday?"

Shrugging, I say, "Yeah, sure. What about you?"

He eyeballs a little girl with long, blonde curls who can't stifle a yawn. "I wouldn't mind one of those."

There goes that fist-clench on my heart again and I can barely breathe at the intensity of the moment.

Back at the hotel, I lie in my bed and replay the evening. I got to see a whole other side to Kyle. There are a lot more layers to him than I originally thought. A lot more. He's kind, sensitive, and respectful. I'm glad we were able to have this time together.

As I fall asleep, I try to conjure up Rory's handsome face and deadly blue eyes, but for some reason, the only thing I can envision is Kyle Nettle's smile and his warm eyes.

I sigh hard and roll over, punching the pillow with my fist.

Damn that fucking Employees Manual.

CHAPTER FOURTEEN

The tradeshow the next day is a bitch. Successful for the company, but a pain for my feet. Stupid me, I wore my kitten heel Kenneth Cole sandals with the strap around the ankles that make me look taller. Very old Hollywood style, Joan Crawford-esque. They're for fashion, not function.

As tired as I am, I'm motivated, too. Watching Kyle give demos of the software is awe-inspiring. He wows potential customers with his smile and humor and he has them asking questions without any prompting. He's the perfect salesman—even though he's not officially one of them—without being slimy or sleazy. All of our clients who stop by to visit and chat are enthralled by his every word. Jiles was certainly smart bringing in someone as savvy as Kyle to head up our client services. I'm totally impressed.

I do about a dozen demos myself through the course of the tradeshow. Two of the people I demoed to had been at the SalesTracker booth and told me they liked our product better. I make note of their names to give to the right sales people for follow-up. It's not about swooping anything from Rory, it's about business.

"I've talked so much my voice has left me," I squeak out toward the end of the show. Kyle reaches into his bag and hands me a bottle of water.

"And that's a big deal for a loudmouth like you," Rick adds.

"Three sales today. Not bad," Kyle announces

"Hey, I satisfied two disgruntled clients. That should get me some kudos. Or at least a beer," Rick says with a laugh.

"Great effort by all of us and I'll make sure Jiles knows when we get home." Kyle closes up his computer case and we head back to the hotel.

By the time the show ends the next day, I want to chop off my feet. Two days of hectic, demanding work and ten hours of standing in my sandals. Must get more sensible shoes for these trips. I long for my own clothes and not the company uniform—black pants and the company golf shirt. Every muscle in my body aches and I want a hot bath. But, it's five o'clock and we've already checked out of the hotel. We're not leaving until 11:58 p.m. on the red eye back to Boston.

"God, I'm so hungry. I could eat Caesar's Palace," I announce when we're back at the rental van.

"Me too," Rick says. "I need a very cold beer with it."

"All right. Vanessa told me I needed to relax," Kyle says. "We're off the company clock. Let's kill time at more casinos. I've got to win back the money I lost last night."

"Wait a sec," I say. "If we're going to be running around all night, we need a designated driver."

"Not it," Rick shouts.

Mr. Professional, Kyle speaks up too. "Me either." He hands me the keys to the minivan and says, "You're it, Vanessa."

"How did I become *it?*" I ask in disbelief. I never win anything. Not a scratch ticket or the slots or online contests anywhere. *This* I win? "You're the one who rented this thing. You drive." I dangle the keys in front of Kyle's face.

"I've been selling all day, come on," he begs and that damn dimple deepens on his cheek. I really wish he hadn't pulled the dimple out as ammunition.

Kyle seems to be comfortable in his non-business mode that I'd encouraged last night. "The prettiest has to drive. And well, look at Rick and me. You're it," he says.

I'm taken aback at Kyle's sudden remark that he thinks I'm pretty. That kind of trumps Rory telling me I'm "cute." I shake out of it, though. Kyle's just trying to butter me up to drive around for them.

"Dammit! That's not fair." My attraction has now turned to resentment. I worked as hard as these guys and I should be allowed to have some fun too.

"It's completely fair," Rick says, climbing into the back.

Apparently, I have no choice.

I inch the rental van down the crowded strip toward the more modern casinos. Our first stop is Treasure Island. Rick spends an hour playing Keno and Kyle is still trying at black-jack. I stand around like a moron with the keys in my hand, waiting for the next destination. Then, we load back into the minivan and head over to the Venetian. The place is gorgeous and it's full of shops and restaurants I'm dying to try out. However, the guys are focused on the casino. In no time at all, I'm resenting the opulent beauty around me. A gondola with a couple making out in it passes by on the man-made water way as I search out a bathroom. I wish I were in a gondola making out instead of playing mother hen while these guys drink and gamble. I'm beginning to choke on the glitter and flash of this all-night town. Honestly, I think if you want to see the glories of Italian art, hop a friggin' plane to the real place. It isn't the lovely hotel's fault that I'm not having any fun.

"Let's hit the roulette wheel," Kyle says when I get back to where they're still sitting. He immediately hits a few times and starts to recoup his losses.

"Awesome man, look at all those chips." Rick takes the time to count his own winnings. "Don't you want to take a turn, Vanessa?"

I'm not very good at gambling, but then I think of Rory's request:

Bet on 22 black for me.

I hand the dealer a twenty dollar bill and take the chips from him. I put everything on twenty-two black and wait while the wheel whirls around and the white ball bounces along.

This is a sign... a determination of my future. I'm betting on Rory and he's got to come through.

Everyone leans forward as the ball pops into one of the numbers slots.

"Eighteen red!"

Dammit! It was right next to twenty-two black. So close. "Sorry, Rory," I mutter under my breath and watch as the dealer scoops up my chips like it's no big deal. It's not to him. He does this all day long when suckers like me walk up to the table.

Maybe that wasn't a sign. Maybe it was just fate telling me not to waste my hard-earned money. Especially cash I can't get a receipt for to get reimbursed.

I won't read too much into the "fates" having some hand in the results.

Rick snickers at me and reaches for his winnings. "Them's the breaks, Virtue."

Kyle tucks chips into his pocket. "Well, I'm feeling much better now that I've got some money back in my wallet." He and Rick fist bump each other.

I only feel worse. Bored, annoyed, tired, hungry, ill and like it doesn't matter whether I'm here or not.

After an hour at the Venetian, we're back in the minivan steering toward Paris. No, not France, although I'd rather be there. All the casinos start looking alike after a while. We stay at Paris for another hour. The guys gamble while I stock up on touristy things like cheesy martini glasses and T-shirts for Griz and William. Then, it's off to Mandalay Bay where Kyle's heard they have the loosest slots in town.

"Loosest sluts? I'm there," a drunken Rick shouts from the back of the Ford Windstar. "Are they as cute as Isabella?" He leans forward toward me, his eyes a bit at half mast. "Vaness'er," he says in his think New England accent. "I'm so into her. Isabell'er that is."

"What about the company no dating policy?" I ask. I don't dare look at Kyle, who's sitting there gazing out at the strip. He's management, after all.

"Fuck the company policy," Rick slurs.

Kyle turns. "Easy there, Churchman." He is, after all, still Rick's boss.

I sigh and shake my head. This is so ridiculous. "I feel like a soccer mom taking her kids to practice."

By the time we reach Bally's, I've had enough. Rick is acting like a complete child, making an ass of himself spilling beer on the blackjack table and Kyle seems morose and focused on the cards. It's not that I need to be the center of attention, but I don't feel like I belong. Last time this happened to me on a trip, Rory showed up and made me feel better. Only, he's in Seattle, not Las Vegas.

I excuse myself and go to the ladies room. When I close the door to the stall, I completely lose it, crying my eyes out. I'm beyond exhausted. And hungry. My body aches, I haven't slept well, and I can't participate in the debauchery because I *am* Soccer Mom. I want my bed, my pillow, and my favorite ratty T-shirt. And, dammit, I want Rory.

After a little while, I take some deep breaths, compose myself, and step over to the mirror to assess the damage.

I reapply my mascara and eyeliner and dab my face with some loose powder, making sure my nose isn't too red. I need to get hold of myself. Only a few more hours and I'll be headed home. I decide to get over myself. I'm acting like a kid and not like a grown up on a business trip. I've just let tiredness get the best of me. I'll go out and insert myself into the fun and enjoy the time I have left here in Vegas.

Leaving the ladies room, I return to where I'd left the guys winning at blackjack.

"What the—"

They're gone.

Nowhere in sight.

I spin around getting the lay of the casino. This *is* the table where they were sitting. Yeah. I recognize the dealer.

"They left a while ago, honey," the dealer says to me.

Terror fills my head and panic washes through me.

They left me?

But wait... I have the keys to the van. There's no need to freak out. But I do. My heart pounds furiously in my chest and I suddenly know what mothers experience in stores when their children wander off. It's nine-thirty and our flight leaves in a couple of hours.

Twenty minutes later I go over to a house phone. "Could you please have Kyle Nettles paged? Thanks." I listen as the overhead announcer says his name.

Nothing.

Then I try paging Rick.

Nothing.

What am I going to do? What if something horrible happened to them? Rick's drunk; Kyle's depressed. Now I'm starting to feel guilty over my bitchy behavior. But wait. Maybe they ditched me because I was being no fun. I honestly couldn't blame them.

Maybe I should call "911" or alert the casino security. They've got cameras watching every person and their every move. I've seen the shows on the Travel Channel that detail the eyes in the skies in casinos. They'd probably snicker at me if I told them I'd lost my drunken co-workers. They'd say, "Yeah, tell us something that's never happened, lady."

Not knowing what else to do, I try my cell phone, but it doesn't work inside here. So, I make my way out of the casino until I have some bars to call out. I dial the first person I know I can trust to tell me what to do.

"Gray Gander," someone shouts as music blares in the back.

"May I speak to William McEwan?" I yell. An older couple walking by looks at me like I've ruined their evening by speaking so loudly.

"Who?"

"William McEwan!" I'm literally screaming into the phone in search of my roommate.

"I can't hear you. The music's too loud."

I hear the click as he hangs up.

"You asshole, that was important," I say to the lost call. Course, what can Wills do from thousands of miles away? "This is insane."

Out of desperation, I dig Rory's business card out of my purse. I want to talk to him more than anything. Maybe he can calm me down. However, all I have is his work number and that won't do any good. I stroke the letters on the card, hoping they'll bring me closer to someone who really seems to care for me. Not these two rude guys who just walked off and left me.

I grind my teeth together, seething at Kyle and Rick for wandering off. Dammit, I'm getting on that plane in an hour and a half with or without them.

They get one more chance.

I scroll through my contacts on my phone and find Kyle's cell number. After a couple of rings, I hear, "We're sorry, the cellular customer you are trying to reach has left the area."

"No shit, Sherlock."

Absolutely disgusted with the entire situation, I walk back to the blackjack table where I'd left them originally when all of a sudden I heard shouting.

Rick calls out, "Soccer Mom!"

"Vanessa, there you are! Over here!" Kyle calls out.

They swarm around, overjoyed at seeing me. Rick, of all people, hugs me to him.

"We didn't know where you'd gone. We thought you left us 'cause I was bein' a drunken asshole," Rick says. "We went out to the parking lot looking for you."

Kyle looks relieved to see me. Very relieved. "We wandered around the casino floor searching. Then I had you paged."

"You did? But I've been here the whole time, I didn't hear anything."

"I heard it. I heard them say your name, Soccer Mom," Rick says, still squeezing me.

My chest hurts, though, at the realization that they were missing me and looking for me. "Did you actually have them say Soccer Mom?"

"Yeah," Kyle says softly.

"I'm sorry, you guys. This is so stupid." I almost start to cry again, which brings them upon me, comforting me.

"This is all because we wouldn't let you drink?" Kyle asks. "Come on, Vanessa, I think you've earned a stiff one."

I look up through my glossy haze and laugh.

"A stiff drink. Get your mind out of the gutter." He winks and I feel like everything will be okay now.

"But someone has to drive."

"Listen," Kyle starts. "MGM is close to the airport."

"I think I can handle that."

"We'll only stay until eleven-thirty. That should give us plenty of time to drop off the minivan and get to the gate." Kyle is sure of it. Or full of it. One or the other.

I have no problem catching up with the guys' alcohol consumption as I stand at the craps table drinking for free. Kyle fills me in on how the game works and even gives me a fifty-dollar chip to play with. Apparently, he's made up for his losses from the other day.

"You keep whatever you make, okay?" he says.

"I can't do that."

"It's my way of saying 'I'm sorry.'"

With a killer smile like that peering down at me, I can't refuse.

Rick's at the other end of the craps table and he has the dice. As I slurp beer, I follow Kyle's lead and place my bets accordingly.

The craps table reminds me—as even the tiniest thing does—of Rory and how he cleaned up on the dice in Atlantic City. He'd tried to explain the game to me that night, but I'd been too into him to understand. Now, I wish he was here instructing me. But Kyle's doing that now. My skin heats and tingles all at the same time when I feel his hand move on the small of my back. I shift my weight into him more until he's nearly supporting my weight. He doesn't seem to mind at all and it feels so...*right*.

"Eight!" the dealer shouts.

I look down and see that's the number I bet on, so I'm a winner. Kyle is too. He wraps his arm around me and hugs me close to him. Man, he's nothing but a rack of muscles. I can sense his rapid heartbeat as we're smashed together. I'm assuming it's from the craps win because the dealer moves over an impressive stack of chips his way. Kyle looks down at me and for a minute, it's almost like something passes between us... a whisper of unspoken words, a moment of understand each other, the thought that things could be different, deeper if we didn't work together, the promise of—

Once again, I get poked with the dice retrieving stick. "Hey lady, it's your roll. Pick your dice," the dealer snaps at me.

My mouth drops open and I tear my eyes away from Kyle's.

"Sorry," Kyle says, letting me go and stepping back as if burned. "Got excited."

The moment's over just as quickly as it happened.

I exhale and play off the tension with a joke. "Hey, I got excited, too. I just won a shit-load of money. Now, I get to roll."

Kyle seems relieved, so I don't press it further. And I sure don't admit to myself how good it felt to be in his arms. Instead, I take a pair of dice and toss them to the end of the table with everyone cheering me on.

An hour later—and four beers in my system—I'm the happiest gal in Nevada with a little over two hundred dollars in winnings. But, it's time to go.

"We're going to miss our flight," I say frantically.

We blow through the cashier line at MGM as quickly as we can and run like greyhounds out to the parking deck.

"Punch it, Soccer Mom!" Rick screams once we're all belted in.

Moments later, we pull up to the Hertz drop-off area.

The representative doesn't seem fazed by our franticness. He just inspects the vehicle, takes the keys and asks, "Would you like to keep all the charges on this credit card?"

"Umm, sure. Whatever," I say. I have no idea what credit card he means and I honestly don't care at this point. I just want to go home.

We lurch toward the airport shuttle with all of our crap in tow. A woman clutches her small son to her as we stagger on and plop into the seats. We must be a sight.

"We're not going to make it," I say, shaking my head.

"Yes we are. Think positively," Kyle says.

I glance around and ask, "Who's got the booth?"

"I've got it, Soccer Mom! Don't worry," Rick shouts, leaning against the large vinyl casing.

The shuttle drops us off at the terminal five minutes before our flight is scheduled to take off. Fuck, fuck, fuckity fuck! Scrambling through the automatic doors, we scurry in and come to a dead stop. The line at the counter flows outside the roped off area. There's no way we're getting on the red eye and I'm in no mood to spend another night in Vegas.

Kyle reads my eyes. "Leave it to me."

He inches his way over to the First Class line and steps forward. He bends his head to talk to the ticket agent. She says something, and then the two of them laugh. I sense the green monster of jealousy creeping up and peering over my shoulder when I see the way she's eyeballing Kyle. Rick rolls the booth apparatus next to me and stretches his arm over the top of it, holding himself up. I'm literally out of breath.

Kyle works his way back over to us and heaves a deep sigh. "Flight 66 to Boston has..." he pauses for dramatic effect, "...been delayed."

I think I'm going to be sick.

CHAPTER FIFTEEN

Our flight from Las Vegas doesn't take off until after one a.m.

Rick, who continues to drink at the airport, is so blitzed he can barely keep his eyes open. He's so out of it that he tips the lady behind the counter fifty dollars to put him in a window seat on the plane. Idiot was already *booked* in a window seat, but she took the tip. (I would, too.)

Finally, we board the oversold flight. Rick takes his seat three rows in front of Kyle and me and promptly passes out cold, wearing his sunglasses.

"Here, Vanessa, you want the window seat?" Kyle asks, moving aside for me.

I step in and all of a sudden the familiar fear washes over me. I'm nauseated and my head hurts. My pulse rattles feverishly in my veins and I can feel my breathing starting to get labored.

"Oh no," Kyle says. "Your fear of flying?

I nod.

"It's okay, Vanessa. Just look out to the horizon, remember?"

The horizon consists of flashing neon lights, twirling spots, and oversized billboards of Criss Angel, Penn and Teller and a revival performance of Celine Dion, like she ever went away from Vegas. Besides, I'm afraid the horizon won't help in keeping down the Burger King chicken sand-wich and fries I crammed into my system before boarding the plane. That's what I get for not eating all day, stress-ing out at the tradeshow, and then pouring alcohol onto an empty stomach.

I know I need to remain calm, but the plane's starting to move and make all of those flaps shifting sounds. My blood pressure begins to rise so much that I feel the seared heat in my face, on my neck, and around my ears. I must look like Violet in *Willie Wonka* when she starts turning purple. They do carry oxygen and defibrillators on airplanes. I just hope I don't need either one.

Realistically, I know the wings aren't going to fall off. Someone at Boeing or McDonald Douglas or one of those other companies spent a lot of man hours welding and rivet-ing the steel beast together. Yet, I can't stop my body from over-reacting to the idea of the plane crashing into the fake Eiffel Tower down below.

"Breath, Vanessa," Kyle says softly. He makes a hissing sound of sucking in and out as if he's my Lamaze partner. "Look at me."

I can't. I have to watch out the window to make sure everything goes properly.

Kyle speaks up a bit. "Vanessa Virtue. Look. At. Me."

Turning, I see his face, dimly lit from the overhead light. His eyes are dark and dilated, but totally zoomed in on me. His fingers form a "V" and he points them toward his eyes and then at me. I do my best to breathe through the panic and instead disappear into the depths of his hazel orbs.

"Good," he says. "Keep watching me."

This works momentarily. Then this horrendous groan-ing begins to sound out from under the 727. "What's that?" I ask abruptly.

"It's nothing."

"It's something."

"Breathe, Vanessa."

"Fuck breathing!"

As we power down the runway, I have my death grip on the armrest that separates Kyle and me. My knuckles are turning white and the veins in the top of my hand are bulging out. This is going to be the end of me. Twenty-five years and what… there's nothing to show the world that Vanessa Virtue was here. I will die a coward in a smoldering heap of charred metal and my parents will have to use my high school senior year dental records to identify me.

Suddenly, there's something warm on my fingers. Something soothing. I glance down and see Kyle's large, strong hand covering mine and trying to wrench it from the armrest.

"It's okay, Vanessa. I'm here for you."

Slowly, I loosen my hold on the seat and let his hand take over. Our hands merge together, disappearing into one another. The rapid rate of my heart increases at his touch, at his care, at his concern. Yet, I'm soothed and starting to think I won't die alone. Kyle's with me. He cares and he won't let me down. Certainly the company handbook wouldn't frown on comfort like this from one employee to the other when it's in a work travel situation.

Peeling my fingers off the seat handle, I rotate my wrist and flip my hand over. Kyle holds on tightly to me. I can't tell if he's uncomfortable with the contact because it's so dark in here. Maybe he's thinking about that damn manual, too. I don't know. Whatever the case, I just appreciate that he's trying to put my mind at ease.

When the plane finally barrels down the runway and then lifts off the ground, I gasp; not so much from the thrust of the jet or the flaps pulling us through the night sky. It's from the heated fire stoking the embers of attraction in my entire body from Kyle's touch. His thumb moves ever so slightly against my hand, as if to say every thing's going to be okay. That he's here to watch over me.

His whisper tiptoes over me. "Just go to sleep. I'm here for you."

"Thanks, Kyle. You're the best."

"I am, aren't I?" he says.

Basking in the warmth of his protection, I lean my head back, close my eyes, and allow myself to fall into a deep sleep.

When we land at Logan at six a.m.—damn Jiles making us take red eyes to save money—I bolt up from my comfortable resting place. Shit! I'd slept on Kyle's shoulder.

"Morning," he says with a grin.

Our arms are still tangled together and I sense a blush cross my face as I pull my hand from his. Wow, he held me the whole flight.

"Sorry. Didn't mean to pass out on you."

"It's okay," he assures me. "If it helps you get through the flight... whatever works."

I run my hands through my hair and cringe at the thought of my appearance. "I must look like something the cat dragged in and the kittens wouldn't have." A stupid saying of my father's. One I can't tamp down before it bubbles out.

Kyle merely laughs and unhooks his seatbelt.

We file off the plane—Rick's still wearing his sunglasses, obviously to mask his hangover—and we head down to baggage claim. We retrieve our bags and the booth and Rick says he'll haul it back to the office in his truck.

Kyle slings his suitcase over his shoulder and walks me out to the curb where I step to the cab queue. His eyes are slightly dilated in the early morning light and he says, "Come on Vanessa, no need for a cab. I'll give you a ride home."

My whole body aches and sings at the same time from the deliciousness of spending the night in Kyle's arms. Strangely enough, I don't I feel like I've cheated on Rory. I just got some comfort from a friend.

A friend who looks like heaven first thing in the morning. Kyle's cheeks are stubbled with dark hair shadowing his stern jaw. I want to reach out and touch his face, but that would be ludicrous. We ride in silence, other than me giving him directions to Porter Square, and the Ministry of Sound CD he has playing.

At the front of my house, Kyle parks the car and turns to me. For a split second, he has that look like he wants to kiss me. I almost want that too. Almost.

"Thanks for the ride home, Kyle. And for helping on the plane."

Kyle merely smiles. "It was a pleasure traveling with you, Ms. Virtue. Let's do it again real soon."

My next trip is San Francisco—to see Rory and have our third (sex?) date—and I realize right then that the last person I want on that trip is Kyle Nettles.

CHAPTER SIXTEEN

"**I** can't leave town anymore," I say to Griz at lunch two weeks later. "Something happens to you every time. And it's the same foot."

So far this September, I've been to Orlando, Tucson, and Atlanta and I've racked up a ton of sales leads, as well as frequent flier miles. Turbulence on the way back from Tucson had me using of the barf bag (thank God I was traveling alone) and two shots of tequila helped me weather the storm down to Atlanta. I've got to find a better way to survive these flights or else I'll get an ulcer.

But my fatigue pales in comparison to Griz's woes.

"Quit judging me," she says, plunging her fingers into her reddish-brown hair. "Fussing at me is a monumental waste of time."

Ignoring her, I ask, "How did your foot get run over?"

"Rick and I went out Saturday night to—"

"—I can't believe how stupid you two are being," I say with my mouth full of tuna salad. Course, who am I to talk, sneaking around under the cover of Miami darkness with our sworn corporate enemy. And napping on an airplane on the Hazel-Eyed Hunk's shoulder.

She harrumphs. "As I was saying, we hailed a cab on Lansdowne, but these X'd out college bitches ran in front of us and got into it. The cab's back tire ran over my foot and I screamed bloody murder."

"Griz, you are the poster child for 'Shit Happens.'"

"I know! Rick told the driver we were going to sue. The cabbie drove me to the hospital for free."

"So, what's the diagnosis?"

"It's pretty swollen, but it'll be fine in about a week." Her face falls and it seems like she's about to lose it. "I swear to God. No decent-looking guy is going to ask me out in this condition."

"Doesn't seem to bother Rick." Because I don't necessarily want to be privy to Griz breaching company rules, I change the subject. "So, what have I missed while I've been out of the office?"

She takes a bite of her sandwich and her eyes grow large as she chews and quickly swallows. "Did I tell you Jiles Chancey said if I'm talking to customers then I need diction tapes to get rid of my Chicago accent?"

"Now you know why Jack calls him Little Baby Jesus."

She waves her hand in the air and dismisses it. "He's a jackass. I'm glad I don't have to deal with him on a regular basis."

"Well, I do." I take a sip of Diet Coke. "I was here this weekend putting leads into the sales system and all he could say to me was 'well, it had to be done, didn't it?'"

"Why do you push yourself so hard to please him?"

"Because I want Jiles to know I'm a team player and willing to do what's necessary to get the job done."

Griz throws her hands up. "God, I'm so sick of hearing that, Vanessa. Why does his opinion matter so much to you?"

I sit up straight and pound the table with my fist for emphasis. "He's the ultimate authority on everything here at work."

"This isn't the only job in town," she notes.

"Don't you listen to the news?" I ask. "The economy is in the crapper. Unemployment is high and companies aren't recruiting like they used to."

"Jiles can't rule your life like this," she says, pointing the corner of her sandwich at me. "It's just a job. You'll have many more before you retire."

I shake with frustration. "I still have to prove myself. Every. Day."

Griz says, "Vanessa, you've got the job; stop interviewing for it."

I lower my voice and laser my eyes at her. "Well, *you* won't have one for long with your little office tryst. What's gotten into you?"

She chews her sandwich and winks. "Rick's almost gotten into me. Maybe on our third date."

I hold up my hands. "TMI. If you're dating, that's your business, but I don't want to be around when you get called into HR for breaking the rules."

"If it's true love, then how can it be breaking the rules?"

I can't believe her *laissez faire* attitude. Obviously, she doesn't have the bills that I do; otherwise she'd be more concerned about keeping her job. I don't have time for this, though. Especially after the guilt of having too much fun on the Vegas trip with Kyle and Rick. I probably wasn't as professional as I should have been. Now that I'm back in the office, I've got to focus. First off is the training for the new version of The Director. It's out of beta testing and ready to roll to the sales and marketing teams.

When I return from lunch, Jack has other ideas and is distracting me from my professional demeanor. In the training room, he hands me a sheet of paper with squares drawn in the middle. Each block contains a buzzword like "synergy," "core competencies," "value added" and "win-win."

"What's this?"

"It's secret office bingo." He sets his coffee next to the terminal. "Whenever one of those phrases is used," he points, "mark the card. When you get a line filled, you win."

All right, I'll admit it. I love when Jack comes up with activities to take our minds off the corporate meeting blather. Most of these meetings are meaningless to us anyway. We're marketing. We just enact the plans, get the leads, and dole them out. No need to play the corporate games.

Kyle walks into the room and our eyes meet. He looks very focus-driven himself. I smile, hoping he'll lighten up. He's so much cuter when the dimple shows.

For over an hour, Jiles prattles on about our new iPhone and Android apps that give clients follow-up (hey, that's a phrase on the bingo card!) information at all times. He sits on the table. "We'll unveil the new features at the tradeshow in San Francisco."

"But Jiles," Ted speaks up. "If I can demo this right now, I'll have at least four sales this week."

Scratching his beard, Jiles says, "Not gonna happen, man. We have to rock and roll in a hot environment. It'll be a win-win situation. We're doing a big splash in San Fran. Hold it in your pants a few more days, and then we'll set the snake free."

Everyone in the room laughs as I stare in disbelief at the obvious penis reference.

Wait, he said "win-win," that's on my bingo card, too.

Jiles continues. "Due to security and the cost of demo disks, we're going to pre-qualify the lead *before* a disk goes out."

"Why don't we just put it on a secure server online for downloading?" Reagan asks.

"No. That's not how I want to do it," Jiles says.

"Primarily we're protecting the data's integrity," Little Baby Jesus says as he shifts his short legs to the floor.

"I've got 'integrity'," Jack whispers to me.

Jiles crooks his mouth. "Bottom line is our procedure is changing."

I roll my eyes. At the meeting. At the discussion. At the game. Sending out a demo disk for our software shouldn't be this complicated. This is an example of management *not* listening to the workers who probably know best.

Kyle pipes up. "Excuse me for saying, but this is bullshit. Customers aren't going to like this at all, Jiles."

My head snaps up and I almost gasp noticeably. *Whoa!* Boy Wonder just went against the master. Pride swells in my chest as I watch Kyle step up for the customers, the sales team, hell, for the employees here at DigitalDirection who have to execute this new initiative.

Jiles holds his hands up. "Lasso the 'tude Nettles. I have my reasons."

Frustration steams off Kyle in a most obvious way. "Sorry. Continue."

Pacing a bit, Jiles says, "A demo disk can be sent to a prospect, but first they must sign a license agreement."

"What?"

"No way!"

"For a demo?"

"It'll slow the sales process down tenfold."

LBJ shouts and stops the cacophony of sales voices declaring their disbelief. "This isn't a democracy. It's coming from the board. Each disk will have a registration number and everyone will sign this"—holding up a document—"agreement saying they won't try to break the code."

"This is asinine. Just to look at software? Most companies allow free demo downloads on their website," Kyle says firmly, his jaw set in defeat.

Jiles doesn't blink. "We don't want any demo disks of this new version falling into the hands of SalesTracker in particular."

I immediately think of Rory and I wonder if his sales team has to deal with the same corporate ridiculousness as well.

"Jiles, you know damn well that if SalesTracker wants a copy of our demo, they'll get it... easily," Ted interjects.

"We can try to stop them, man," Jiles says. "If needed, we'll arm everyone here with the knowledge of a S.W.A.T. team."

I shake my head. Kyle's right. This is going to be a bloody nightmare. If leads are slowed down, it will hinder the entire sales process. If I've learned anything since joining DigitalDirection, it's that the pipeline of potential customers has to stay full. And it's marketing's job to see to that. My job.

I peer across at Kyle who is taking assiduous notes on iPad. He runs his hand through his thick hair and slumps in his chair. Our eyes hook up and he shakes his head slightly.

Jiles wraps up. "It'll all work out to enhance our bottom line for value added benefits. Now, everyone get back to your training."

As Jiles leaves the room, Jack leans in and stage whispers, "Value added put me over the top. Bingo!"

I brush him off. "Like that was hard."

Our trainer, Morgan stands up and starts working through the new bells and whistles of The Director. I try to follow along, but all I can think about is the InfoTech Show. Five thousand attendees will be at San Francisco's famed Moscone Center. It's a lot of pressure now that we're unveiling the new version. A lot of continued publicity and marketing, which Jack and I have been diligently working on in preparation for the show and the launch. I'll need our top sales people to help pull off this show. And even though I've got plans for the all-important third date with Rory, I know the only way to have total success for the launch there's only one person who can really make it happen.

The training wraps up and I gather all of my notes. Kyle stops and holds the door for me and I step through, our hands brushing accidentally. My insides ache for a moment and I know it's best to make distance.

"Everything will work out." He winks and turns down the opposite aisle. His confidence is infectious. Somehow I know everything will be okay.

At my desk, I notice my voice mail light is on. It's probably Griz calling to say she fell out the window or something.

I press "1" to play the new message and gasp when I hear, "Hey, Vanessa. It's Rory." I snag the receiver, taking it off speaker. The message continues. "I can't wait to see you." He pauses and I swear my breathing stops to take in the meaning of his words. I get a tingly feeling hearing his deep voice. "Hey, I heard there's a new version of The Director. Maybe you can give me a demo? Call or e-mail and let me know."

Here I thought I was going to use him to get information and now he wants to see *our* demo. Maybe I should simply steer clear of business talk with him altogether. DigitalDirection doesn't need me dabbling in any kind of subterfuge or intrigue. I don't want to be disloyal to my company, but I don't want to be rude to Rory. Won't he be able to see a demo if he simply hangs around our booth? Or will *he* have to sign the new license agreement?

I start to call, but my palms get sweaty and I don't know what to say. I want to discuss our kisses, our touches, not our software. But Rory's a rule breaker. He likes to win. And while I admire that, I don't want to be a bump in his road to success.

I send him an e-mail instead:

Sorry I missed your call. Perhaps we can arrange a private viewing of the software?

What a tart, I think, as I re-read the unsent message. Maybe not. I delete the last line and type, *When do you get in town?*

An hour later, his response reads: *I'll be in Thursday. Can't wait to see you. R.*

Relief cascades over me. He's not talking business; he's talking us. Maybe he was merely using it as an excuse to e-mail. Yeah, that's it. It won't jeopardize my position to hang out with him—when no one else is around—and explore these niggling feelings I've got. No one needs to know.

One of the tech guys drops off a CD-ROM demo disk.

"I need you to sign the license agreement," he says, handing me a form.

"Are you kidding me?"

Humorless bastard that he is, he flattens his mouth. "Rules are rules."

"I work here." I say quickly.

"Either sign it and get your disk or take it up with Jiles Chancey."

"Fine." I scribble my signature, Hollywood star style, and hand it back to the guy. Jiles has just made working here even more difficult.

The things we'll do for a paycheck.

CHAPTER SEVENTEEN

"I'm not going down there, Wills," I shout out across the apartment Tuesday evening as I pack for San Fran.

"Vanessa, don't be such a pussy," he says.

"I can't help it. Sort of comes naturally."

I tread down the hall to William's room and flop on his bed. He's stretched out in boxers and the Paris Las Vegas T-shirt I'd brought him from my trip, reading "Pride and Prejudice."

"Why are you washing your slinky underwear?" He digs through the pile in my arms and produces a see-through pair of panties. "Is it because of that gorgeous guy from Cuchi Cuchi?

"Who? Kyle?"

"Yeah, Kyle," he mocks in girly voice. "The one with the killer body and gorgeous eyes.

Yep, that would be Kyle. "He's just a co-worker. Nothing more." I don't care what Griz thinks she's doing with Rick. Rules are rules and *I'm* not breaking them.

"Uh-huh... sure. Kyle, Kyle, Kyle, that's all you talk about."

First Griz, now William. All I want is to get my clothes cleaned so I can finish packing for my trip. "William, please. I can't go down into that basement."

"Just do it for her," Mia shouts through the bedroom wall.

I lay my head on William's shoulder. "Oh, all right. How many loads do you have?"

"Two." I try not to gloat. "You're a doll."

As William heads for the basement, I continue packing. Okay, maybe I have selected the best underwear sets. I've got my new black lace bra and thong panties—which feel like dental floss up the butt—and my black one-piece hold-everything-in-place thingy with the snaps between the legs (for smoothing out purposes.)

I can't wait to wake up in the morning, hop a cab to Logan and wing out to the Left Coast. Ted and Reagan get in after me, so I'll get the booth built and then try to find Rory.

"Vanessa!" William calls up from the basement. "I don't know if these pants can go in the washer. Come down here."

Every hair on my body stands on end. But William is with me; I'll be okay. I put on my flip-flops—the basement floor is *nasty*—and head into the dark recesses of our house.

It smells like old furniture, wet cardboard, and laundry detergent. There's a triple bolted cellar door to the right at the bottom of the rickety, narrow staircase. Dan Paulsen—the land lizard, as William calls him—is the only one allowed to use the door since he's paranoid about someone breaking in.

"No problem. They can go in," I say when William holds up the two pairs of pants in question. "So, what should I do?"

He stuffs the clothes into the washer. "About what?

"About Rory?"

"We were talking about Kyle a minute ago."

I grit my teeth. "No. You were. Focus, would you?"

"Do you like him?"

"Who? Kyle?" I asked, feeling a bit defensive.

William laughs. "No, dumb shit, Rory?"

"Oh, right... Rory. Yes, I do. There's mystery to him. He's got an edge."

"And Kyle doesn't?"

"Kyle's not part of the equation." God, he's as bad as Griz.

Sighing, William says, "You're not answering my question. If you could get down and dirty with anyone in the world, would Rory be at the top of the list?"

Remarkably, the first image that flashes in my mind is of Kyle. I'd seen him at work today bending to retrieve a soda from the machine. He caught me looking at him, so I laughed it off and said he had something on his pants. The look on his face made me blush as this sort of moment passed between us. My brain screams out that it's Rory I want, but my body ignites every time Kyle is around. I don't understand why I'm so sexually "on" all of a sudden. Maybe it's because I've been out of the game so long.

I need medication.

Which reminds me that I have a prescription for Atavan that's supposed to help calm me down on the flight. I have to remember to pack it in my purse

Getting back to William's question, I say, "Sure Rory would be at the top of the list. Don't you think so after everything I've told you?"

"I don't know," he says. "I've never met the guy. All I have to go by is what you say." William pours detergent on top of the clothes. "Is there something more than physical attraction?"

"Sure, he's a risk taker. Doesn't play by the rules. I admire that. And he makes me feel good about myself."

William faces me. "He's got a dimple too, doesn't he?"

"Sort of. He has a cleft in his chin. How'd you know?"

He stops and then says, "I know what it's like to fall for a dimple." After a moment, he says. "Just go for it."

I try not to think of the professional repercussions if we were to be discovered by anyone at SalesWanker or DigitalDirection. Then again, I be a risk-taker, too.

"Just take care of yourself, Vanessa. I don't want to see you get hurt," William says, pointing a finger at me.

I reach over and hug him. "You're the best, Wills."

He pats me on the back. "Did you bring the next load down?"

"No, I left it by the kitchen door."

"No worries," he says, brushing past me.

"William... I... "

The lazy chug-a-chug-a-chug of the washer reverberates off the stone walls of the basement. My crazy heartbeat echoes along in a syncopated rhythm.

Okay, I'm a big girl. I can sit here for one freaking minute while William goes upstairs. Nothing's going to...

There's a pounding on the window.

"AHH!" I almost jump out of my skin. When I look up to the glass panel, all I see are beady eyes inside a helmet. My heart slams in my chest and I make a mad dash for the stairs.

William bolts down the wooden staircase. "What's wrong?!"

I point at the window and scurry behind him for cover. "There's some sort of helmet-clad monstrosity out there. He's trying to break in."

"Hold on." He reaches for the snow shovel hanging on the wall.

"Like that's going to help," I hiss out.

"Shut up," William scolds. "Who's there?"

We see a finger tap on the windowpane. "I locked myself out. Let me in." the muffled voice says.

"Oh no you don't!" I shout, pulling at William's waistband.

He turns and laughs. "It's the land lizard."

"Mr. Paulsen?"

William lays the shovel against the wall and shouts up, "Come around to the side door. I'll let you in."

The helmeted shadow disappears from the window.

"I don't want to see him." I gather the clothes strewn on the floor and hand them to William. "You deal with this" —plopping the clothes in his arms— "and him" —pointing to the cellar door—" and I'll get you anything you want for dinner."

"Yes, but is Johnny Depp available on such short notice?"

Of course I can't get out of town without a late night visit from Griz following a call from my mother.

"Mom told me when I was a little girl, I couldn't say San Francisco. It always came out Fran Sancisco," I relay to Griz.

"That's adorable," she says, munch on the pita chips and hummus on my dresser.

"Talking to my mother is not adorable. She thinks I should move home and go into business with her."

"What kind of business?"

"Hairdressing."

She screws up her face. "You?"

I look over into the mirror at my messy ponytail. "Why would you say that?"

"You *are* looking at yourself in the mirror, right?"

"Thanks a lot."

Griz plops on my bed and starts her own line of questioning.

"What's the obsession with San Francisco?" Griz asks.

"I don't know. I've always thought it looked cool in movies and on television." I fold my blue jeans neatly and place them in the suitcase. "When I was a teenager, I went through a Journey phase."

"I thought they were from Philadelphia?"

Here she goes again. "Nope. San Fran. They sang about it."

"Don't they have the one-armed drummer?"

"No, that's Def Leppard."

"And they're from Austria, right?"

I plunge my fingers into my hair. "I can't do this tonight."

She follows me to the bathroom where I pile toiletries into my bag.

"Are you going to look up your old boyfriend while you're out there?" she asks without a care. Two days ago, I'd gotten an e-mail from a Delta Gam sorority sister saying my former college boyfriend, Alan Partridge, now lives in San Fran. He works for one of those Silicon Valley companies that managed to survive the dot.bomb era.

"I don't think so." I have enough men haunting my every thought as it is without adding an ex into the mix.

Griz follows me back to my room and flops on the bed while I continue to cram items into the suitcase. "I'm nervous as hell about this product launch as well as seeing Rory," I tell her.

"What're you going to do about it?"

"I don't have a game plan, per se. Any advice?"

"It ain't nuthin' but a chicken wing," she says with a laugh.

"What the...? Please speak English," I beg.

"You know Marcell in accounting? He's from South Carolina. Says it all the time. It means it's no big thing. Don't make such a huge hairy deal out of this trip. Get your job done and then show Rory you want him," she says. "Guys have to be told these things."

"But, do I know what I want?" Yeah, I want a plate of Buffalo wings with bleu cheese dressing on the side. "You're right. You know me, though. Doesn't take much to set off my self-doubt."

The fact that Rory's e-mails have been more "business" in tone makes me think he's not looking forward to seeing me as much as I've been looking forward to seeing him. There's something weird there... something distant. I don't want to feel this way. I know it's just the elves of self doubt. I need to tell them to fuck off.

"Talking to your mother didn't help."

I brush aside her armchair psychology. "I don't want to lose my job for having an affair with Rory."

"The rules say no dating within our company, not dating *between* companies. Besides, who has to know? I'm not telling."

"I'd hate for Jiles Chancey to get wind of it." *Or Kyle.*

"Screw Jiles," she says with a laugh.

"I'd rather not." I have someone much more desirable in mind.

She stares off, like she's watching a movie in her mind. "You know the intrigue of an illicit affair kind of like what Rick and I've got going is totally hot."

I want more than an illicit affair. I want a connection. Something *real*. I want a relationship, not a one-night stand. I just haven't told Griz that yet. "This isn't a reality TV show, Griz. This is my life!"

"What do I always tell you, Vanessa? Go with the flow. Don't make me say it again."

"You just did."

When my plane touches down the next morning and I loosen my death-grip on the armrest, I decide to listen to Griz and go with the flow. Why not, the Atavan has certainly taken off the rough edges and I feel like I'm floating in Marshmallow Fluff.

I'll let San Francisco captivate me and move my emotions. And I'll see where things go with Rory.

First, I need a cab, though.

I haul my suitcase into the taxi and head into town. I had no idea the airport was so far out of the city. This explains why I haven't seen the Golden Gate Bridge yet. The cab pulls up in front of the Sir Francis Drake Hotel on Powell Street. A friendly doorman dressed as a Beefeater opens the car door and takes my bags. I check in and am very pleased to have a corner room overlooking Union Square, full of sketch artists and pigeons. I wonder if I'll have the opportunity to show off the leopard-patterned comforter to Rory. My heart accelerates at the thought of being with him and it's like my body is on fire for his touches and kisses. Dammit, I'm so ripe, I'm about to fall off the tree.

I change into jeans and a black sweater and head back downstairs to get directions to the convention center from the Beefeater who's standing at the door. Thankfully, it's only a short walk from the hotel.

Once there, I descend into the bowels of the Moscone Center via one of its many escalators. My exhibitor badge allows me access into the great hall before the show officially opens. Inside the concrete giant, I see that DigitalDirection's ten-by-twenty booth is going to be upstaged by the massive, flashier tech displays being constructed all around me.

I check in at the show decorator's blue-draped area to inquire on my work orders. The lady behind the counter is most helpful. "Our system shows your shipment is on the loading dock. The handlers will bring the crates over to your space. Go on over and register for your union labor."

After completing all of the paperwork, I go to my booth space to wait. And wait... For an hour and a half. Finally, a small forklift deposits my booth case and boxes into space number 2222.

"There you go, sis," the man says and drives off.

That's when the trouble starts.

I didn't know I wasn't allowed to *touch* my own boxes. When I do, a union boss charges over and shouts, "You can't do that!"

"It's my stuff," I yell back.

A harsh woman, missing a bottom front tooth, steps forward. "That's unions' job to open those boxes. Didn't you contract help?"

I don't like being talked to like this. I produce my forms. "I've been waiting forever for someone to show up."

She snatches the paperwork from me. "Be right back."

Witchypoo, the boss, reappears ten minutes later with a one-armed man named Sid. This has to be a joke. I'm paying by the hour for a laborer and they send me a guy with one arm.

"Now, missy... you may direct Sid and..."

"Don't talk to me like that. My name is Vanessa." I cross my hands in front of my chest and tap my foot.

She eyeballs me and continues. "As I was saying, you can instruct Sid, but he's to do the work. Those are the rules."

Two hours later, with hardly any of the booth pieces in place, I've had enough. Sid's nice enough—even though he's taken two cigarette breaks—so I go straight to the show organizer.

"I don't mean to complain," I say, "but the union guy they sent me only has one arm and it's taking forever to assemble our booth. I refuse to continue wasting my company's money like this."

The organizer radios for the union boss to come to her office. Witchypoo appears and glares at me. When the organizer explains the situation, Witchypoo won't budge.

"I have an idea," I say. "Why don't you send me another one-armed man so we can get this thing up before the show starts tomorrow." I flatten my mouth to let them know I mean business. I may be young, but no one's going to walk all over me.

"Now you listen here you little—"

I take a challenging pose. "Look, I'm going back to my booth to work. I've lost a great deal of time and money this morning."

I sigh at the mess in space 2222. "Okay, Sid. We have to step on it." He shrugs with his nub of an arm.

We struggle, but work in tandem. I'm sweating to death in this sweater and I wish I'd worn something lighter. The sleeves are stretched from pushing at them, so much that they won't stay above my elbows. My makeup is smeared, my hair is a clumped mess, and I've broken three fingernails. And people think working in marketing is glamorous.

Just when I think I'm at the end of my rope, I hear a soft, husky voice from behind.

"You look like you could use an extra hand."

"Oh, Rory!" I exclaim in surprise and relief, coupled with silly heart palpitations that threaten my consciousness. "You're a knight in shining armor."

He lifts an eyebrow. "Now that's a role I could get used to."

Chapter Eighteen

I'm so glad Rory showed up when he did. With his help, we finished the booth in twenty minutes flat. When Witchypoo tried to make an issue of it, Rory sauntered over, whispered something to her that made her laugh, and then acted like it was nothing at all. I turned in my paperwork, tipped Sid well, and downed a bottle of water.

"So, what's on your agenda now?" Rory asks as we cross Market Street near the cable car stop on our way to the hotel.

I look down at my disheveled appearance. "A shower."

He smiles down into my eyes with fierce sapphire ones of his own. "After that."

I swallow the lump that's quickly formed in my throat. "Well, I want to ride the cable car and hang off the front, like the people on the Rice-a-Roni box."

Rory throws his head back and laughs. "You're adorable."

I sense a blush creeping up my throat, but I continue, thinking about Ted and Reagan. "The only other thing is I'm meeting up later with people from work for dinner."

He's fixated on me as we tromp up the hill.

"What?" I ask, feeling a bit self-conscious. "Is something wrong?"

He stops and turns me to look at him. His finger traces down the side of my face from the temple to my chin. Every nerve ending on my body is on alert and I'm riveted into place on the sidewalk. People grumble as they walk by, bumping me. It does nothing to knock me out of my trance. I'm unaware of the city life shuffling around us because I'm absorbed in the depths of his face.

"It's good to see you, Vanessa."

"You too, Rory." I say breathlessly. He holds my gaze for what seems like hours. I bask in the adoration, although there seems to be something almost regretful in his eyes. As if he has something to tell me, but won't just spit it out.

Then he surprises me when he says, "You have great eyes. There must be a lot behind them."

My heart flutters in my chest and goose bumps run up and down my arms. That's one of the smoothest lines I've ever heard. I wonder if he's been practicing that one.

"Thanks," I say, gulping. "There is. I mean, if you want to spend the time to find out." I surprise myself with my boldness.

Before I can say anything else, his lips connect with mine in a scorching moment that I sends zaps of energy through my body all the way down to my toes. My senses soar to heights I've never experienced before and I know for sure that I want even more.

When I open my eyes, Rory's beaming at me. I smile brightly and we lace our fingers together as we continue along. I like the way my hand fits inside his. Warm and protected. At the hotel, we break long enough to go to our rooms, freshen up, and check messages.

I have a voice mail from Ted. "Hey, Virtue. Reagan's with clients and I'm in my room making calls. We're meeting up in the lobby at seven for dinner. See ya then." It's not so much an invitation as a must-do sort of thing.

Forty minutes later, Rory and I board the cable car at Market Street. I push my way to the car and nab the spot up front on the left. I spend the whole ride hanging off the front of the car like I've always wanted to do.

"Don't fall," Rory says, clutching my waist from behind. I like the way his fingers curl into my hips protectively and I feel like Leonardo DiCaprio... well, *Queen* of the World, anyway.

The view from the trolley is amazing with the Pacific Ocean stretching out for miles. But, wispy clouds and haze ride low over the Bay, blocking my view of the Golden Gate Bridge.

"Well, that sucks. I wanted to see the bridge," I say in disappointment.

"It's typical," he says. "San Fran's weather is consistent year round—a bit on the chilly side, with overcast skies."

"Thanks for the update, Al Roker. Now, what about wishing happy 106th birthday to granny in Wichita?"

Rory first sneers at me, then he can't help but laugh.

We hop off at Ghirardelli Square and walk along the waterfront to Fisherman's Wharf where we watch the fishing boats unload their fresh catch of the day. Restaurants line the street; as do vendors selling chili, crab legs, and delectable and aromatic foods. Rory buys clam chowder in a sourdough bread bowl and we sit at an open table. "Wanna share?" he asks, handing me a spoon.

"Sure. Thanks." I'm a huge chowder snob, considering I live in New England, but I relish the contact with Rory. I want to savor every minute of it. As we eat, he tells me about his first visit to San Francisco five years ago.

"I had this crazy idea of working on a fishing boat," he says, licking his spoon. He stops for a moment when he sees me watching him. My face heats and I drop my eyes to the soup as he continues. "A buddy told me it was amazing here—you could blend in and never be seen."

"I love cities. Being an Air Force brat, I've lived in some out of the way places. That's why I love Boston," I say. "I get the atmosphere of a big city without losing my identity. I can't stand small town Generica where everyone knows your business and all of the stores and restaurants are the same."

"I know what you mean," he notes. "I need to be in a place where I can disappear into a crowd. I hate to bring attention to myself." He tosses a crust of the bread bowl to a flock of pigeons who bound in and attack, fighting each other for a nibble.

The man can't help but bring attention to himself with his six-foot plus athletic frame and blond hair that's a bit too long right now. His eyes alone stand out like two sapphires in the snow. There's an edge to him, a danger, a roughness. I'm indisputably drawn to him and there's nothing I can do to stop it.

A bit bowled over by this realization, I try to slow my crazy pulse and find out more about this man than I'm falling for. I ask, "Did you grow up in a small town?"

"Yeah, Everyone Knows Your Business, Indiana," he says with a sneer. "Couldn't wait to escape. You all done here?" Rory clears his throat, shifting his stare back to the bowl of chowder for one last bite, thus ending our brief "get to know me" chatter.

"Um, sure. Yeah." Usually men love talking about themselves; it's in their testosterone. Rory doesn't want to seem to open up at all.

He takes my hand in his and tucks it into his coat pocket. "Let's walk down The Embarcadero and see the sea lions."

He wraps his arm around my waist and brings me so close that I can almost feel his heartbeat through his windbreaker. I like that I have an effect on his metabolism, too. I'm certainly no wanton sex goddess, but he makes me feel sexy. And wanted.

We wander into the touristy Pier 39 area filled with specialty shops, bay view restaurants and other fun attractions. The pier provides visitors with postcard views of Alcatraz, the Golden Gate Bridge—when the fog lifts—and the skyline.

"I need to get some batteries for my camera," he says. So, we pick our way through the crowd and into a shop of knickknacks, jewelry, and San Fran memorabilia. He wanders off and I take in the jewelry display. My eyes fall to a pair of silver and opal dangle earrings. I hold them up to my ear and notice Rory's reflection in the mirror behind me.

"Those are dazzling." He wraps his hand around to rest on my stomach. "Or maybe it's just you," he whispers.

My stomach lurches uncontrollably in a lovely ache of need and want. His eyes say everything his words won't. There's desire smoking in his eyes. Especially when he's looking at me like that.

I can't put a name on my feelings. Is it love or just lust? Or is it the high from the intrigue we've got going on with our stealth interaction. I give the pierced earrings back to the sales girl and turn to Rory. "Did you get everything you needed?"

"Actually, I need one more thing. Why don't you look around?"

I go over to the postcard rack and pick out one for William: a semi-clad, buff, beefcake guy stretched out over the Golden Gate Bridge with the caption, "Open your Golden Gate." Perfect for him. I pay for the card and shove it into my purse, looking around for Rory.

He surprises me. "Wanna go see the sea lions now?"

"Sure thing." He takes me by the hand and leads me out through the innumerable shops and hordes of people to the end of the pier. I luxuriate in the feel of his fingers pressed against mine, protectively guiding me through the hordes of people blocking our way.

We round the corner and I lean over the wooden railing to look at a pile of slick sea creatures, who, according to the sign, took up residence here after an earthquake. Several sea lions slide up onto the pier, pointing their noses up as they bark gleefully.

"They're so adorable," I say. "I wish I could take one of them home as a souvenir."

Rory turns to me. "Why don't you take these home instead?"

He places a small tissue-wrapped item in my hand.

Hastily, I unfurl the paper and gasp.

Out pop the precious opal and silver earrings.

CHAPTER NINETEEN

Ted has dinner reservations for us at a restaurant not too far from the hotel. He and I hop a cab and Reagan's supposed to meet us there. When she walks in, though, my treacherous heart trips and falls when I see who arrives with her.

Kyle.

I had no idea he was coming to San Francisco.

"Well, this is a surprise," I say, barely able to comprehend that he's here.

"Vanessa, you look great tonight," he says, pulling the chair out for me. The man has manners, I'll give him that.

I want to tell him he looks amazing, too, but I can't find the words that seem to collide in the back of my throat no matter how nice those gray slacks fit his legs or how soft his skin looks from the obvious fresh shave. I've got to break the tension in the air hanging in the midst of his spicy cologne that curls its fingers out to tempt me.

"Who let the dog out?" I ask with a grin, even though my pulse is trilling away.

"Jiles and the Willies thought it'd be a good idea for me to meet with customers, especially with the big demo launch," Kyle says. His smile is bright and genuine.

The four of us share a quiet dinner, indulging in a semi-expensive bottle of Chianti, compliments of Ted's expense report. I sense Kyle smiling at me through my dinner of swordfish, Cabernet and shallot reduction, and mashed potatoes. I'm slightly self-conscious when he looks at me in such a soft manner. Then, before the tiramisu arrives, I have that vision of us together again. Clear as day, as if I'm looking at a memory instead of a possibility. A house, 2.3 kids, a dog, and a minivan. My throat hitches and I start to cough. I reach out desperately for my glass of water.

Reagan moves toward me. "Are you okay, Vanessa?"

Ted starts to smack me on the back, but Kyle stretches his arm and does it instead. Reagan hands me her water.

I'm not interested in Kyle Nettles.

I'm not.

I can't be.

I'm interested in Rory.

What the hell is wrong with me? Must be residual affects of the Atavan.

"Something went down the wrong way," I manage to say.

My hands shake a bit as I regain my composure. I shift my eyes to view Kyle out of my peripherals. His hand rests on the table so close to my arm that I can almost feel the heat radiating from him. He smells so damn good, intoxicating my senses.

I've got to ignore Kyle and his... everything he does to me.

Fortunately, Ted's all business for the rest of dinner, carping about customers and software updates. "The demo numbers aren't as high as predicted because of that damn license agreement. You've got to get rid of it."

"I can't do anything about that," Kyle adds. "I've talked to Jiles, but his mind is made up."

"Yeah, man, but you've got to get rid of this stumbling block. It's slowing down the sales process," Ted adds.

To block out the corporate babble, I play with the dangly earrings Rory bought me. My secret connection to him. We're supposed to hook up later at the Starlight Room on the top floor of our hotel. If I can break away and get there.

Outside after dinner, Ted lights a cigarette and asks, "Where to next?"

"I thought I'd turn in early," I say.

"No way," Reagan says, wrapping her arm around me. "This is our first trip together and we're going to do it up right." She holds out her cell phone and start moving her finger over the screen, checking possibilities on Yelp, Foursquare, and UrbanSpoon.

If I'm not able to get away from my co-workers, I have to at least find a way to get to where Rory will be. I don't want him to think I'm ignoring him.

Wreathed in a miasma of Ted's cigarette smoke, I wave my hands about and quickly suggest, "Why don't we try out that bar at the top of our hotel? Looks pretty cool and we won't have far to go to our rooms if we get blitzed."

Kyle laughs, "They have dancing up there, too." He smiles at me and I wonder why chill bumps graze my arms, my body betraying me. Must be the evening air.

"Sounds like a plan," Reagan says with a smile.

When we step off of the elevator into the Starlight Room, Rory is one of the first people I see. Good thing I'm decked out in a new red wrap-around Anne Taylor dress because this place is like a swanky cocktail party. The 30's style glamorous nightclub has luxurious high-back booths, red curtains, and mirrors. The classy crowd is grooving to the swing sounds of the small six-piece orchestra.

We take a booth, date-like: girl, boy, girl, Kyle. Impatiently, Ted signals for the waitress, who is wearing a long, formal evening gown. He pretentiously asks to see a cocktail menu.

When he moves to light a cigarette, our waitress stops him. "It's against California state code to smoke here, sir."

Ted swears under his breath, pushes out of his chair, and asks us to order him a Dirty Martini. Then he makes his way back to the elevator to go outside for a smoke. I order a yummy drink called The Cable Car, made of lemon, sugar and Captain Morgan's.

I watch Rory moving to the music with a woman I assume to be his client. He's doing much better than he did in Atlantic City, not flailing his lanky legs as much. The woman laughs up at him. I'm jealous, but it's because I want to dance with him. Should I cut in? Probably not or someone will accuse me of hobnobbing with the enemy.

"Great, there's the guy from SalesTracker," Kyle notes.

"SalesWanker, more like," Reagan corrects.

"Which one?" I ask coyly.

"Give it up, Vanessa. You know who I'm talking about," Kyle says. "The one you're staring at."

Oh. I paste a weak smile on my face and am relieved when the waitress sets my drink in front of me. I've got to play this down and not rouse any suspicions. "Oh, right, that's Rory. We met him in Atlantic City, remember?"

"And Miami Beach," Kyle adds.

I finger the rim of my drink. "Right, he was there, too."

Kyle raises an inquisitive eyebrow. "He seems to be everywhere you are."

I must turn the tables, so I spin to face Kyle. "Say, what are you doing here anyway?"

His dimple pops when a devilish smile crosses his face. "At this club or in San Francisco?"

"On this trip. It seems weird that you're here, out of the blue, without my knowing. I plan these events, after all."

He leans in closer; the heat from his body warming me. "What, you don't like my company?" he teases.

"Sure. The more, the merrier," I say, playing off his proximity. Thing is, I don't need my office distraction, well, distracting me, when I'm making plans with Rory. With Kyle sitting here, I feel like I'm being disloyal—to whom?—by associating with Rory.

"I like being here, Vanessa," Kyle whispers. There's an ache in my stomach that resembles a craving or a longing and I quickly gulp at the sweet cocktail to wash the sensation away.

Reagan watches us curiously and reaches to the middle of the table for handful of peanuts. "Don't mind me over here."

Kyle reaches for his beer, his skin reddening over Reagan's comment. Very un-Kyle-like.

I glance at the dance floor at Rory. He throws a crooked smile my way and I nod, not really caring at this moment who sees it. I need to fan myself from the spiced rum warming my insides. Or maybe the heat is from the look in his eyes?

He excuses himself from his dance partner and makes his way through the crowd right to my table. Looks like Rory's not playing games anymore, either.

"Hey there DigitalDirection people," he says, sliding into the booth next to Reagan. "Rory Ellery. And you are?"

"Reagan Vanbiesbrouck. You work for SalesTracker, right?"

"He sure does," Kyle says, sitting tall in the booth.

Rory points an accusatory finger Kyle's way. "Aren't you the guy who stole EG Venture Capital away from me?"

Kyle is ice cool. "Not my fault if they weren't happy with your customer service and promises of product enhancements that don't exist."

Rory picks up the dirty martini the waitress left for Ted and pops an olive into his mouth. "Trust me, our enhancements will shake the industry if I have anything to do with it."

Kyle and Rory both adjust in their seats and puff their chests out at each other. If I didn't know better, I would've thought they'd sprouted feathers, beaks and combs, and were about to go at it like fighting cocks. *Roosters, that is.*

Reagan goes into saleswoman mode. "I spoke with Young Electronics and they said you've been out to see them."

Rory snags a couple of cashews from the bowl. His gaze touches mine briefly and he starts to answer Reagan.

"Reagan, don't talk business with this guy, he's trouble," Kyle says firmly. "No consorting with the enemy. Right Vanessa?"

I give Kyle a bit of a curious look, wondering exactly what he's getting at. Rory seems perturbed and Kyle is in gloating mode. I have to admit, I dig that Kyle swooped that account from SalesTracker. I don't want to talk business, though.

Instead, I answer Kyle's question. "I don't want to consort, but I do want to dance. Rory?"

"Absolutely," he says as he winks at Kyle in triumph.

We groove to a jazzy Glenn Miller piece the band sounds out. Rory spins and dips me and I swear Kyle is watching us with a keen eye. I'll probably get a lecture about dancing with the competition, but I don't care. I know I need to be cool, but I simply want to be with Kyle... er, I mean Rory. Jesus! What is wrong with me? Must be too much rum in that drink.

We stay at the Starlight Room past one a.m. when Ted disappears again in search of more cigarettes. Rory and I dance on and off the whole time, doing our best to be stealthy of our attraction to each other while we're on display for all to see. I want more from him. My own one-on-one meeting. I've got to get away from my work buddies.

We pile onto the elevator, but Reagan is a sloppy drunk, punching all the buttons and singing along with the Musak overhead. Kyle holds Reagan around the waist, steadying her as we descend.

"I wanna goodnight kisssss," she says with a slur. "How 'bout it, Nettles? You're cute. You, too, SalesWanker guy."

Rory lifts a brow.

"I think you've had too much to drink, Reagan," Kyle says, intervening. I feign a smile, but the green monster of jealousy has jumped on my back as I see the way Reagan is holding on to Kyle. Her hands are everywhere and she's making no bones about wanting to get him back to her room.

"Hey... Vanessa..." she says. "Look at us with two hot guys."

I don't respond.

Kyle braces Reagan against him. "I'll help you to your room."

"I can do that," I snap. "I mean, I'm a girl and all."

"That you are," Kyle says. "You're going to need help, though."

Rory catches my eye and holds up his cell phone. I glance at mine and see a text from a 206 area code.

Room number?

Anticipation circles around me and fills my nostrils as I breathe in. With one hand, I text back: *Room 1424.*

Rory winks and my stomach lurches in tantalizing expectation.

"Goodnight folks," Rory says as he steps off of the elevator.

I hope I'll see him soon.

Kyle and I nearly drag Reagan to her room on the eleventh floor. She's playful and fights us a bit, trying to get her fingers inside Kyle's shirt.

"Now now, Reagan."

She rolls her eyes at him and tries to open her door.

Inside her room, Reagan reaches for the front buttons of her blouse. "Okay then, you can help *me* take my shirt off, Nyle Kettles?"

"All right," I say sternly. I step between them.

"Whoa there, Reagan. Let Vanessa help you." Kyle runs his hands through his hair and takes a pace back. "You got this under control?"

Pleased that I cock-blocked Reagan's move on Kyle, I smile. "Yeah, I'm fine. I've got her."

He steps to the door. "I'm in 1409 if you need me for anything." He emphasizes *anything* a bit too much.

When he leaves, I get Reagan undressed as she swings her arms around in protest.

"He duzzzn't know what he's missin'," she slurs out. You'd think she would have learned her lesson with the server room fiasco. Apparently she's a glutton for punishment. I don't even try to get her to wash her face or brush her teeth. I just get her to bed, tuck her in, and put her on her side. Before I leave, I nab the wastebasket and put it near the bed.

"I didn't get my goodnight kiss!" she yells.

Dammit, I want *my* goodnight kiss from Rory. I reach over the bed and place a quick kiss on her forehead and vamoose.

Kyle is standing in the hallway waiting for the elevator. "She okay?"

"All set." I need to get to my room in case Rory's waiting. I step in the car with Kyle and we both reach for the

"14" button. "Ooh, sorry." My skin sings deliciously from the brief touch.

When the door slides open, I look down the hall. Thankfully, Rory's nowhere to be seen. I feel so dishonest. So sneaky. So conniving.

"Looking for someone?" he asks.

"No, just couldn't remember which way my room was." I bite my bottom lip at how quickly I'm able to come up with a cover story. "Goodnight, Kyle." I wave to him and I rush to my room.

I know in my heart of hearts there will be a knock on my door soon, so I've got to prepare. I kick off my shoes and run to the bathroom where I brush my teeth and splash some perfume on the appropriate pulse points. Then, I go to the desk and turn on my computer. Windows hums upon startup. I plunder through my CD case. What to choose? I have vintage JLo and Cher, several House mixes, and a Ministry of Sound Best Of. I choose something fast paced, with pulsating rhythms? Might drive a man insane. I pop The Director demo disk out of my drive and toss it onto the desk. As I click on the multimedia player, there's the knock I've been waiting for.

I can't see through the peephole because it's too high and I've lost three inches by tossing my shoes aside. I know who it is, though. I open the door and see his sexy smile and twinkling eyes. I reach forward and pull him in by the hand and the next thing I know, he has me pressed up against the yellow and green wallpaper as he goes on the offensive.

"You've been teasing me all day, Vanessa."

"I didn't do it on purpose."

"You didn't have to," Rory says as his lips close in.

We kiss like we've never done it before, breathing heavily and moving our hands everywhere to touch each other.

His tongue traces my mouth, fingers lacing through my hair. He maneuvers me until I feel the soft mattress on the backs of my legs.

I knead my hands into the firm flesh of Rory's back and slide them down to the waistband of his pants to yank his shirt free. His hands are on my shoulders, tugging at my dress. I rotate and push him to sit on the bed. My fingers trail the buttons on his shirt until his broad chest is revealed to me in all its glory.

I can't believe I'm being so forward, but I've been thinking about this for a while. A new Vanessa who lives on the edge, takes what she wants, and demands attention. This man wants to be with me. There are no rules. No regulations. No judgment.

Rory peels my dress off my arms until it hangs at my waist. His eyes take in my lacy black bra, and then his hands skim up my midriff to capture both breasts. My head falls back as the breath nearly leaves my body. His hands knead away gently, teasing my turgid nipple with his deft fingers. I don't think I can take anymore. I've waited long enough. Taking the initiative, I dive on him, laying us on the bed as we resume our foreplay.

He rolls me over and lowers his head to leave hot, wet kisses down my neck. Then, he nips at the lace of my bra with his teeth before dipping his tongue underneath the fabric. My back arches up off the bed to provide him with more of a playing field.

The blare of the room phone makes me jump.

"No!" I scream, and then cover my mouth in horror. Rory laughs and moves aside.

On the third ring, he says, "You better answer that. Might be important."

"Who's calling this late?" I sit up, adjust my dress, and snag the receiver. It's way too late—or early, depending on how you look at it. "Hello?"

"Vanessa..."

Kyle? My heart rate slams into overdrive. "What's wrong?"

"I wanted to make sure you're okay. You looked kind of panicked on the elevator. You weren't sleeping yet, were you?" he asks. "Sounds like you're having a party."

I push my hair out of my face. "Umm, no, I'm just playing some music on the computer."

Rory's weight lifts off the bed and he starts pacing. I mouth, "I'm sorry." He waves me off and goes to sit at the desk.

Kyle asks, "So, is everything all right?"

"Yeah, I'm fine." My heart accelerates hearing Kyle's concerned voice. I'm touched that he's checking on me.

"That was really nice of you to take care of Reagan."

"She would have done the same for me." At least, I hope she would.

I slice my eyes over and see Rory's fiddling with my music CDs. I turn away to try and finish this private conversation. My blood is coursing through my veins so much that I can hear my pulse reverberating in my head.

Kyle clears his throat. "So, what time are we supposed to be at the booth tomorrow, well, today actually."

"We start at nine," I say. "Be there early to help set up the laptops, if you can."

"Sure. Whatever you need me to do." He pauses. "You're doing an awesome job, Vanessa. You're really an asset to the company. I wish we had more people as dedicated and professional as you. You're a real team player."

Guilt washes over me like the surf. Yeah, a team player with the competition in her room.

"Thanks. I appreciate it. That means a lot to me."

"I mean it and I intend to tell Jiles how great you are."

I slump forward and hold my head in my hand while the other holds the receiver. I wish Kyle hadn't reminded me why I'm in San Francisco. It's not so I can have sex with someone I barely know. All of a sudden, this is tainted and just... *wrong.*

What else is weird is that part of me wants to curl up on the pillows and talk to Kyle all night or until one of us falls asleep. There's something about his soothing voice. No wonder the clients love him. But, Rory's still here and I have to figure out what to do now.

Kyle continues. "That guy from SalesTracker wasn't bothering you, was he?"

Taken aback, I don't say anything. I'm concerned about what Kyle thinks about me. Were Rory and I obvious about our attraction on the dance floor? "No, not at all," I lie.

His voice lowers, as if he's sharing a corporate trade secret. "Look, I've heard he'll do anything to make a sale and to get ahead."

I'm touched that Kyle is concerned and I feel guilty lying to him with Rory—who seems to be public enemy number one—sitting a few feet away.

This isn't right. None of it. It isn't responsible or professional. It's *not* how to get ahead in business.

"You don't have to worry about me," I say quietly.

"So you're okay?" he asks one more time.

"Umm, yeah, everything's cool." I hope the alcohol in his system dulls the hesitation in my voice.

"Well, you have fun, Vanessa." He laughs. "See you in the morning."

I return the receiver and expel the breath I've been holding.

Great. Now what the hell do I do?

CHAPTER TWENTY

I turn to Rory. "I'm sorry about that."

He shrugs as he sits there with an open shirt and gray boxers, his trousers draped over the chair. "Don't worry about it. Nosy co-worker?"

I scoot up on the bed against the headboard. "Something like that."

He lets out a long stream of air. I do the same. Everything's changed. The mood's been killed. His appetite for me has faded and suddenly I'm not amorous either.

He stretches out on the bed next to me, burying his face in the pillows. "I'm so tired," he mutters.

"The show starts in like seven hours."

"I know," he mutters. Frustration steams off of him like a hot shower.

I tug my dress up over my shoulders to cover myself. My voracious craving for him is gone. I can't even imagine picking up where we left off. It would be… wrong. My stomach growls and I feel nauseated that I lied to Kyle, after he's been nothing but nice to me.

I want Rory to leave.

Now.

I don't know how to tell him that, though. I don't want to be labeled a tease.

Rory looks up and smiles. "Your hair's all messed up."

"Gee, I wonder why?" I reach over to run my fingers through my unruly hair. "Rory..."

"Uh-hmm..."

It seems wrong to be with him now. I feel dirty. Totally deceitful. I'm a disappointment to my company, to my colleagues, to professional women everywhere, and especially to Kyle.

As Rory's lips move across my neck, I tense up. I can't do this. Not after hearing Kyle's caring voice on the phone. To sleep with Rory now would be a huge mistake. Tantamount to professional suicide.

It's not who I am.

Rory obviously doesn't feel the same way. He begins to nibble my ear and his tongue sweeps the sensitive flesh of my lobe. I close my eyes for a second, and try to unwind, but the image that comes into full view in my mind of the man stretched out next to me, caressing me, is Kyle, not Rory.

I bolt straight up.

"What's wrong, Vanessa?" Rory asks, sitting up, too.

"Nothing, it's just— Look, Rory, I'm sorry. I don't think it's a good idea to—" I focus on my hands in my lap, unable to meet his stare.

"Getting cold feet?"

"I don't want you to think I'm an easy lay."

"There's nothing easy about you," he says with a crooked grin.

"I'm serious, Rory. I'm not a one-night-stander. I'm a relationship gal. I can't just—"

He stands up and moves toward his pants. "Don't worry, Vanessa. Your virtue is safe." He fastens the slacks, bends down, and cups my face in his hands. "I should go."

"Yeah, I think so." Surprisingly, I'm relieved. Now I'm not being disloyal or unfaithful to anyone.

Rory blows me a kiss as he heads to the door. "Get some sleep."

When the door closes, I roll over and pound my fist into the pillow and groan. That's what I get for answering the phone. Late night calls are always trouble.

The next morning, after fitful sleep filled with images of Rory and Kyle melding in to one person—*I'm going insane*—I shower, dress, and head over to the Moscone Center. Reagan's obviously hung-over. Kyle nods at me and returns to setting up his computer in our cordoned off conference space.

I'm glad Rory left last night because I could never look Kyle in the face if the deal had been consummated. "Everyone feeling okay?" I ask to cover my uneasiness.

Reagan groans. "I feel like ass. What was in those drinks?"

I pat her on the back. "A lot of alcohol." I peer in at Kyle. "What's up with you?"

"Client meetings. Hope it's okay that I've taken over this space." He's dressed to the hilt in a black suit, tan shirt and silk tie. He looks like a million bucks. And ready to get down to business, as per usual.

"Good luck to you. Knock 'em dead." I swivel back around to Reagan. "Either of you seen Ted this morning?"

"Called his room twice last night, but no answer," Kyle says.

Hmmm, so maybe I'm reading too much in to my late night phone call. Perhaps Kyle was simply checking in on all of us?

The booth is soon packed with people, but we're short-handed because Ted doesn't show up until almost noon. He gets a healthy glare from both Kyle and me when he finally crosses into the booth.

"Where have you been?" I demand.

Kyle steps up. "Dude, we've got clients looking for you."

"I'm sorry. Really I am." Ted's eyes are beet red and he reeks of cigarette smoke.

Kyle waves his hand in the air. "Ever heard of a shower?"

"What happened to you last night?" I ask.

"I was so wasted. I went to my room, changed into my swim trunks, went and got in the hot tub, and fell asleep.

Kyle isn't thrilled with this news. "Passed out, you mean."

Ted shrugs. "A security guard making rounds found me this morning and rousted me out. I'm sorry guys."

I shake my head. "Ted, you could've drowned."

"No, there wasn't any water in it."

Suddenly the tension in the air over his lateness cracks like veneer and Kyle and I almost fall over laughing.

"I'm never gonna let you live this down, man," Kyle says with a smirk and slaps him on the back.

Ted scowls and moves to his demo station. "Go fuck yourselves."

By the end of the day, I want to cut my feet off. Reagan's back hurts and Ted's itching for nicotine. Kyle has had a steady stream of unhappy customers in the conference room, but they all withdraw smiling. Gorgeous, and he's good at his job.

Ted is wrapping up a final demo when his computer battery is finally exhausted. "Oh man, I left the power cable in my room. Vanessa, can I use your laptop over here?"

"No problem." I dig my computer out of the bag and quickly set it up. When the power comes on, the techno-dance CD blares out.

Mortified, I hurry to click it off. "Sorry, I was listening to music last night." That means my Director demo disk is in my hotel room. "You'll need a CD."

Ted pops the disk out of his computer and doesn't miss a beat. Fifteen minutes later when the show closes, he's made a sale. "Thanks Vanessa." He ejects his CD. "You saved my ass."

"Anything for the team."

Thoroughly depleted of energy, I rejoice when the last booth panel is in the crate, labeled for shipping, and sent off with the union handlers. Now, I might have time to find Rory before our flights. I don't want to leave things like we did last night.

First, I have to settle my tradeshow bill. I'd given them my corporate card when the show started, so it's only a matter of signing off and making sure I get a discount for the one-armed man, Sid.

Reagan and Kyle accompany me to the decorator's desk. The woman at the counter takes my forms and then announces, quite boisterously, "DigitalDirection. Your credit card was declined."

I spin around; horrified that my fellow exhibitors might think I'm skipping out on my bill. That's when my eyes meet Rory's steely blue ones. I had no idea he was in line next to me. Is that a smirk on his face? Son of a...

Think fast.

"Oh, there must be some mix up," I say in a hushed voice. "It's a company card and there shouldn't be any problems."

"Well, there *is* a problem because we've run it twice."

"Do you have another one?" Reagan asks.

I bite down on my bottom lip wondering how to solve this. "No. That's it."

Rory slides along the counter. "Everything okay, Vanessa?" I see a yellow receipt in his hand. Apparently SalesTracker doesn't have any problem with *their* company credit cards.

"Oh, err, no, nothing at all."

"You call not being able to pay your bill 'nothing at all?'" the woman snarks off.

"Do you need help?" Rory reaches for his wallet.

"We're fine, Ellery," Kyle interjects.

I put my hands up. "No, it's not a problem." My labored breathing is going to give me away. I have to take control. Can't let the competition see me sweat. "You know what? I accidentally gave you my *personal* credit card. Of course that's not going to work." I glare at the woman behind the counter, daring her to contradict me.

"Are you sure, Vanessa?" Rory presses. Reagan and Kyle watch, knowing damn well what it will mean if Rory thinks we're having financial trouble.

I laugh it off, though. That college elective drama class in is about to pay off. "No, I'm serious. I gave them my Visa. You think someone like me has that much credit?" I make a big deal to laugh it off like it's the stupidest thing I've ever done.

Kyle flips open his wallet. "Here, we'll use my company card."

I look down to see that it's his personal MasterCard. My eyes lift to his, no words need to be said as an understanding passes between us.

When Rory saunters off a bit too gleefully, I turn to Kyle. I can't resist laying my hands against his face. "My hero."

A smile curls the side of his mouth and his dimple pops. "Pleased to be of service to you."

"That was smooth, Vanessa," Reagan says. "I'm impressed."

I watch Kyle sign the receipt. "Do you have two thousand bucks on there?"

"Don't worry about it," Kyle says.

I let out a frustrated sigh. "Jiles will be pissed at me if this gets out."

"He should've thought of that when he didn't pay your AmEx bill," Reagan snaps.

Kyle stuffs his credit card into his wallet. "You were quick on your feet and no one's the wiser. Not even Ellery."

"Kyle...I don't know how to thank you."

His jaw is stern and set. "You handled yourself well in front of the competition. You can bet Jiles will hear about this."

We double-time it to the hotel to check out of our rooms. Reagan pays for mine since my card obviously doesn't work. Rory and his co-workers are checking out and he and I share a smile across the lobby. My emotions are mixed over him. He's such a fierce competitor as apparent moments ago, but I know there's a softer side. He's only doing his job by looking for the company's weaknesses. I would have done the same thing if I had been in his position.

I want to at least say goodbye because I don't know when we'll see each other again. How can I give him a proper sendoff with Ted, Reagan, and Kyle hanging out in the lobby?

Walking to where Rory stands in line, I whisper, "Meet me downstairs."

I wait outside the ladies room on the bottom level where Rory quickly shows up. "Everything straightened out with your charges?"

I shrug. "Oh, yeah. No big deal. My mix-up." I take a deep breath. "Listen, about last night, I—"

"Don't think twice about it, Vanessa. I understand." He looks around for a moment as if he's searching for something. "Well, this is it for a while for me as far as tradeshows go," he says.

"What do you mean?"

"No trips for a couple of months. I do hope we can pick up where we left off. Very soon." He advances and draws me to him.

His index finger lifts my chin and I glance up into those perilously blue eyes. He lowers his head and places a sweet, short kiss on my forehead. I'm not sure what it means. It feels like goodbye.

"So no more tradeshows," I manage to say through my emotional choke.

"I'm going to be swamped working on our product enhancements, so it'll be hard to take phone calls, texts, or stay on top of e-mail."

This feels like a brush off. I know, I've been there before.

He lifts my face with his finger again. "Maybe I'll visit Boston when I'm done with the project."

I smile at the notion. "I'd like to show you my city."

He places my hair behind my ear and plays with the silver earrings he gave me that dangle next to my neck. "Hey, there's another show here in San Francisco in November."

"I know. We're coming to it."

"I should be done with this project then. Why don't we say it's a date?"

I don't know what tomorrow will bring, let alone months down the road. I want him to remember me. My pulse accelerates; anxiety courses through my veins. I have to stop worrying about what will happen next while he's still here. There'll be plenty of time for analysis on the flight home. I close my eyes and take pleasure when Rory layers his lips over mine in a whisper of a kiss.

"Hey, Ellery, we're getting ready to—"

Rory and I jump apart as Gene Cappucci stands there grinning at us. I step back hastily and straighten my shirt.

"Sorry," Gene says. "Didn't mean to interrupt." His dark eyes move from Rory to me as he scratches his bushy black mustache.

Rory steps away. "No big deal."

I must be six shades of crimson by now.

"Well, I've got to go." Rory follows Gene to the staircase, but stops and turns back to me. "Take care of yourself, Vanessa."

As I watch him walk away, there's something inside me that tells me I'm never going to see him again.

CHAPTER TWENTY-ONE

Two weeks after the San Francisco trip, Jiles Chancey's panties are in a knot and the proverbial shit is hitting the fan.

"SalesWanker contacted one of our clients to pitch their new iPhone application," he screams to the assembled group of sales, marketing, and client services people.

"They don't have an iPhone app," Ted counters, picking up his SmartPhone to start looking for it.

"They do now." Jiles' face turns fiery red. "It's the quickest fucking product enhancement release in the history of software." He slams his hand down on the tabletop and coffee and pens go flying.

I wonder if this was the big project that Rory said he'd be working on.

Reagan drums her fingers. "How could they have gotten it done so fast after our big splash in San Francisco? There weren't any SalesWanker people in our booth, but that doesn't mean they didn't send a client over to watch a demo."

Ted speaks up. "I gave out five disks at the show. I have the signed license agreements from all of them, so we can track them down."

Jiles throws his pen across the room, nearly hitting Kyle, who's deep in thought. Little Baby Jesus rails on.

"SalesTracker is touting enhancements that are exactly like ours. Even the fucking graphics are the same as our in-house designs. They don't give a shit that they stole it directly from us!"

Kyle speaks up. "The only way SalesTracker could've busted the code was if they *have* an actual demo disk. I told you the programmers shouldn't have made it so easy."

Oh... shit...

My mouth turns arid and I nearly begin to gag. My demo disk is missing. Last I'd seen it was when I popped it out of my computer in my San Francisco hotel room to play music. It was lying on the desk next to the envelope where I kept my travel receipts. I'd looked everywhere for it before checking out, but figured it must've fallen into the trash. No big deal... right?

Oh, but it *is* a big deal.

Our competition is making a huge splash in the marketplace with our enhancements and I'd hosted their top sales guy in my room for a slumber party. My breathing grows sparse and I focus on Jiles, trying not to black out as the reality of my actions sinks in.

Jiles sweeps his notebook off the table, sending papers and business cards flying.

Kyle goes over to him. "We can figure this out. We just need a game plan. Everyone needs to remain calm." He's so professional, never missing a beat. I can't believe Jiles is letting a subordinate tell him to chill, but it's working. It's that smooth voice of Kyle's that makes you want to do anything he says, like give a pint of plasma, bake homemade brownies, or roll over on your back and beg for more.

Then my heart nearly stops. The realization hits me like ice cold water in the face. Rory was only into me for this one purpose. He probably took the disk out of my room, right underneath my nose. I don't want to think the worst, however, it's hard not to.

My pulse slams into overdrive and I know for certain that I'm going to have a myocardial infarction here on the conference table. Just my luck, it'll be someone like Ted, or God forbid, LBJ, who'll give me mouth-to-mouth resuscitation to save my pathetic life.

A voice inside my head screams "wise up, fool! Rory used you!" I want to fight it and tell it it's wrong. "No. He wouldn't have taken the disk from my room," I mutter.

"What did you say, Vanessa?" Jack asks.

"Nothing, I just... This is really weird, don't you think?"

He shakes his head. "Someone screwed up and let SalesTracker get our new version. There's going to be hell to pay."

I have to think. Reenact everything. Knock at the door, heavy kissing, third date-like petting and then the phone rang. I talked to Kyle and that must've been when Rory swiped the disk from wherever I'd tossed it on the desk. He was sitting at my computer, after all.

Wait a sec, Rory had been undressing. His hardware was on the brain, not my software. It was about our impending corporate merger. Then again, he didn't exactly fight me when I told him I didn't want to have sex. He seemed ever so happy to just... leave.

Little Baby Jesus' voice returns me to the room. "I want a check on every new demo disk that's out there. Reel them all in. Contact the clients, the prospects, everyone."

A nervous tide rolls through the conference room.

Kyle holds his hands up in protest. "Don't you think you're overreacting, Jiles? Clients are going to want to know what's happening. This is going to be one hell of a PR nightmare."

"I don't care. I pay you to triage shit like this. Earn your goddamned paycheck, Nettles."

Kyle's mouth opens and closes and then he stares across the room in disbelief. Our eyes meet and I lower my face into a pout to let him know I feel for him. He's got his work cut out.

And it's all my fault!

"Everyone on this staff who has a demo disk must turn it in," LBJ says.

What am I going to do?

Jack notices my sporadic breathing. "What's up with you?"

"This makes me nervous, that's all," I manage to say.

"This is the programmers' fault," Jack says assuredly. "Nothing marketing could've done to prevent it."

Yeah, marketing could have prevented it by keeping the competition out of her hotel room.

Jiles continues. "We'll match up the license numbers and see if we can track this down. I'll be damned if those jackasses in Seattle are going to do this to us."

An unfamiliar rumbling starts in my stomach and a sharp pain spreads across my belly. My heart triples its rhythm and I have to concentrate to breathe.

I am completely screwed.

Tears sting the back of my eyes and I fear I'm going to have an emotional outburst. I can't believe what I've done. I'm a horrible person and I've ruined everything. I'm a disappointment to my company. I've failed at the corporate game. I'm a disgrace to the marketing team, to my friends, my family. To women everywhere.

Even if Rory didn't take the disk—if it truly had been thrown out or misplaced—I still have a lot of explaining to do because my copy of the software is missing. That points the finger of blame straight at me, no matter what.

The meeting breaks up. I grab my stomach and I feel like I'm going to be sick. Turning the corner, I dash to the Ted Williams conference room and shut the door. The tumultuous feelings roiling through my body come to a boiling head and I completely lose it. I can't stop the flow of hot salty tears as everything cascades around on me. I'm blanketed in shame, spiraling down to the lowest point in my life.

The creak of the door brings me back to my senses and I quickly wiper-blade my tears.

"Vanessa?"

Oh dear God. It's Kyle. I can't look at him. I can't lie to *him*. Not again. He's so professional. Forthright and honest. I want him to think I'm smart, with-it, together. Not a sobbing, runny-nosed mess.

He shuts the door and then reaches into his jeans for a white handkerchief. That's classy; I didn't know guys still carried those. I accept it and wipe at my face, trailing mascara on the crisp white fabric.

Kyle kneels in front of me. "Let me do that. You're making it worse." He takes the cloth and gently sweeps it over my face. The material is soft and worn and smells of Downy freshness.

My eyes sync with his and suddenly my body is covered in a warm sensation. Like a warm fire and hot chocolate on a winter's day. Like being away for a long time and finally coming home.

"Sorry you have to see me this way," I say, finally getting my lungs to capacity with some air. "Real mature, huh? I've never cried at work before."

"There's always a first time." He dabs under my eyes. "Want to tell me what's going on?"

I don't know if I can trust him, especially since he's so tight with LBJ. What if he whistle blows on me if I admit my wrongdoings? Then I gaze into his eyes that are so kind. And his smile. I could get lost in that dimple for a week.

Look what happened the last time I got involved with a dimple.

Taking a brave breath, I strike out. "I lost my demo CD."

He doesn't bolt to go tell LBJ. Instead, he flattens his mouth in a "thinking about it" gesture. "Where?"

"When I was in San Francisco."

He smiles. "No, I mean specifically."

"I think the maid threw it away when she cleaned my room." I leave out the tiny detail of Rory being in my room.

"That's not worth crying this hard over." He trails his thumb under my chin, watching me intently with his clear hazel eyes. Every fiber of my being is on fire from his caring touch. The concern on his face is overwhelming and my chest actually hurts.

I get a good breath and look away. "Jiles is going to blame me for all of this and I'm going to get fired." The reality of my words seeps in. I won't have a job and I'll be living on a grate in Harvard Square. I'll beg people to pay me for holding the ATM door open. I'll have to collect bottles and cans just to eke out enough to buy cat food for my dinner.

I collapse, my head in my hands, not caring if Kyle sees my continued breakdown. I'm a really strong person, but my immediate future is on the line.

Kyle's strong hand curves around my neck and he begins to rub. God, that feels so good. I'm not supposed to be attracted to his warm eyes, his reassuring hand, or his silky voice. Perhaps not all men are jerks who use you for what they can get out of you.

Then he says, "How can I help?"

I sit up. He drops his hand to his knee, which is covered in denim stretching across his fine-toned hamstrings. "Thanks Kyle, but this is my mess and I've got to clean it up."

I'm drowning in a sea of guilt battering me over and over again with another wave. Kyle's offering me a life jacket, and I don't deserve it at all.

"I'm here if you need me," he says with a smile. "Anytime. I mean that, Vanessa."

I compose myself, take a deep breath. "I might take you up on that."

"Heard from Rory?" Griz asks later that afternoon, setting a Diet Coke on my desk. She's asked me this every day since I returned from my trip. Today is not the time to continue the line of questioning.

"Nope."

"Aren't you mad?"

"Yeah, but not because of that."

"What then?"

"He's a jerk. Typical male."

She maneuvers to sit on my desk. "I hear SalesTracker's kicking our ass in new sales these days. Their marketplace downloads on Android phones are one of the top purchases this week according to the office gossip."

"It would seem so."

Griz squints at me. "You all right, Double-Vee?"

Do I dare tell her about the missing disk? Everyone in the company is whispering about SaleTracker's swoop of us, accusing this, that, or the other disgruntled customer of selling us out. I trust Griz, but I don't want to drag her into the corporate quagmire with me. "What do you mean?"

"I think you're hiding something from me, Vanessa."

Am I that obvious? "No, I'm sick of thinking about Rory. It's not worth it."

She screws her face up. "I thought he was Mr. Right."

I take a sip of soda. "More like Mr. What Was I Thinking?"

"All of this attitude because you haven't heard from him?" She reaches around me and picks up my phone. "Call him. Right now. This is stupid."

She's right. Maybe I should at least give him the opportunity to deny that he swiped my disk. Convince me it's all a bad misunderstanding. I shouldn't immediately jump to conclusions before giving him a chance to explain. "I'll take care of it. Now let me get back to work."

I have to get to the bottom of this. There's more at stake here than my heart. My career and way of life is on the line.

I dash off an e-mail: *Rory...I know you're busy with work, but we need to talk. Vanessa.*

There. Short and sweet. Non-committal. Challenging.

Ten minutes later: *Vanessa...I'm swamped, but it's good to hear from you. I can't wait see you next month. R.*

Okay. I'm feeling a little bit better. Maybe I'm reading too much into all of this corporate hullabaloo.

My response: *Did you take a CD from my room when you were there?* That's a roundabout way of getting to the issue.

Rory: *The Jennifer Lopez CD? Not a big fan of hers. Why?*

Me: *Do you remember seeing one next to my computer?*

Could I be more obvious?

Rory: *All I remember is you in that dead-sexy red dress.*

All right. Nice dodge. He's squirming his way back into my good books, still something doesn't feel right. Maybe it's only a terrible happenstance. Bad timing. Screwed up karma or biorhythms. Perhaps I've convicted Rory on circumstantial evidence. Still, a gnawing ache in my brain tells me my first instincts might be right. I can only solve the puzzle by talking to him. I'll definitely get to the bottom of this in San Francisco. He's not out of the doghouse yet.

I am, though.

I still have to deal with turning in a disk. My ass is on the line. Jiles is out for blood and anyone with a missing disk will be a target.

That night, I wake up in bed drenched in sweat after a nightmare starring Little Baby Jesus. He was dressed as Freddy Krueger chasing me down a long hallway. Only, instead of razors on his fingers, he had shiny silvery CD-ROMs. I need psychiatric help.

I can't lose my job. If I do, I'll have to go back to Virginia to live with my parents. My mother will insist I learn to give perms, blow-outs, and prom/wedding "up dos." I'll spend time cutting Safeway coupons, shelling butter beans, and trimming the rhododendrons.

No. That can *not* happen.

I'm an honest person, so I need to fess up. Face the music. Pay the piper and all those trite sayings that never make sense when you're the one trying to get out of a situation.

At work the next morning, I'm about to knock on Jiles' door and confess the loss of the disk when Kyle heads me off in the hallway. He pulls me by the elbow into one of the Willies' offices and closes the door.

"I thought of you in the shower this morning," he says.

The thought of Kyle Nettles naked, wet, and soapy makes the walls of my mouth water. The thought of Kyle Nettles naked, wet, and soapy and thinking of me makes my legs wobbly.

"Rather, I had an idea."

I wash away the mental image with sarcasm. "You decided soap-on-a-rope needs to make a comeback and you're just the entrepreneur to do it?"

He snickers. "No, but thanks for the marketing tip." He drops his hand from my elbow. "You can make a demo disk."

"Why? To cover my butt?"

"Exactly. And to make sure you don't get blamed for something that's the programmers' fault to begin with."

This is actually quite ingenious. I perk up. "The template for the disk label is on the server," I say.

"I know where the disk labels and CDRs are," he says proudly. "They're in the storage room next to the letterhead. Everyone has access to them."

The pieces of my life are starting to come back into place. "I have the number of my 'real' demo disk from the copy of the license agreement I signed. All I have to do is get a new disk, add the label with the proper info and turn it in."

Kyle smiles with a raised eyebrow. "Now you're catching on."

"Wait." Hitch in the plan. "It won't have the software."

"Can you say your demo disk never worked?"

"Sure. The IT guys burn so many of them, I'll bet some of them slip through that aren't formatted properly."

This plan could work. However, it's manipulative and it makes me a lying coward. Here I am dragging Kyle down with me. I have no idea if I'm actually responsible for this breach in security. I can't prove anything. Maybe I should just tell the truth. Then again, would anyone else in a similar position? No. And they probably wouldn't walk in front of an eighteen-wheeler.

"Let's get to it," he says.

As he opens the door, I stop him. "Why are you doing this?" I thought he was corporate through and through, yet he wants to help me buck the rules.

His smile is damn near heartbreaking and I actually feel butterflies pounding their wings inside my chest. Silly insects.

"Vanessa, you're a hard worker and you don't deserve to lose your job over this. Jiles is putting his focus into this instead of keeping the customers happy. I've got to deflect his attention elsewhere by solving this mystery. If he doesn't get back to the basics of running this company, there won't *be* a company to run."

Okay. No undying love in his confession. It's all about business. All the same, I appreciate Kyle's camaraderie.

Two hours later, I hand over the counterfeit disk to LBJ, trying not to retch as I stand in front of him.

"Here you go, Jiles. Don't bother with mine, it never worked anyway," I say, testing the waters.

He tosses it onto a pile of other CDs on his desk. "You're the third person who's said that. Damn IT guys not checking their work."

I stand rooted in place in front of his desk.

Jiles pops his head up and glares. "Is there something else?"

I take two steps back, blown away that my feet are moving. "Nope. That's it. Thanks."

My heart pounds away in my ears and I feel I may faint from the overpowering relief. Our little plan worked. Yet I don't feel any liberation. I'm a bad employee and I have to somehow make this up to DigitalDirection by working my ass off even harder.

In business, it's oftentimes admirable to screw the competition. However, I came too close. Have I committed the ultimate corporate sin? If so, whom do I make a confession to?

Of course, with sin comes guilt.

Guilt I'll have to live with.

For now.

CHAPTER TWENTY-TWO

"Hello, Vanessa. I trust you're feeling okay?"

I cringe as I'm about to put the key in the front door of my apartment. Instead, I turn to the land lizard and say, "What can I do for you, Mr. Paulsen?"

"I'm concerned about what's going on in your apartment. There are regulations you must abide by and I'm legally responsible."

"For what?" This guy's been eating too many Fruit Loops.

He points at our window. "You and that boyfriend of yours."

"William's not my boyfriend. He's gay."

The land lizard either doesn't believe me or he's not listening. "I found something in your trash," he says.

"You were digging through our garbage?" This guy needs a hobby. One that doesn't include my life.

"I was sorting recyclables and your pregnancy test popped out."

"My what?" I haven't had sex in forever. "It's probably the girls downstairs. Have you asked them?"

His brows lower. "It was next to some of your mail."

Someone call a cop.

I don't have to stand here and take this. I have packing to do. I've got to get to San Francisco. I've got to talk to Rory. Suss out what's going on. Face-to-face so I'll know the truth about the disk. "I'm not now, nor have I ever been pregnant."

Mr. Paulsen doesn't falter, though. "This house has lead paint. If there's a child in there, the apartment will have to be de-leaded at the tenant's expense."

I push open the front door and wave him away. "Whatever."

He follows me inside. "I wouldn't be a responsible land-lord if I didn't give you these, Vanessa." He places a stack of pamphlets in my hand. "Call me if you have any questions."

"Thank you?" I ask more than say.

"What was that all about?" William asks when I step inside. He's stirring brownie batter, so I dip my finger in and suck the chocolate gooiness into my mouth.

"Freakazoid upstairs found a pregnancy test in the gar-bage and thinks you knocked me up."

William beams at me. "Darling! I'm so happy."

I bat him away. "Get over yourself." Then I pause. "Do you think it's Mia's?"

He shakes his head. "She hasn't been on a date in six months. Too busy with school."

"Then I don't care," I say.

"Actually, it's me," he says with a laugh. "I had phone sex the other night and now I've missed my period."

I swat at him with the stack of brochures.

"What are those?"

"They're from the land lizard," I say. I look at the pam-phlets in my hand and double over laughing: *Lead and Your Baby – a Guide to Lead Paint Removal*, *Massachusetts Tenants Responsibilities*, and in 72 point red bold type, a tract from the Catholic Church entitled: **HELL**...*Is that your next residence?*

Probably so, but not for the reasons Mr. Paulsen thinks.

I've got to right everything in my life. ASAP.

⚜ ⚜ ⚜

The next morning, I decide Mr. Paulsen's bad karma is screwing with my life.

Before I leave town, I check my biorhythms. The website states my health is "getting worse," I should "avoid communication" and relationships are "unstable." Lovely. The gods are laughing their asses off at me. This whole trip has "natural disaster" water-colored all over it.

At the airport, I smile when I see Kyle's friendly face. A nice distraction in the not-so-friendly skies. As we stand in line, he asks, "How's that pteromerhanophobia going?"

"I'm impressed. That's a big word to memorize."

"Well, I do have a Master's degree," he says with a smile.

"I took an Atavan." The two cups of coffee will probably counter-balance the sedative, though. "If the flight's not full, I hope to stretch out and wake up on the Wrong Coast."

Kyle takes the row opposite me and goes straight to work even before we take off. He's such a diligent employee, trying so hard to keep our clients happy. He puts the company first and his efforts are paying off. He's saved some big accounts this week with the whole SalesTracker calamity. With his customer service plan, we're bound to get plenty of renewals. I admire Kyle's work ethic and dedication.

My medication is starting to relax me when suddenly the captain announces, "Folks, we've got to turn around because of a small technical difficulty."

"What difficulty?" I ask the passing flight attendant, a wee bit of dread in my voice. "I'm not good at this flying thing to begin with and I'm certainly not good with 'difficulties.'"

She flashes a plastic smile. "We've popped a hatch and the cabin is slowly depressurizing. But, nothing to worry about."

I can't breathe. I need air. I want to get out. I paw at the window like a trapped animal as marshmallowy clouds mock me with their free-floating independence. "We're going to crash and burn. They'll be nothing left of me for my parents to bury."

Kyle slides into the aisle seat of my row to comfort me. "Don't panic, Vanessa. Everything's cool. No need to worry."

"Like hell there isn't anything to worry about!" I pull out the bottle of Atavan and down another one dry. Looking around, no one else seems fazed by this announcement, but readily accepts our doomed fate.

Suddenly, a baby starts crying.

Flights with babies on them never crash. It would be wrong. Just then, the plane banks hard to the left, turning back toward Boston. I grip the armrest and close my eyes. "Oh, dear God." Prayer. The last refuge of a scoundrel. I feel a nudge against my arm and glance over. Kyle is offering his hand again, just like on the flight from Vegas.

"Feel free to hold on."

Well, that's sweet. I need to feel secure. I need strength. I need to know I won't die in a fiery ball. I need to not reach out to him. Or feel the heat of his skin. Not a good thing. "I'll be okay. Thanks." I don't want to run the risk of enjoying the way his hand will surely feel.

When we land in Boston, fire trucks, police and Federal Aviation Administration authorities meet our flight. We have to get re-booked and wait another two hours before finally taking off. By then, I'm so woozy from the extra medication that I pull the tray table down, lay my head on it, and sleep the entire way across the country.

More karmic retribution when we check into the Fairmont Hotel. My corporate AmEx is rejected.

"Here, Vanessa. I can take care of that." Once again, Kyle and his magic credit card save the day.

I trudge to the furthest end of the hallway and open the door to my room. It smells like an old man who hasn't bathed in a month. Since the hotel's totally booked, it's this room or a park bench. I breathe out of my mouth and begin unpacking.

Twenty minutes later, there's more bad news.

"Our booth hasn't arrived yet," Reagan reports when I step into the ballroom.

"Of course, even if it had arrived, I forgot to bring the fucking key with me again," I rant. I should buy stock in that biorhythm website. They know their shit.

My head just isn't in the game. It's on talking to Rory face-to-face. I've got to get to the truth, find out what happened in my room last time I was in this city. I have to take charge. I have to be strong. Because, after much anxious consideration, I've decided I'm breaking it off, no matter what he says about the disk. The fact that I even think he was capable of taking it means he's not the guy for me. Trust is the foundation of all relationships and something about Rory now screams out, "Beware of Dog."

Plus, Kyle just totally saved my professional ass.

I'm doing the right thing. And I'm doing it on my terms.

Reagan hugs me to her side and knocks me back to the here and now. "Maybe we can pick the lock with a paper clip?"

"Ted's done it before," I say. Only Ted's not here.

The boxes of collaterals I'd arduously packed and shipped are actually here, so I spread the marketing materials from them over the table, along with business cards and a wicker basket to gather leads. Kyle and Reagan set up their laptops on each corner to give demos. That's when I see the familiar teal SalesTracker logo across the ballroom and decide the time is now. I make my way through the box-strewn clutter toward it.

I hear my heart thundering in my ears.

The blood in my body is rushing to every vital organ.

Perspiration coats the back of my neck under my hair.

Yet, I'm strong and read for the necessary.

This is it. Time to get this over with.

Rory and I'll get everything settled, part as friends, and move on.

No more sneaking around behind closed hotel room doors.

I can do this.

I take a deep breath and step into the half-built booth. "Hey there, Gene."

The Italian Stallion is bent over a carton, but stands up when he sees me. I'll be professional, even though SalesTracker is a big turd in my company's punchbowl.

"Hey Vanessa." A smile spreads underneath his mustache.

I glance around. "I'm looking for Rory. Is he here?"

Gene rubs his chin and his face pales instantly. He glances around, seeming to search for the right thing to say.

"What's wrong?" Did something happen to Rory? Okay...I know I'm breaking up with him, but I don't wish the guy any harm.

Gene scratches his bald head. "Hell, Vanessa. I don't really know how to tell you this."

"Tell me what?" Hot blood courses through my veins, rushing throughout my body in that human animal natural fight or flight reaction.

"He's... ahh... well, there's no easy way to say it."

"Gene, you're scaring me."

He takes a deep breath. "Rory's been arrested."

"Arrested? When?" My rapid pulse throbs in my temples and nausea roils through my intestines, which are cramping for good measure.

"Two days ago. These guys with the State Attorney General showed up at the office and cuffed him."

"Why would the AG arrest him? I didn't know they had that authority."

"Well, they do."

"What for?"

"Seems he abandoned his wife and six-year-old son in Indiana and owes court-ordered back child support. You know, deadbeat dad sort of thing. His wife's been trying to track him down for four years, but every time she got close, he disappeared again."

Oh my God... oh my God... oh my God.

Breathing becomes a task as I struggle to hear Gene's words correctly. How ignorant of me for not knowing something wasn't right with Rory. Blinded by lust. Fooled by his charm. He has a wife. He has a kid.

Gene pours out the rest of the worms from the can. "I know you two had something going, but you should also know he was living with our receptionist at SalesTracker. Scuttlebutt is he fathered her kid too."

Jesus, it just keeps getting worse.

"And, it turns out his name isn't Rory Ellery. It's Rodney Elmore."

My heart rate accelerates; my ears ring like Sunday church bells. That does it. I wish I had a paper bag to breathe into as the choppy pants stuck in my windpipe threaten to overtake me. The walls of the ballroom close in and I get a tingly feeling all over, like ants crawling on my body. I can feel bile rising in my throat.

I have to get out of here.

"I'm sorry to be the one to tell you this, Vanessa," Gene calls out.

I breeze by Reagan and Ted. "I've got to run an errand," I say quickly as I grab my purse and bolt through the lobby.

"Hey Vanessa, I tracked down the booth," Kyle says, trying to impede my flight.

"I'll talk to you later, Kyle." Then I fly out the front door of the hotel.

"Do you need a cab, ma'am?" the doorman asks.

I spin around, my hair flying in my face. "Yeah. That'd be great."

He whistles for a taxi and I wait for a moment for the yellow car to pull forward. I can't see for the blurred ripple before my eyes. I sweep the tears away as they plummet down my cheeks. I crawl into the cab and it pulls out onto Mason Street. The uncontrollable floodgate releases and I can't breathe as childlike sobs rack me.

Rory betrayed me in the worst possible way. I don't care about the demo disk disaster anymore. I only care that I became a pawn in his games. The other woman. Hell, the other, other woman. And, I'd allowed it.

"Do you see a ring?" I mock his lie in Atlantic City.

Jackass. Phony. Fraud. Manipulator.

Boy, was I wrong. Wrong! The opposite of right. That'll teach me. At least I was about to end things.

"Where to, lady?" the cabbie asks.

I sip a deep gulp of air and say, "Boston."

CHAPTER TWENTY-THREE

O kay, so the guy doesn't drive me to Boston, but he offers me a handful of Kleenex. Then, he drops me off on a corner near a coffee show. I need to reach out and touch someone. I'd call Griz, though I think this requires a more feminine viewpoint.

William answers on the third ring and I dive right in.

"A deadbeat dad. Hell, a dad, period. And a husband. With a live-in girlfriend and another kid. A thief. Definitely a liar."

"Vanessa, calm down and tell me everything." William's voice is soothing over the long distance.

When I finally exhaust the story, I take a deep breath. "An imposter on top of everything else. And now, a criminal."

William clicks his tongue. "Fine. He'll be convicted and serve jail time."

"He owes it to his family to pay what's due them. I hope his girlfriend with the kid slaps him with a lawsuit, too," I say. What's due to me, though? I feel like I've earned some sort of compensation or restitution. "Oh my God. I'm going to hell for adultery."

William chuckles. "He's the adulterer, Double Vee, not you. Besides, you have to actually have sex to be an adulterer."

"You're splitting hairs."

"You're teetering on the edge," he retorts.

"How could he have walked away from a marriage, a family, and a commitment?" Apparently as easily as he'd walked away from me after he got what he wanted.

Prime directive: DigitalDirections' software.

"It's a blessing in disguise, Vanessa. If this hadn't happened, you might've gotten more involved. What if he kept lying... or worse got you pregnant? Would you have wanted that?"

"No. Certainly not. I was breaking up with him, remember?" I wipe my hand under my nose. "He played me like a fine-tuned instrument. I let him. Ready, willing, and able. And completely fucking naïve." William remains quiet, although I can hear his breathing. "I was so enthralled by the attention and thinking I was mature enough to handle an adult relationship, I couldn't see the forest for the fucking lying trees. I was blind to the signs, deaf to the clues, and dumb toward the entire situation."

"We all make mistakes, Vee. Man has free will. He just doesn't know what to do with it. Besides, you were calling it quits."

"I was. But on my terms, not like this."

I don't understand how I could I be so galactically stupid. I graduated *Suma cum laude*. I suppose my university will be wanting their degree back.

I finish up with William and realize I've walked back to the hotel. I slip back in, freshen up in the ladies, and then rejoin my co-workers. Kyle's eyes connect with mine and I can read the alarm on his face. Thank heavens he's classy enough not to ask me what's wrong.

I've got to get a grip on my emotions and get to work.

A warm grin spreads from the corner of Kyle's mouth as he walks toward me. "The booth was delivered across the bay to the Fairmont in San Jose by mistake. It'll be here in an hour."

"Thanks for taking care of that, Kyle. I had a personal matter to attend to."

"You okay?"

"Umm, yeah. Sure. Just needed some air."

He nods. "I understand. That's what teamwork's all about."

Ironically, a calming sensation passes through me like a ghost of a breeze. Something inside me wants to confess the whole dirty affair to Kyle; to come clean and ask his advice. He's my co-worker, not my confidante, advisor, or even a priest.

The booth finally arrives and we set up in time for the cocktail reception. I try to get into the spirit of things, but that damned SalesWanker logo taunts me from across the room. I stand anesthetized, rooted in place by shame and guilt.

Near the end of the reception, I signal to Kyle. He looks pretty damn sharp in his gray fitted knit shirt and black dress pants. His dimple is quite prominent tonight, but I try not to let it distract me. After all, he's just a guy like the rest of them. Look at him flirting with female customers. He probably has a girlfriend back in Boston, too. All men are scum.

He turns away from the slender redhead and meets my stare. He excuses himself and saunters over to me with a glass of wine.

"Thought you might like this."

I eyeball this spokesman for the male race and wonder if he's too good to be true. I'm in no frame of mind to try and figure it out. "Thanks. I've got a splitting headache. I think I'm going to go lie down."

"Get some rest. We can cover things here. Tomorrow's a long day." As I turn to leave, I can feel Kyle's eyes on me. I appreciate that someone actually gives a damn.

Around eight p.m., sick of the melodrama, and, quite frankly, sick of myself, I decide to buck up, get dressed, and go out for some food. William's a dorky Hard Rock Café fan, so I decide to go have dinner there and buy him a souvenir.

I step into the elevator dressed all in black, to match my mood. At the next floor down, a man gets on and looks me over.

"What?" I snap.

"You're from the East Coast, aren't you?" he asks.

"Yeah. How'd you know?"

"Your outfit. Don't get a lot of that where I'm from."

"And where would that be? East Bumfuck, Egypt?"

Thank goodness the elevator door opens immediately and I bolt from the man's sight, not able to meet his horrified gaze. I've gone from crushed to depressed and now I'm bordering on livid. Angry at the situation. Angry at Rory. But most of all, royally pissed off at Vanessa Virtue.

Someone's going to get it.

I take the cable car down California to the Hard Rock on Van Ness Avenue. The hostess seems appalled that I'm alone and escorts me to a table in the back. The waitress can't get me out of there fast enough, nearly shoving my food at me. Fine. I can take a hint.

I head to the T-shirt counter and pick out a Hard Rock logo shirt for William. The checker rings up the order and takes my credit card. Before running it through, he asks, "Would you like to crank it up for the kids?"

"Would I like to what?"

He picks up a canister sitting next to the cash register. "Crank it up... for the kids. We're raising money for area kids from single parent homes. Would you like to crank it up?"

Goddamn brainless marketing people coming up with stupid-ass phrases like "crank it up for the kids."

"No, Tim," I say, peering at his nametag. "I don't believe I would, but thanks anyway."

"Come on, everyone wants to help out the kids," he presses.

"I'm all set. Thanks."

But he won't take no for an answer. "Does that mean you'll crank it up for the kids?"

That's the last drop. "No, Tim. It doesn't mean that." I can't take anymore. My biorhythm chart was a hundred percent right. Communication *is* a dangerous thing. "You see, Tim, I believe it's the parents' duty to crank it up—whatever the hell that means—for their kids. People shouldn't have children if they're going to walk out on them. They shouldn't run away and avoid paying child support. Then they shouldn't pursue other people, knowing damn well they're not available. That they're big, fat, *fucking* liars. Then, you hit me up for money, asking me to pay for other people's mistakes. I'm not going to do it, Tim. So, no, I won't CRANK IT UP FOR THE KIDS!"

Dozens of eyes sear through my back and I want to disappear. Tim stares at me in disbelief and his mouth hangs open for a second before he says, "that'll be $29.90."

Feeling guilty after he hands my credit card back, I stuff a ten dollar bill into the charity canister and flee the Hard Rock through a veil of shame.

I wish someone would crank it up for me.

I go through the motions of existing the rest of the trade-show, putting on a strong front and trying to be a professional. No use losing my job because of my bad attitude toward everything.

It pains me to think about the whispers, secret touches, and hot kisses Rory and I shared. It's all so cheap and dirty now. I know in my heart of hearts that he swiped my demo disk. No doubt about it. I don't have to be a CSI detective to figure that out. I simply have to accept the reality in my own head. My own heart.

Looking back now, it explains the computer being on in New Jersey and my room seeming like a disaster area (more so than usual) in Miami. I was too blinded by lust to realize what was going on around me.

I hate Rory Ellery.

No, I hate Rodney Ellmore.

And I hate myself.

What a manipulative genius. I wonder if there are other places where he pulled off a con job like this. At least he was caught. Nabbed. I hope he fries for what he's done to that poor woman and her son. Rory, no *Rodney* is no good to women everywhere.

I have to stop dwelling on him and get away from the games my mind is playing. I can't, tough. Reminiscences splash over me like dirty bathwater. Emblazoned in my memory bank. Seared on my heart. Rory. The disk. His promises and kisses. His wife. His kid. His lies. His exploitation.

I focus on the tradeshow, shining my best smile for all to see. Admit it, it's my fault that everyone at DigitalDirection now has to bust their asses daily because of our competition getting our software code. They got it from *my* disk. I gnaw on my tongue to stop from screaming my guilt out to everyone.

"We've generated a hell of a lot of leads," Kyle says at the end of the show. "Jiles will be pleased."

Well, at least I'm helping the company now. "Just doing my job," I say flatly, trying to ignore the curving smile he flashes at me.

"We should take in the sights. Go out dancing." Kyle moves along with music that's apparently playing in his head. The guy is always upbeat and positive. He must be on a heavy dose of Zoloft. I wonder if he'll share.

Visions of my last trip to San Francisco gel in my mind and suddenly nausea coils around me like a dank cloak. "I think I'll stay in tonight."

"Come on. There's a club on Folsom called Holy Cow. Great bands. It'll be a blast." Kyle's jazzed about being here and the success of the show. I'd only be a party pooper.

"I won't be any fun. Take Reagan and Ted. I'm going to take a hot bath and go to bed."

Kyle pulls his hand through his hair. "Nothing I can do to change your mind?"

My stomach echoes a hollow kerplunk and I smile weakly. Maybe not all guys are first class assholes. "I'm afraid not. You're nice, though. Some gal in Boston is pretty lucky."

I rub his arm for emphasis and turn for the door when I hear him mutter, "She would be if she paid attention."

I wake up at o'dark thirty the next morning with someone pounding down my hotel door. "What is this? A raid?" I have a bit of a headache because I'd ordered a bottle of wine from room service and promptly polished it off, along with some cherry cheesecake.

Reagan parades in, screwing her nose up at my ratty American University T-shirt. "Come on. It's a gorgeous Saturday and I insist on fresh air and exercise."

She's done the Boston Marathon twice and is the type of person who thinks rock climbing in Thailand is a relaxing vacation. Not me. Give me the Caribbean and a frozen fruity girl drink any day of the week and twice on Sundays.

"Fresh air is overrated," I say.

"Come on. Kyle's down in the restaurant waiting for us."

"What about Ted?" If I have to go, he does too.

Reagan digs my jeans out of the suitcase and tosses them at me. "He got this inner ear infection thing and changed his flight. He's already gone."

We're taking the red-eye home. Jiles always says it saves money. I'd prefer to go home with Ted rather than go traipsing through town. The city I long loved has a stank that smells of Rory's deceit. Damn him for ruining yet another thing for me.

Once downstairs, Kyle hands me a coffee, just the way I like it, hot, lots of cream, and two pink packets. "Thanks," I say.

Reagan drags us to Fisherman's Wharf where we rent bicycles. Kyle seems flummoxed all of a sudden. "I should be working. I've got to get going on the customer service plan."

"There's no use arguing with her," I say, tugging at my knit top that keeps riding up. "She's not our top salesperson for lack of persuasive skills."

Kyle laughs and glances at the map she handed him. "Guess I can work on the plane tonight."

The curling chill in the air seems to be a hindrance for a bite ride through the city. However, that doesn't stop Reagan's enthusiasm. When she plops an electric-pink helmet on my head, I balk.

"Why do I have to wear this? I'm not riding in the Tour de France," I smart off.

"You should never ride a bike without a helmet," she says, zipping up her fleece jacket.

"That's crap," I say. "I rode a bicycle my entire childhood without wearing one. I never crashed my head like these kids today."

Reagan's mouth drops open and Kyle laughs heartily.

"I'm serious," I continue. "It's whacked out, over-protective parents who've caused this helmet phenomenon. Kids are so molly-coddled they can't even enjoy riding a bike." I flatten my mouth and put my hands on my hips. "Anyway, it'll make my hair go flat." Why do I care what my hair looks like? It's not like I have a date. No, he's in jail. I swallow hard, feeling Rory's deception blaze through me like nasty heartburn. Treacherous shit head.

"Vanessa Virtue, I can't believe what's coming out of your mouth," Reagan scolds. "Children have *died* not wearing helmets."

"Do I look like a child?" I don't know why I'm taking out my Rory-wrath on nice Reagan.

Kyle leans against his bike. "Vanessa, you need to wear it. It's like a state law or something. We don't want anything to happen to you," he says with a manipulative smile.

I plop the fuchsia monstrosity on my noggin. "Sorry, Rea. It's not you. It's me," I say, not wanting to elaborate.

"That's okay, girlfriend." She buckles the strap under her chin. On her, it looks cute, hip, and adventurous. It makes me look like a flathead worm.

"It's not like you're going to run into anyone you know," she says with a laugh.

"Exactly," Kyle agrees.

I straddle my bike. "You both better hope not."

According to the map, it will take four hours to traverse the western shore of San Francisco Bay, cross the Golden Gate Bridge, and ride down into Sausalito. From there, we're supposed to take the ferry back across the Bay. Because Reagan has to stop and take pictures every one hundred feet, we'll never be done with this.

"You guys pose over there," she instructs, waving Kyle and me toward the duck pond at the Presidio.

Awkwardly, I lean on Kyle and he wraps his arm around me. I'm suddenly crushed against his steel frame and it feels way too good. I must be exhibiting something similar to panic because Reagan yells, "Smile for Christ's sake, Vanessa."

Never have I been so cold in my entire life, yet there's a warm after-glowing tingle across my shoulder as Kyle pulls away. It's probably pheromones on overload. I hop back on the bike and try to pedal faster so I'm not behind Kyle, looking at his behind.

At Baker's Beach, Reagan wants to photograph the wind surfers, so Kyle and I wait on the sandy path. My cycle is propped on the kickstand until a gusting wind blows it over, knocking me to the ground. The pedal cuts a nasty gash in my jeans and blood oozes from my calf.

"Dammit all!"

Kyle tosses his bike down and is immediately at my side. He pulls out a familiar handkerchief and presses it to the wound. "I've got to put pressure on it."

My fingers are so cold, my teeth won't stop chattering, and I fear I'm going to start weeping like a baby. I bite my quivering lip with my teeth and will the bleeding to stop.

"It's not as bad as it looks," he says, his warm hazel eyes comforting. He's acting more like my friend than a co-worker. Isn't he worried how Reagan might interpret his attentiveness?

Somehow, I don't care though. I stifle a feigned laugh. "I'm more upset that my new jeans are ripped." I take my helmet off and run my fingers through the clumped mess. I hope I don't look as bad as I feel. This is not the cool, city girl image I try to project. Cold. Bleeding. Annoyed. Bad hair. Seriously, I don't know what else can happen.

That's when I hear...

"Vanessa Virtue? Oh, my God. Is that you?"

I cringe, not wanting to turn around.

"I think that guy's calling you," Kyle says.

I crane my head around to see a wet surfer approaching.

No. It couldn't be...

Alan Partridge. College boyfriend.

Oh right, he does live here.

"Vanessa! It *is* you," he exclaims, trotting toward me with surfboard on his hip. "It's been forever"

Man, I'm going to kill Reagan for making me wear this helmet. One always wants to look sensational when running into an ex.

Kyle helps me up and lowers his brows in Alan's direction. He stands by possessively while I fake an excited look.

"Alan, I can't believe it's you. How are you?" I try to sound composed. He's just as adorable as he'd been in college. Only more muscular. His black hair is slick from swimming and his green eyes shine out from his smiling face.

"I'm fantastic. What are you doing here?"

"I'm in town on business. We're flying out tonight, so we thought we'd kill time and bike around the city."

"That's fabulous. And you happened upon my beach. I come out every weekend, no matter the temperature. The waves are amazing." He smiles past me and looks approvingly at Kyle.

"Hi, I'm Alan Partridge. Vanessa and I went out in college."

"Kyle Nettles," he says, stretching his hand out. "We work together." There's a bit of an irked off tone to his voice.

"So, last I heard you were in Dallas," I say to Alan.

"Yeah, but I met someone and he wanted to move here."

"He?"

"Yeah, Josh. My boyfriend. We've been together almost three years." Alan must read the shock on my face. "I guess you didn't know I'd come out of the closet."

Kyle covers his uncomfortable laugh by clearing his throat. I can't look at him for fear I'll throw up right here, right now. "Umm, well, no," I stutter.

"Come on, you guys," Reagan yells from fifty feet away. "We've got to keep going."

"Look, it was great seeing you, Alan. I'm happy for you and, err, Josh," I say. We hug awkwardly and then I give him my business card, telling him to keep in touch.

My history with men sucks. My college boyfriend is gay and my last fling is in jail. Two strikes. One more, I'm out.

I look into Kyle's clear eyes and wonder about him. About his kindness. "You keep rescuing me and I don't know why."

He gazes at me softly, almost too softly, and says, "Maybe one day you'll figure it out."

CHAPTER TWENTY-FOUR

"**I**'ve been beating a dead date dad," I slur to Griz at Cuchi Cuchi's over my third Godiva chocolate martini Sunday night after returning from San Francisco.

"You're doing what?" she asks over the loud music. "You're beating off? Vanessa, really."

I bang my head on the table, trying to erase the memories of the last three days and Griz's current attempt at humor.

"Stop that!" She pushes my shoulders back.

I'm emotionally drained and I don't give a rat's ass about anything. I've been foolish in my judgment and I deserve to suffer. I want to drink until I don't feel pain. Until my brain can make sound decisions again. Until I can exterminate everything about *him* from my system. The lying sack of human excrement.

Griz signals for another cocktail. "Start from the beginning.

I enunciate slowly. "I'm. Dating. A. Deadbeat. Dad."

"Well, that's a new one."

After relaying the sordid details to Griz, I realize I'm going to have a hell of a hangover tomorrow, so I order a Diet Coke. "What idiot allows bars open on Sunday anyway?"

"People who know other people need to sulk and feel sorry for themselves." She looks at her watch and then notes.

"You officially have three days to that and then you have to get the hell over it."

I think what happened with Rory qualifies for the need to wallow in a huge vat of self-pity. All this time, I've tried to be professional—and follow company rules—around Kyle when he's the one who's been on my side. Supporting me. Rescuing me.

"So do you think Rory's going go to jail to stay?" Griz asks.

"I don't care."

"So that's it? You'll never hear from him or see him again?"

"Would *you* want to see him again?"

She thinks for a moment. "I suppose not."

"Besides, I was calling it quits anyway." I poke at my chest. "*I* wanted to be in control, though."

"'Because of all the sneaking around and stuff?"

"It didn't feel right, Griz. He didn't seem right. Don't I look smart now? I hope they put him under the fucking jail."

"Vanessa…"

"No, seriously. Pour concrete over him and seal him up for all eternity so he won't do anything manipulative or harmful to another person."

Sipping my soda, I hope it will sober me up. I slump in the seat, my shoulders feeling the weight of my head. I can't hold it up. Don't want to. Sitting tall means I'm proud and sturdy. Those words don't describe me right now. I can't believe what a dumb shit I've been. "This whole thing was a salmon trip, Griz."

"I don't know what a salmon trip is," she says.

I squint at her and point my index finger. "It's when you spend your entire life swimming upstream only to get screwed by someone you barely know and then die in the end." I let my head fall back to the tabletop.

"Vanessa, you're not dead. You're only beaten up. Like Grizabella the Glamour Cat. Everything's going to be okay."

If she breaks into a song from the musical "Cats," I'm going to get up and leave without paying my bill.

She doesn't, so I pull myself up and smile weakly. "I let this happen," I say. "Rory got what he wanted."

"What are you talking about? He abandoned his family and messed around with you. If he hadn't got arrested, he was going to mess around with you some more!" Griz doesn't know about the demo disk. And she never will because it's a spotlight on my own idiocy. "He's a duplicitous salesman."

I nod. "Yes, he is. I don't want to talk about him or what happened anymore. Guys aren't worth the effort."

She sips her water. "You should become a lesbian. It's very 'in' these days."

I shake my head and laugh. "I'm sure I'd screw that up, too."

"What about Kyle?"

My heart betrays me with a quick skitter. "What about him?"

She moves my empty martini glass away. "He likes you."

"He thinks I'm pathetic."

Griz sighs. "You know, maybe you're not so smart. You need to look around and see what's right in front of your face, woman."

I don't understand why Griz is doing this to me. I'm vulnerable. Weak. "The last thing I need is to throw myself at Kyle. I have no chance with him. Unlike you, I don't want to jeopardize my job."

"Rick and I are discreet. You and Kyle could be, too."

"We're working together on this project."

"All the more reason to see where things could go," she says. "Jiles knows you spend time together anyway, so what's the big deal? Just say you're working when you're really dating."

"No. Maybe. I don't know. Perhaps in another lifetime." I'm warmed by the thought of Kyle and me. Hell, I've been attracted to the guy since Day One. I don't know if it's worth the risk, though. Bottom line, I have to make myself happy. Work. That's where I'll bury myself. Aislin's on maternity leave and it's my chance to shine.

Starting tomorrow morning.

I down the rest of my soda and signal for the bill. "I can't talk about this anymore, but thanks Griz. I really appreciate it."

She lays money on the table. "You're not wearing those earrings Whatever-The-Hell-His-Name-Was, gave you. What happened?"

Straightening up, I laugh at my last melodramatic act related to the Rory Incident. "I gave them to William to put on eBay. Last I saw, the current bid was twenty-eight dollars."

I pulverize my keyboard while adding leads into the sales system from the San Francisco show. An Outlook alert pops: *New mail has arrived. Would you like to read it now?*

"No, fuck off," I mutter out loud. "I would not like read it right now." Still, I Alt+Tab to my e-mail. It's a multi-for-warded urban legend from Jack. I respond: *I'm busy.*

Two minutes later, he sends: *Why do you hate your keyboard?*

Bad weekend. Don't mess with me, I reply.

What are you, Texas? he sends.

I crack up laughing, silently blessing Jack for staying on me.

"Up to no good?" a velvety voice interrupts my shenanigans.

I look up into the hazel eyes that always make me feel at ease. "Can't get away from you, can I?"

Kyle leans against my cube. "I hope not."

I swallow the knot in my throat that his smile produces.

"Listen, are you ready to roll on the customer service plan?" he asks. "I can't do it alone."

A smile crosses my face. "Whatever you need from me. I owe you."

"Let's talk about it over lunch. Paparazzi?"

Eek. That's a nice restaurant. Kyle's dressed in a black shirt and tan pants. I, on the other hand, am cultivating the Boston sports fan look wearing a Bruins hockey jersey and my blue jeans.

"Maybe not somewhere so fancy. How about Boca Grande?"

He points toward the door. "Lady's choice."

We walk in silence in the chilly November air. What a depressing time of year. As a kid, I loved the holiday season, but now it's all crass commercialism. We pass the Galleria, decorated to the hilt for the season. Christmas sales and ads already consume the city and it's not even Thanksgiving. The aggressive chain store marketing is everywhere you look...the T, the newspaper, on cabs. Hell, Santa and his elves are sponsored by Dunkin Donuts and are all wearing Gap T-shirts.

In Boca Grande, we each order a chicken burrito with extra sour cream—we like the same things—and head for the top section to discuss the customer service plan.

"So, we'll go with the classroom style seating for the meeting in New Orleans," I say, taking a bite of the messy meal after I jot down some notes.

"You aren't from here, are you?" Kyle asks with a glint in his eye. If he's not careful, he's going to convince me that not all guys are jerks. That and I can disregard company dating policy rules because if his sexy eyes, deadly smile, and that goddamned dimple.

I smile at his query. "No *hah-sh* New England accent. I'm a military brat. I'm from everywhere."

"Ahh. I'm a local boy, myself. Grew up in Wellesley Hills."

I lift a brow, listening. Wellesley is one thing, but Wellesley Hills means his family probably has money. You'd never know by looking at him, though. He's not nearly as pretentious as Ted Spencer thinks he is.

"Where'd you go to school?" I ask, wanting him to keep him talking about himself. Suddenly I crave more knowledge about him. Nice Kyle who's always been on my side. I'm finally opening my eyes wide enough to see what's there underneath the corporate image.

"Boston College. Undergraduate and graduate school. Triple eagle, in fact."

"What does that mean?"

"Oh, just that I went to BC High, too... the mascot's an eagle... never mind," he says with a smile. "Local expression."

I take another bite and contemplate. "Haven't you ever wanted to get away from here?"

"I travel for work all the time, but my family is here. This is home."

I harrumph. "My childhood was a moving truck existence, living in six states and two countries."

"You turned out okay from what I can tell," he says with a grin.

Damn that dimple.

Changing the subject, I note, "You have a reputation as a compassionate customer advocate." I gaze at the top of his spikey black head as he pores over the papers strewn on the table.

Looking up, he says, "I enjoy what I do, but I get frustrated when companies don't see the importance of customer satisfaction. Some CEOs don't recognize how vital client care is." He picks up his burrito and gnaws on it a bit more. "Jiles doesn't understand. All he sees is the bottom line. Money. Dollar signs. If I can change that, then I've earned my paycheck."

"I'll help you any way I can," I say, nodding.

Kyle points at my mouth. "You've got a little sour cream right there..."

Without thinking, I waggle my tongue to get at the rogue dairy product. "Did I get it?"

"No... it's... umm... down a little." His eyes watch my every motion and suddenly the chicken and beans settle hard in my stomach into something similar to a delicious ache of desire for this guy seated next to me.

I retract my tongue and wipe furiously at my mouth with a napkin. Lovely. I'm such a slob. And in front of the Hazel-Eyed Hunk. "Sorry."

His eyes crinkle at me. "Happens to everyone."

When we finish, he does the most courteous thing a thirty-year-old guy can possibly do: he stands and pulls my chair out for me. And back at the office, he lets me go in the elevator first and opens the office door for me. Come to think of it, he's been doing this on all of our travels together, only I just now realized it.

Griz is waiting at my cube when we return.

"See you later, Vanessa," Kyle says, walking away.

"Thanks for lunch," I add and retake my seat.

She watches him walk away and says in a hissed tone, "Something going on with you two?"

"Just lunch and work," I say quickly. I don't want her to know I've actually come to my senses. That I'm seriously letting my attraction for Kyle Nettles take over my better judgment.

"He is mighty gorgeous to look at," Griz says.

I sit at my desk. "Please don't drool on my marketing plan." Then I ask, "Do you need something"

"Who me? No. I was leaving you a note that Jiles Chancey is looking all over for you."

"Oh."

Right then, Little Baby Jesus marches down the aisle like a Storm Trooper. "Vanessa, I needed that lead pipeline spreadsheet ten minutes ago," he shouts as he passes my cube. "Where've you been?"

Griz hightails it back to her desk.

Trying not to stammer, I say, "Discussing the customer service plan with Kyle."

"Well, get this done," he snaps. "Now."

I bust a gut on the Excel table, making it perfect, print it out, and proudly deliver it to Little Baby Jesus' office.

"Sit down. We need to talk," LBJ says as I attempt not to shake in place. I don't want him to know he scares me, so I slide into the chair in front of his desk to give my knees relief.

"With Aislin out on maternity leave, I want to see how you think outside the box and how proactive you are." LBJ crosses his legs. "You should step up to the plate and show us what you're worth."

I thought I'd already shown what I'm worth with all of the travel, late nights, and sacrificed weekends that I spend here instead of at home. I'm not exactly sure what *more* I can do to prove myself further. Work is a good thing and it keeps my concentration occupied instead of focusing on the tomfoolery with Rory or Rodney. I wish I could download the memories of our interaction together onto a thumb drive and then erase it for all eternity.

Then Jiles knocks me back to the here and now.

"You're a real team player, Vanessa. I want you and Nettles together twenty-four/seven getting these client meetings set. No excuses."

I blink hard, trying to comprehend his words. He's ordering me to spend more time with Kyle. It's all about work; however, the little niggle inside me feels that it's a tad bit coincidental and convenient. While I continue to do my job to the best of my abilities, I'll admit being in close proximity and contact with Kyle Nettles isn't going to do much to stop me from exploring these feelings for him. All that time I put into giving Rory my attention and Kyle's been right under my nose.

So, I'll do as ordered by supervisor. More time working with Kyle.

Geesh, I guess that means I need to start dressing better.

Apparently Griz and William agree, because when I get home, they surprise me with an emergency makeover and fashion intervention. I guess I haven't been suffering as silently over Rory as I'd thought.

Thanks to my friends' efforts, my closet is now free of unfashionable, baggy clothes. They sealed them up in a Hefty bag to be carted off to Goodwill. Never to be seen again, thus ending my four-week pity-party.

My makeover consists of a facial, pedicure, and manicure. They even color my hair with Clairol's Apricot Rapture from the Herbal Essences Spicy Collection—*sounds sassy*—the one that makes the woman shout out orgasm-like in the TV ad. It enriches the golden tones in my hair. I have to admit, they did a great job.

Griz organizes my black clothes like a department store. Pants, skirt, and shirts all sectioned off. We come up with several outfits both she and William assure me compliment my figure.

"Look at this." She's up to her elbows in my underwear drawer. "You've got all this sexy underwear. What the hell are these?" She holds up a pair of oversized, worn, cotton panties.

I snag them from her. "They're comfortable. So sue me."

"You won't feel sexy if you're wearing granny panties. You'll feel like the frump you've been looking like."

"I haven't been looking like a frump."

William nearly spews coffee and then reaches for his phone. "Griz has been sending me pictures of your daily work attire. Do I need to go through all of the photos and give you my real opinion?"

I glare at Griz. "You took pictures of me?

"This isn't about me. It's about you, Vanessa, and getting you out of this funk."

No, it's actually about two of the best friends a girl can have. They care deeply and won't let me wither away in the corner all because one horrid man trampled my heart.

I can't help but feel like things are looking up.

And why wouldn't they with help from friends like this.

CHAPTER TWENTY-FIVE

A week later, my Android beeps during the sales, market-ing, and client services meeting. I ignore it at first while I listen to Jiles' presentation. But the notifications persist.

I pull the device into my lap and pull my finger over the screen, clicking on the messages icon. It's from Kyle's cell phone and it reads: *You did something to your hair.*

It beeps again.

"Virtue, turn that damn thing off," Jiles snaps.

"Sorry, the battery must be running low." Hastily, I click the sound off only to see another text message: *So, did you?*

I pan the room and then I catch those spectacular hazel eyes, smiling at me from the back.

Trying my best to act like I'm listening to Jiles instead of texting, I write: *Shouldn't we be listening, Mr. Manager?*

Nothing I haven't heard before, is the next text.

What's the point? I write back.

Blamestorming.

What's that?

Less creative brainstorming?

I thought that's why they hired you.

I do my best.

Okay, maybe he's not the non-stop Mr. Corporate I origi-nally thought he was. Maybe he's not a Jiles wannabe, either. He's just a hard worker. Like me.

Guys love compliments, so I text: *You're the Miracle Man.*

He writes: *Whatever. So... the holiday party...*

DigitalDirection is holding its annual event at the Royal Sonesta hotel tomorrow night.

I respond: *You going?*

Like he has a choice. Everyone is required to go.

Yep. Let's have a drink together, okay?

My heart skips a beat and it's all I can do not to break out into a beaming smile. Kyle is sort of asking me out. It's a safe environment. A work thing where flirting can mix in with forced socialization.

Before I can hit send on my "*Okay*," I get another text: *Meet me after this.*

Following the meeting, Kyle is deep in conversation with one of the Willies—I don't know which one is which. I don't want to loiter, so I head back to my desk. Ten minutes later, I hear a creak as someone leans against the partition of my cube.

"What color is that?" Kyle asks, pointing at my hair.

I sit up tall. "It's apricot."

"It suits you. It's soft and pretty." His smile and compliment warms me from head to toe. I wonder if he thinks that I am soft and pretty, or just my hair. Men should learn to be more specific.

"Thanks, Kyle. So, what's up?" I ask, changing the subject away from me.

"Mind if I sit?" He hitches his black clad hip up onto the top of my desk. I shake my head and watch the smooth fabric stretch over his muscular thighs. Charcoal spidery eyelashes, that are way too long to be wasted on a guy, frame his hazel eyes. It may be cliché, but his features *are* chiseled and precise. When I feel the overwhelming desire to reach up and run my finger along his lips, I sit on my hand to keep it from acting out on its own.

"What's up?" I repeat, trying not to stare at his... everything. I'm livid with myself for letting Rodney Elmore fool me when Kyle has been the one all along that I've had this dormant attraction to. And all because of some asinine employee handbook and my pre-conceived notions, I pushed toward the wrong person. However, like a fresh summer breeze bringing warmth and freshness to me, I suddenly realize I don't care about DigitalDirection's rules or regulations. Maybe after spending so much time with me, Kyle doesn't care about them either. Or so it seems by the look in his eyes.

He clears his throat and the moment's over. For now.

"Our first client meeting is after the holidays in Newport Beach, California," he starts. "I was thinking it would be nice to have a 'thanks for your business' flyer inside the portfolios."

I smooth out my short black skirt. This is one of those "you better wear this to work" outfits Griz and William picked out. "We don't really have time to get anything through the design and printing phase here."

"I was hoping you could design it," Kyle says, smiling, exposing the dimple. I want to place my index finger in the dent.

"I don't know about designing it myself. I mean—"

"You know the basic layout design software, right?"

"Well, sure. I suppose I can take a stab at it."

"Here's what I'm after." He leans across my desk. For a second, I think he's after my left breast, rather he reaches past me for a notebook and pen. I take a deep breath and steady myself. I watch him sketch. He's a lefty with a really nice handwriting. He adds squiggles where the company logo should be. I open my drawer to get another pen and add a couple of thumbnail sketches to his ideas. "We're on the same wavelength," he says, cheerfully.

Looking at our sketch, I can do this. "Give me a while to play with this, okay?"

An hour later, Kyle's standing by the printer when I go to retrieve my masterpiece. I hand him the flyer. "How does this look to you?"

"Pretty good. I have an idea, though. Do you mind?"

He points toward my cube and follows me there. He snags the empty chair from Jack's area and pulls it into mine. I scoot my chair under the desk to make room for him as he edits the text. At one point, we both reach for the pen and our hands brush before he relents and allows me to claim the tools. My skin burns where it touched his. It's nice to know that after a month and a half of my self-imposed nunnery my libido is still alive. My whole body reacts in a relaxed, lazy, liquid way. Goose bumps run over me and I hope my excitement doesn't show through my white shirt.

Remarkably, for the first time in a long time, I'm not over-analyzing things. I'm not worrying about what people will think, or who will see us. I'm actually going with the flow.

Kyle moves from the chair and plops his hip on the desktop. He leans in toward my computer screen, pointing at graphics and text boxes. But, I'm gone; immersed in the smell and nearness of him. He has a slight citrus scent to him and I wonder what cologne he wears. Happy? Escada? Tommy? His long-sleeved olive polo stretches across his broad chest and highlights the expansive curves of his forearms. The pants fit him perfectly, accentuating his trim physique.

I gasp unknowingly.

He's simply the most gorgeous guy I've ever met.

"See if that works," Kyle says, running his hand through his hair. I wonder what the texture's like. Stiff and bristly? Or soft and inviting?

"Sorry?" I try to key in on what he just said. Then, I notice he's looking down my shirt. He doesn't see me catch him, but it's apparent. There's a mellifluous reaction throughout me once again and I fidget to control it. He is interested in me, despite these idiotic company rules. Maybe... just maybe Kyle Nettles is a rebel after all.

His hand is on the back of my chair. He's so close I can feel the warmth emanating from him. "We make a good team, Vanessa."

"I think so, too." I finger my hair behind my ears and his eyes follow the movement of my hand. Then, they move to my mouth. His lips part slightly and he takes a deep breath. We bend toward each other and I feel my head tip to the side.

Dear God, he's going to kiss me and I'm going to let him.

"Yo, Nettles."

We jump apart. Surely my face registers my shock and awe. My eyes shift over his shoulder to see one of the Willies.

"What's going on here?" he asks sternly.

Kyle rocks back and clears his throat. "Nothing, just working on a flyer for the customers."

Will doesn't seem convinced. "That's not what it looked like to me," he says with a bit of a sneer.

I can't look up. I can't meet his stare or his judgment. Holy shit! I can't believe what we were thinking of doing. We were almost busted.

"I'm, umm, finished here," Kyle says, standing up.

"Will needs to see you," the other Will says, then turns.

I stare at the computer screen and queue the final version to the printer trying to swallow down the reality of what almost happened. Not at being caught. Over what could have been. My pulse is going triple time under my skin. I don't want Kyle to go meet with a Willie. I want him to stay right here. For the rest of the day. I want to put him in my pocket and take him home with me. Kyle almost kissed me. In the office. Here for everyone to see.

He seems reluctant to leave, but scratches his head. "Look, I'm sorry I—"

Please don't let him have regret. I switch back immediately to professional business mode. "I'll get copies of the flyer into the portfolios and ship them to the hotel in California."

He smiles in relief. "You're the best, Vanessa." Then, before leaving, he leans over the cube divider and says, "Don't forget that drink tomorrow night at the holiday party."

As he rounds the corner, I grab the phone and buzz Griz's extension. E-mail's too slow for *this* development.

CHAPTER TWENTY-SIX

Kyle is into me.

Or so I'm trying to convince myself as I sit at the pre-holiday party Board presentation (bored, more like) with my mind wandering to Kyle. That scene in my cube yesterday was enough to whack out my sensibilities and damn near throw a Molotov cocktail at the "no office dating" rule.

When the meeting finishes, we move into the main ballroom of the Royal Sonesta, overlooking the Charles River. The setting sun throws an amber glow over the banquet room, decorated with tables in fine linen, plain white holiday lights, and with several buffet stations lining the walls. One of the HR ladies hands me two drink tickets when I walk in. I work my way into the room and see Aislin with her newborn, Caitlin.

"Oh, Ais, she's adorable." The little bundle has fuzzy red hair just like her mother.

"Do you want to hold her while I get a soda?" Aislin asks.

Even though I'm not very good with babies, I take the squirming bundle into my arms. "You're such a lucky little girl, you know that? You have a great mommy." I prop Caitlin up slightly and show her where Paul Honan stands at the bar. "Look, there's your daddy over there." A dull knot stabs me in the gut. "He's a good guy. He'd never abandon you, leaving you to wonder where he is and when he'll return or not pay child support—"

My breath catches in my throat and I want to run from the room screaming. Just when a cloud of contentment and self-assurance hangs over me, I've let *him* back in.

"Here, Jack, can you take her?" I pass Caitlin to my Nordic co-worker who happily accepts her.

I clench my fists at my side and turn away.

Rory.

Damn him. Damn everything about him. Damn anyone who won't damn him.

My physical makeover may be complete, but I can tell my soul still needs some work. I need to get out of here.

I spin quickly on my heels and bump square chested into Kyle.

"Whoa! What's the hurry?" he asks, smiling down at me.

"Sorry, Kyle. Just needed some air."

He nods over at Caitlin. "You looked good with her."

"She's a little doll," I say, feeling my anger draining.

Kyle looks me straight in the eyes. "Takes one to know one."

Man, his timing's good and my heart springs back to life, diving straight to my feet and back with his blatant flirting. I open my mouth to speak, but one of the Willies pulls him aside. Those men are always interrupting at inopportune moments.

"Hey, I heard that," Griz says, stuffing a carrot stick into her mouth.

"Heard what?"

"Kyle's compliment. He's really into you and you like it."

I shrug, not wanting to give away my game. "Around Kyle, I feel empowered. Not like I'm some useless little woman who's nothing without a man. I don't harp on my failed relationships or my work stress."

Griz is right about the stupid Section seven edict. Who are these people—this employer—to tell us how to live our personal lives? We should be able to test interactions with people we find attractive, freely, without judgment or repercussions. I'm a grown up. I don't need anyone's permission to explore my feelings toward Kyle.

I glance about trying to relocate the Hazel-Eyed Hunk. There he is… leaning against the bar talking to Paul Honan, Aislin's husband. I take in Kyle's smart outfit of gray pants and a long-sleeved black dress shirt with a gray T-shirt underneath.

Not wanting to stare, I move to the hors d'oeuvres table and pile a couple of baby quiches, some cold shrimp, and something vaguely meatball-shaped on my plate. I love free dinner.

Griz and Rick have scoped out a table and saved some seats. When I approach, their hands break apart quickly. Maybe they aren't as irresponsible as I think. This is an official work event, after all.

I set my plate down, eyeball Griz, and then go stand in line for a glass of wine.

Suddenly, Jiles is behind me, breathing down my neck. "Are you having fun, Vanessa?" LBJ asks. I force myself not to cringe hearing his grating voice.

"So far, Jiles. And you?"

He scans the room with his beady little eyes. "Well, it's a waste of money to do something this extravagant, but I got over-ruled by the HR people. They said it'd be good for morale. I think the morale booster should be that you still have a job, right?" He knocks me on the shoulder to make his point.

I truly hate him. I don't understand how he got so high up the corporate ladder having so few social skills I want to smack him on his furry little chin. Instead, I fake a smile and face forward.

I no sooner make camp at the table with Griz and Rick, sipping my Chardonnay when I hear, "Can I sit with you guys?" Kyle settles his cute self down. Our gazes touch and I swear I see a sparkle in his.

"Yeah, but we're going be drinking this place dry, so you'll have to come along for the ride." Griz toasts him with her glass.

Reagan and Ted join us and I realize all of sudden that everyone seems to be shucking off the company rules and, as Griz says, going with the flow.

When the drink tickets run out, we decide to take turns buying rounds. If I'm lucky, the party will end before they make it to me. Only one lone Lincoln in my Kate Spade knock-off. Our socializing is interrupted when Jiles taps his glass to get everyone's attention. The conversations subside so we can hear what the president has to say.

"I want to rattle off what a great job you're all doing. We've got a great team, a fantastic product and we're going to kick major tail feathers in the New Year."

Everyone claps politely, although I can tell my fellow co-workers want to get back to the free eats and not-so-free drinks. I glance over at Reagan and Ted and note how comfortable they seem, almost snuggled up together with his arm draped across the back of her chair. Rick, too, has his arm flush against Griz's on the table, not caring who can see their not-so-subtle public display of affection. Then there's Kyle and me. I wonder if people think there's something going on with us.

Feeling warm and fuzzy, I'm suddenly knocked back into the here and now when Kyle taps me on the back and points at Jiles.

LBJ raises a large, shiny, silver spatula and announces, "I'm happy to present the 'Chef of the Year' to the employee who has contributed the most winning ingredients to the company's recipe for success. Vanessa Virtue!"

"What?" I exclaim, my hand to my heart. "Is this real?"

Kyle wraps his arm around me and squeezes. "I knew that was coming," he whispers.

Goose bumps cover my arms, even though I'm clad in a Gap sweater. Did Kyle nominate me for this? The look in his eyes says he was in on the decision.

Griz jostles me. "Double-Vee! You need to get up there."

I stand and inchworm through the tables to accept my award from Jiles. "You're cooking with gas, Virtue," he says.

As I make my way back to the table, the DJ spins hits from the 70s and 80s. Folks get up on the dance floor. Reagan and Ted make a spectacle of themselves gyrating way too friendly-like. All around me people are pairing off and I wonder if someone's slipped a love potion into the Cambridge, Massachusetts water system.

I see Nancy Mendelssohn, HR Director, frown as she watches our two top salespeople. Reagan needs to watch herself, especially after the "sex in the server room" incident a while back that put her on warnings.

I look at Griz and Rick, who have their heads bent together in an intimate conversation. I follow Nancy's judgmental eyes as they settle on our table. Rick leans in and whispers something to Griz and then goes to get her more wine.

Griz smiles and slides her eyes back and forth between Kyle and me. I give her a "don't even think about it" stare, although I wonder what exactly she sees. I hope Nancy Mendelssohn doesn't note it, as well.

Kyle picks up the spatula and swats at me playfully. "I knew what a great asset you are to this company. Now you have proof. How about that drink I owe you? You drink white, right?"

It's nice that he's taken notice all this time. "Chardonnay thanks." I watch him move through the tables to stand in line at the bar. My heart lurches and my breath hitches. Treacherous heart and double-crossing breath telling me it might be worth "getting caught" to have him in my life.

"Somebody's got a huge crush," Griz whispers.

"No I don't," I say a bit too quickly.

"I'm talking about *him*, Vanessa."

"Don't be ridiculous." It does make sense, though. The flirting in my cube. The come-hither looks and complimentary comment. Not to mention the innumerable flutterings in my body whenever Kyle's near. I can't tell Griz any of this because she will make too big a deal out of it and make it into something that it really shouldn't be as long as we're all employed under the same roof.

"Vanessa, I thought we'd gotten over the bitter stage. I mean, you're bathing again every day and you're not dressing like a frump anymore. Kyle's a wicked little flirt."

"He's only being nice. We've done a lot on this client services plan." If I admit the flirting to Griz, it'll become real. Then I'll screw it up or get caught.

"Well," she says, fiddling with her napkin, "I think it's more than that. There's chemistry."

"I'm sure he has a girlfriend. I mean, please, would *that* not have a steady thing?"

"Rick said he doesn't." She pauses, then adds. "Show him the charming side of Vanessa Virtue. Bat your eyelashes, cross your legs toward him, stick your tits out."

"You did not just say that."

"You heard me."

"Yeah, and so did half the room."

"Here he comes. Be nice," she says. "Remember, where you tend a rose, a thistle can't grow."

"What the...?" We both collapse on the table laughing.

"What's so funny?" Kyle sets a full glass of wine in front of me.

Instinctively, though, I lean toward Kyle. "Griz just says the strangest things sometimes. Like she's a female Confucius or something."

Rick returns, wrapping his arm around her and tickle-teasing her. I see her reach under the table and place her hand on his thigh. There's no doubt how Rick feels about her. Smitten.

Seeing Griz and Rick, I'm fueled by a burning jealousy. Not that I want Rick, but my heart aches for... *that*. What they've got going. The gut-wrenching attraction. The need to touch the other person. Even secretly. The desire that eats you up inside. Closeness. Comfort. All of it.

I slump in the chair slightly. I want that too.

Griz looks at her watch. "Oh! I've got to get going."

"Why? Hot date?" I ask more sarcastically than intended.

"No, my favorite Christmas movie is on tonight."

"Rudolph or Frosty?" Rick asks, grinning doe-eyed at her.

"No, 'It's a Wonderful Life,'" she says. "It's the best movie ever."

Something inside me clicks and an emotional maelstrom rolls up my chest causing me to spew my resentment. Annoyed that Griz has something I don't have. Irritated that I'd gone for the wrong guy before. Frustrated that I can't have the one sitting next to me because of stupid work regulations. The floodgate is open. "*It's a Wonderful Life?* You've got to be kidding me." I pick up my glass and slurp the wine in an unladylike gulp.

"You don't think it's great?" Kyle places his arm over the back of my chair, but it does nothing to stop me.

"No."

"But it's widely recognized as the most joyous holiday classic of love and hope," he says. Did he get that from *TV Guide?*

I put my wine glass down on the table. "Looking at the events of George Bailey's life, they certainly paint a different picture," I state.

Griz looks puzzled. "What do you mean?"

"It is *the most* depressing example of shattered dreams ever committed to film. The movie begins with George contemplating suicide. And no wonder! His life has taken one grim turn after another since boyhood. He never went to college, never saw the world and never built things. He was goaded into taking over a failing S&L and was almost jailed because he hired an inept relative. He missed out on the plastics revolution, and because he was 4-F, he couldn't even leave to fight Hitler."

"I never thought of it that way," Griz says, disappointment lacing her voice.

I'm on a roll and can't stop myself. "To the best of our knowledge, George never left the town he was born in, which he clearly and consistently states throughout the movie as his one wish in life. For whatever reason, Bedford Falls owns him and keeps sucking him back into its vortex." I'm teetering on the edge. "When God intervenes, even He, in saving poor George, keeps him within the city limits. Then they sing, bells ring and we're supposed to believe everything is okay? That George is finally happy enough?

That his meager existence in that town will cut it? I don't think so. It's the most depressing movie ever."

Kyle, Griz and Rick all stare in disbelief.

"Holy shit, Vanessa," Griz says. "Thanks a lot. I'll never be able to watch it the same way ever again."

Someone please stamp an "L" on my forehead. I'm a complete loser.

Kyle moves his arm to my shoulder, his eyes brimming with concern. I don't blink as he gazes at me. He probably thinks I should be committed after a speech like that. And I should be.

Then, he moves close to my ear. In a voice where only I can hear, he says, "Someone hurt you something awful, didn't they?"

The pity in Kyle's voice continues to ring through my head as I recount everything to William post-party. It continues through the weekend of no phone calls from Griz and sleepless nights, tossing, turning and listening to Mr. Paulsen's upstairs snores penetrate the thin ceiling. Kyle's words reverberate Monday morning at my desk while I try to focus on banquet orders for the Newport Beach, New Orleans, and Tucson client services meetings.

Maybe I should apologize to everyone for my tirade. It wasn't right of me to rain on Griz's happiness parade.

I sit back and reach for a jumbo paperclip from the magnetized holder on my desk. I straighten the long bit of metal and shape it into a "U" formation. When I was younger, I used to do this and pretend they were braces. Not that I needed them; I was just a strange little kid. Now, I roll the metal around my desktop with my left hand while my right holds my chin. I concentrate intently on what to do next in my quest to be a grown up.

The answer lies in Kyle Nettles. I need to ask him about that near kiss in my cube. I must find out if he feels anything for me. I have to know if he's interested enough to take the risk and see if this emotional magnetic pull we've got is for real. You can't fight what's natural. You can't legislate attraction.

I pick up the phone to dial his extension when I hear him next to me, "Hey Vanessa. You got a minute?"

I swallow hard and face him. "Listen, about the other night—"

He holds up his hand. "That's why I stopped by."

"I'm sorry," we say in unison.

I furrow my brows. "You're sorry? For what?"

He props his hip on the top of my desk and leans in. "That was rude of me to say what I did. You know, that thing about someone hurting you."

I drop my head and toy with my hands in my lap for a moment. "I'm sorry for going off on one of the most classic movies of all time."

He chuckles. "You know, I'd never thought about it before. You do have a point. George Bailey got screwed. It can be a depressing movie."

I lift my head and let a soft laugh escape. "Thanks, Kyle. Sometimes I don't think before I speak."

"It really is a movie of love, friendship, support, and hope." He pauses and then reaches out for my hand. My fingers curl automatically into his and the zap of electricity sizzles all the way down to my double-socked, boot covered toes. "Your assessment was cute. You're cute," he says.

My insides do one of those crazy loop-dee-loops while I let his words soak in. If I'm going to make a go at this with Kyle, it's confession time. "You were right, Kyle."

He rubs my knuckle with his forefinger. "How so?"

"Someone did hurt me. Wicked bad." I gulp hard and wonder if I should clarify. Not just yet. Keep it generic for now. "I've been a little bitter about guys lately."

Kyle's smile is warm and endearing. "We're not all bad."

This is the first time I've allowed myself to enjoy the sensation of his skin on mine. Before it was for fear of flying purposes. This is something more. A pressure low in my belly makes my body ache for him. It feels so right sitting here with our fingers weaved together to the point where I can't tell whose is whose. This isn't wrong, although company procedures would disagree. Apparently Kyle, the guy I thought was Mr. Corporate through and through, agrees that some rules just need to be broken since he continues to rub my hand.

"Dude, there you are," Rick shouts out as he approaches.

Kyle pulls away and stands up. "What's going on?"

Rick's face is ashen and I have a horrible feeling something bad has happened. I hope it's not more problems with losing customers from SalesTracker's shenanigans. I thought things were going better now that we'd rolled out our enhancements to the customers. Something's making Rick's eyes bug out though.

"Isabella and I just got out of Nancy Mendelssohn's office. Shit's hitting the fan big time."

I stand up. "Why? What did you do?"

"Too much fraternization at the company party," he says flatly. "Nancy reminded us of the policy against dating and said if we wanted to keep our jobs, we'll keep our socializing to a professional level as to not 'endanger' the customer base."

Kyle runs his hand through his hair, making it stand on end. He shifts his eyes over to me and lets out a long sigh.

"Doesn't this company have anything better to do — like make customers happy instead of torturing employees?"

"Is Griz okay?" I ask.

Rick lets out a puff of air. "She was put on warning. We both were."

I shake my head to try and rearrange my scattered thoughts. I told her. I said she and Rick had to be careful, but did they listen to me? Now they're on some sort of probation and at risk to lose their jobs. All for the pleasure of the flesh.

My eyes graze Kyle's as my heart pings in sympathy over what Griz and Rick are going through. I want Kyle so badly, yet I can't have him. I need this job. I have to have the money. My student loan won't get paid on its own. I refuse to rely on unemployment to get me through. I can't be a failure.

Rick interrupts my thoughts. "It gets worse, though."

"How can it get worse?" Kyle asks. He seems most frustrated, like he's searching for a solution to this dilemma.

"After the holiday party, Reagan got a room at the Sonesta and charged it to her company AmEx card."

"So?"

Continuing, Rick says, "Seems like she had some company."

I cover my mouth with my hand. "Tell me she didn't..."

"She and Ted Spencer used company money for their sex romp."

My chest tightens. "She's going to get fired."

Rick sneers. "She *got* fired. Nancy and Jiles are updating the company manual to reflect harsher 'no dating' policies. Something like, if you break the rule, not only do you lose your job, but you forfeit your vacation pay and stock options, as well."

Kyle slams his fist down. "This has nothing to do with running a profitable company, taking care of customers, or providing quality products. It's about controlling people's lives."

I'm relieved to hear Kyle stand up for employee's rights and buck Little Baby Jesus' way of management. I don't know what we can do about it, though. We have to play by the rules or suffer the consequences. Or find another job, which is easier said than done these days. Reagan knew she was already walking on thin ice, yet she defied the rules. Now she's paying the price for her actions. Our top salesperson—the woman who's brought in more new business this year—is fired over being attracted to someone.

"What about Ted?" I ask.

"First offense," Rick says. "Warning, just like us."

I look at Kyle's profile and see the frustration cross his beautiful face. He can't change this any more than I can. If we want to keep our jobs, we have to stay away from each other. I'm here to work. Not entertain my hormones.

Good thing I'm going on Christmas break soon. Time away from the office and away from Kyle will do me some good. It'll give me time to put the Hazel-Eyed Hunk out of my mind.

Time to put my priorities back in order.

Griz, Rick, and Reagan took the chance and have marred their professional fate.

Well, Vanessa Virtue is *not* making that mistake.

CHAPTER TWENTY-SEVEN

"What on God's green earth is that on your nose?" I ask Griz our first day back at work after the holidays. Time away has done me good and I'm ready to attack work—not my stymied sex drive—head on, living up to my "Chef of the Year" award.

Griz points to the diamond chip on her left nostril. "I got it pierced. I think it's sexy?"

"No, it's not. I want to flick at it. What made you do that?"

She shakes her head. "I got into a fight with my mom over Christmas and I needed to rebel. She said Boston's ruining me, so I did this. I call it my nose jewel of defiance."

"Well, that'll show her," I say with a snicker.

I spent Christmas with my parents, little sister, Victoria, and Sergeant, our faithful German shepherd. It was good to be "home" around the people who have to love me. I was able to forget about all of the work turmoil. I put aside—the best I could—thoughts of Kyle and his hazel eyes. I dodged my grown-up responsibilities for a week and luxuriated in my sister's teen angst, my mother's less-than-light cooking and my father's recycled jokes before returning to my urban family.

Griz, who seems unfazed, prattles on about her mother. "I did this when I got back, so she didn't even see my pierced nose. How insolent is that? But she'll flip when she sees it for the first time." Griz twirls the diamond chip around with her finger. "She cried when I got my ears pierced because of the religious overtones. She says the Bible tells you not to pierce your body because it's a temple for God. You're not supposed to get tattoos either. They're the mark of the beast"

I clap my hands together and laugh. "Sounds like a raucous good time at the Perry household this holiday season."

"That's what it's like growing up a minister's daughter."

We laugh together, until Griz winces. Her hand goes to her nose. "That hurts so good—like acupuncture—when I laugh too hard."

"Well," I say, "you can never underestimate the power of a perfectly placed prick."

"Is this a post-holiday party?" a male voice interrupts.

My Lord, it's Kyle. I hope he didn't hear what I said!

Looking at him brings to life the floodgate of emotions toward him I thought I'd dammed up over Christmas break. His hair is still damp from his morning shower and he smells lightly of musk. His skin is bronzed; toasted like a slice of wheat bread, not pasty-white like most New Englanders.

"Happy New Year, ladies. How's it going?" he asks politely.

"Obviously not as good as you," Griz says.

"Yeah, where'd you get that tan?" I say a bit too flirty, hoping Darth Nancy doesn't bound around the corner.

Kyle's deep tawny color continues down his throat to the base of his neck, exposed by the open collar of his royal blue shirt. This man looks more delicious every time I see him. The color only makes his eyes stand out even more. I realize I've missed talking to, working with, and just being around him, even if it was only for a week.

We can't pick up where we left off with the near kiss and the sensual hand holding. No more. Griz may not care that she's on probation, but I'm not going to be so irresponsible.

Kyle leans on the partition. "I went to Hawaii with a college buddy. It was amazing."

"And you didn't send me a postcard?" I say, not recognizing my own voice.

Griz nods approvingly and slides off my desk.

"No, but I got you this." He hands over a wrapped package.

"I'll catch you later. Bye, Kyle," Griz sings out.

"See ya, Isabella."

I take the shiny package and flip it over in my hand. It's bulky and round. Too big to be a three carat diamond. I rip the paper off and out pops a Magic 8-ball.

"I haven't seen one of these in years. Why'd you get me this?"

Kyle smiles and my toes involuntarily wiggle inside my shoes. "I thought it would be an entertaining conversation piece to the rest of your office toys. A 'thank you' for all the great work you've done. Besides, with our client meetings about to start, we need all the good luck we can get."

"That's for sure," I say, holding the 8-ball in my palm. "Will our meetings be a success?" I shake the ball and turn it to see the message in the window. Kyle moves around and places his head near mine to get a better look. I try not to breathe in the scent of him or acknowledge that my body is on fire with his nearness. "AS I SEE IT YES."

"Hey, that's good," I say, almost backing my chair into him.

"Let me try," Kyle says, smiling. "Will Vanessa Virtue go out with me?" I swallow hard and look up at him.

"Yeah, right..." He's kidding, isn't he? Surely he remembers what happened to Griz, Rick, Reagan and Ted before the holiday break.

"And the 8-ball says, 'OUTLOOK NOT SO GOOD.'" Kyle tosses it on my desk. "What the hell does it know, huh?"

"Umm... ahh... Kyle..." Holy shit. I don't know what's wrong with me. I've never had a problem talking before now. My dad called me "Motor Mouth" when I was little kid. Lowering my voice, I say, "You know that's not allowed. Against company rules."

"Some rules are meant to be broken, Vanessa."

I put my hand on my hip. "Some of us enjoy that direct deposit every two weeks so we can do pointless things like make rent, buy groceries, and pay off exorbitant student loans."

"There's more to life than money."

"Easy for you to say, Kyle. First off, you make a lot more than I do, so you have the luxury of saying that. Secondly, you're a guy, so you get to bend the rules more. Women can't. That should be evident from Reagan's firing. I'm not willing to take that chance." No matter how cute you are, I almost add.

His eyes crinkle as a smile spreads across his face. "You forgot the third thing."

"I don't have a third thing."

He holds up three fingers. "Third, I'm stubborn and don't like to take no for an answer. I will wear you down."

My skin heats at his words. Swirls of desire encompass the two of us and I can't guarantee that I'll be able to withstand his advances without eventually caving in. Cockiness becomes him. Kyle *is* a rogue after all. This might be hard, but I'm sticking to my guns.

"Nettles, there you are." It's the older one of the two Willies. "Jiles needs us pronto."

"Oh, okay. Catch ya later, Vanessa," Kyle says with a wink.

So much for my holiday mental cleansing. There goes Kyle sweeping in and taking over my thoughts again. As I watch his gorgeousness round the corner to Little Baby Jesus' office, I pick up the 8-ball and toss it from hand to hand.

He won't give up, huh? Doesn't care about company rules? I'm flattered that someone like Kyle would find me worthy of a challenge like this. I look at my new toy and ask, "Is he for real?"

My heart skitters along while the hazy blue liquid settles. The 8-ball reads, "BETTER NOT TELL YOU NOW."

"Oh, the hell with you," I say, flinging it to my desk.

I'll figure this out on my own.

January is over and done with before I know it. My time in the office increases as my time at home wanes. I've hardly seen Kyle or had the chance to talk with him since that morning in my cube. The Willies constantly have him out at customer sites throughout the country. Also, I've been to Dallas and Chicago for tradeshows.

Work—and lots of it—is good. I'm staying busy and focused and I'm not even thinking about the fact that Kyle wants to date me. We both know it's impossible, especially with the updated Employees Manual that was passed out two days ago with what I call the Reagan Rules and Griz Amendments.

Griz and Rick are still dating. Sleeping together to be more precise. They do a good job keeping it cool at work, but I've barely seen her off-hours because she's practically living with Rick.

"Why do you do it?" I ask her over lunch of our halved tuna, Muenster, and bacon on wheat. "Why are you risking everything?"

She chews carefully and waits to speak. "It's really quite simple, Double-Vee."

"Nothing's simple, Griz. Not work. Not life and certainly not love."

"I risk it because Rick is... *the one.*"

I nearly gasp. "How do you know?"

She shrugs. "We mesh well. And he makes me laugh."

"But you work together and it's against the rules." I can't seem to get this through her head. Griz lives in Back Bay, for heaven's sake, where rents aren't cheap. She has to be afraid of unemployment and not having any money.

"It is what it is," she says, wiping her mouth. "So we were sloppy in the beginning, but it was because of that first love, can't get enough of each other feeling. You want to be with them and let them know you're thinking about them twenty-four/seven."

I want to feel that too. I'll admit it; I'm scared.

I press. "Are you afraid that you're being watched?"

"Yeah. Course, I figure Jiles and Nancy don't have anything better to do than to legislate our private lives. Honestly, Vanessa, you worry too much about what Jiles Chancey thinks. You have to take charge of your life. Do what's best for you."

I take a bite of the sandwich and think for a minute. "Kyle sort of asked me out."

She bolts to attention, nearly dropping the remains of her sandwich. "It's about damn time. I told you he likes you."

"I know he does. I'm the one who doesn't want to do anything about it."

"Are you insane?"

Probably. "No, I'm being smart. Besides, the client services meetings have kicked off, he's going to be on the road a lot. The company's watching expenses and I have to do everything I can to make sure marketing is doing their part for the bottom line."

Griz folds her hands on the table and cocks her head to one side. "Vanessa Virtue is the cause you have worry about. Work is work. We're still in our twenties. There will be other jobs. There will be more important jobs. Quit stressing over this one. Someone like Kyle doesn't come around every day. Don't fuck it up."

My mouth forms an "O" and I stare at her. "Did you just say the 'f' word?"

"You're goddamn right I did," she says and then takes another bite of her sandwich. She means business.

Deep down, I don't want to admit that she's right.

When I get home that night, weary from trying to manage the myriad emotions and thoughts swirling in my head over Kyle, my responsibilities at work, and what's right or wrong, Mr. Paulsen is shoveling the remains of the latest New England snowstorm out of the driveway. He's bundled up in a hooded orange parka with only his creepy eyes.

I crawl out of my Cabrio and the land lizard stares at me. "Hi, Mr. Paulsen. They say we're supposed to have an early spring," I babble. If I'm nice, maybe he won't mess with my karma again.

He sets the shovel in front of him and rests his pointy chin on the handle. "I see you're wearing a rather large coat, Vanessa. Are you hiding something?"

"Hiding something? What do you mean?"

"Like all the weight you've gained?"

"Excuse me?" Yeah, I gained some poundage over the holidays, but this idiot should know you never mention weight to a woman. Then it hits me. "Do you still think I'm pregnant?"

His mouth flattens out in a disapproving grimace.

Other than the innumerable times I've had secret sex in my head with Kyle, I am so chaste it hurts. "You're a freak, you know that? I was *never* pregnant. Get over it."

I hear the window upstairs open and see William peek out.

"I don't appreciate that tone of voice," Mr. Paulsen says.

"And I don't appreciate you sticking your nose into my business. Listen up, bub. We pay our rent on time and we don't cause any problems. You need to back off."

Next thing I know, William's beside me and pulls me by the arm up the front stairs. "You'll have to excuse her. She hasn't been getting any lately. You know, sexually frustrated. All built up inside needing to explode."

"William!" Great, tell the whole street how pitiful I am.

"You better watch yourself," Mr. Paulsen yells after me.

I snap back. "Freak of nature."

William closes the door, wraps his arm around my shoulder, and chuckles. "I guess when our lease is up in June, we'll be looking for a new place, huh?"

A new place would be lovely with no milk crates for shelves, no squeaky floor, no Mr. Paulsen, and as much as I love William, I'd love a new roommate.

I'd love for it to be Kyle.

CHAPTER TWENTY-EIGHT

"Rockin' good time in Chicago, Virtue," LBJ says out of the corner of his mouth as I sit at his conference table with my marketing reports two weeks and three thousand air miles later.

Travel has kept me focused on work. I've gathered a ton of sales leads, the client services meetings are going off well (Kyle e-mails me to let me know what's up—and we do some harmless e-flirting) and the tradeshow in Chicago netted the greatest number of business cards yet this year. I'm proving to Little Baby Jesus that I can handle the extra duties dumped on me since Aislin's maternity leave. More than that, LBJ seems to be taking note. I'm about to get up my nerve to ask about my review and yearly raise. Armed with stacks of paperwork, I'm confident and ready to plead my case.

"Thanks, Jiles," I say. "The clients loved the party we threw at the Sheraton and Ted even made a new sale. We kept the costs on budget and everything seemed to work out for the bottom line."

"Yeah, well, any time you spend a dime, it's bad for the company, but what can you do?" He rubs the hair under his nose.

"I adjusted the marketing budget on the February events and I think if we reallocate a couple of the line items everything will be—"

"—Move along," he interrupts, slurping from his Snapple Half and Half. "We've got to think big picture here."

"I thought that's what I was doing?" My agenda is blown.

"I'm thinking we need something huge to knock the customers on their collective asses." He snaps his fingers. "I know! A party in Denver. It's in the middle and we'll draw lots of customers."

I shuffle through the pages of my marketing plan and see nothing on the schedule for Denver. The last client meeting Kyle and I planned is Salt Lake City on February twenty-sixth.

"Jiles, I'm sorry but you're losing me. Can we start over?"

"Keep up, will you?"

He's all over the place, fluttering around like a hummingbird on Dexatrim. I look at his desk where two empty mega-ounce Starbucks coffee cups sit. God only knows what all of that caffeine does to his mini-man system.

Jiles stands and begins to pace. "The party in Chicago went the distance in tending the wounds of our whiny clients. We've done all these touchy-feely Dr. Phil sessions and where has that gotten us? Nowhere. I want more from this Denver meeting. We've got to distract the clients. Wine them, dine them, set them up with hot women."

I don't understand what he's getting at. "Are we running a house of ill repute?"

"You're funny. I like creative thinking. Stick with me."

He scratches his hairy blond chin and flicks something off his finger that he harvested from the depths of his beard. Then he leans forward and pounds in an extension on the speakerphone.

I hear, "This is Kyle," and there goes my rascally heart, hammering away at the sound of his voice.

"Get in here, Nettles."

"Be there in a sec, Chance."

Kyle has a nickname for Jiles? *Oh, Kyle... gross.*

"Sit," Jiles says when Kyle walks in. He takes the chair next to me and I scoot closer in case I need him as a shield.

Over the next ten minutes, Jiles shuffles through papers, flails his arms, and rips apart the remaining portions of the customer service plan. "Cancel Salt Lake and have those clients gather for a customer appreciation party in Denver."

I let out a long sigh. Great, now I'll have to get out of the hotel contract, but apparently, LBJ doesn't care.

Jiles keeps railing. "I want everyone there; dressed to the hilt, ready to service the clients any way possible." I don't believe he actually intends to prostitute our sales force, but being the materialistic creature he is, he probably thinks pleasing eye candy will ease customers' tensions.

The throbbing vein in Kyle's neck indicates his mood. He tries to defend the plan we've come up with and the effectiveness of the feedback we've already gathered. "Shouldn't we run this by Will and Will?" he asks.

"Nettles, you have a case of the Willies," Jiles says, and then laughs at himself. "I should've been a comedian. Don't you think I'm funny?"

No, not funny. Psychotic more like.

I look at Kyle and he scratches his head. He throws his hands up in surrender. "So what do you want, Jiles?"

"I want an open bar, food, and music. We'll give attendees two months of service for attending. That'll ease the moaning and will seal the deal on profitability."

"How will giving away our services make us profitable?" I can't help but ask. Jiles isn't making any sense.

"We'll bill them for our time in Denver. They're used to client services billings, so we'll pass the cost off to each company. Unless they compare bills, they'll never know."

"That's double-dipping and it's illegal," Kyle snaps. I respect him for standing up to the president like this. I've always thought he was another one of Jiles' lap dogs. Obviously not. Kyle marches to his own drum.

Jiles waves his hand, as if to dismiss Kyle's protestation. "It's only illegal if we get caught. Besides, these clients don't deal with each other. We'll feed them, booze them, schmooze them, and be home free. I have calls to make—starting with Dyno Technologies. They're our biggest client and they're the lynch pin. Don't sit there looking at me, get on this!"

Before we can get out of the chairs, Little Baby Jesus taps on his speakerphone and starts autodialing.

Kyle ushers me by the elbow. "Let's go."

So many unanswered questions cyclone around in my head. What about the lead report I worked on all weekend? What about the revised marketing budget? What about my raise?

"Oh, and Virtue," LBJ adds.

I turn. He's going to tell me about my raise now. "Yes?"

"Fed Ex this for me." He tosses a small box my way. I catch the package and tuck it under my arm, apparently not having a choice in the matter.

I sigh when we get into the hallway. "He's mental."

"Completely whacked," Kyle whispers. "He's letting the pressure get the best of him."

"What pressure?"

Kyle looks around and then leads me toward the Bobby Orr conference room where he closes the door. "Don't tell anyone, but the Board gave Jiles an ultimatum two weeks ago. Profitability by the beginning of March... or else."

"Or else what?" My heart pounds frantically in my chest.

"I don't know. It's up to the Board. Jiles is only their mouthpiece. Don't fool yourself into thinking he has more power."

"He's a tiny little jerk." I clasp my hand over my mouth.

Kyle laughs. "You're so cute. Don't worry about what you say to me." He reaches out and strokes my upper arm. "Besides, I don't know how much more of this company's alleged leadership and idiotic rules I can take. Nothing but seagull management."

"What's a seagull manager?" I can barely concentrate with Kyle's hand on my arm and his eyes peering through me like laser beams. My skin heats where his fingers are and I try not to give in to the desire to toss him onto the conference table.

"Oh, you know, Jiles flies around, squawks a lot, craps on everything, and then flies off. Then, we're the ones who get to clean up his mess."

Unfortunately, Kyle removes his hand and my senses fall back into place. I furrow my brows. "Has Jiles made a mess?"

"Nothing we can't handle, right? We make a great team, you and me," he says, knocking me playfully with his elbow. "We can pull off an impromptu meeting with a hundred clients."

Although he's smiling, I see the concern in his face. He knows more than he's telling.

"Well, it's back to the drawing board. There's a lot to do," I say. Work's not my priority at the moment. My mind is on his full lips. I wonder what they'd feel like brushing over mine.

"Let me check my voice mail, grab my client files, and I'll meet you in the Larry Bird room to start from scratch." Kyle pulls me next to him for a half hug.

We break apart and I go to my desk for my conference folders. I'm so lost in thoughts of trying to please LBJ coupled with the recognition of these forbidden feelings for Kyle that I bump into my cube, dropping Jiles' package.

When I reach over to nab it, I read the address label. It's addressed to Little Baby Jesus' parents in Mashpee, Massachusetts: *Mary and Joseph Chancey.*

"Jack! Come quick! You won't believe this!"

But the irony is squashed when Janine, our receptionist, buzzes my intercom.

"Vanessa, there's someone here to see you. I've shown him to the Larry Bird conference room."

I toss LBJ's package to my desk and grab the meeting folders, a pen, and my Android. God, I hope this visitor isn't that annoying printer guy who calls every other day to "touch base."

I step into the conference room and nearly gag on my hitched inhale. My well-organized folders cascade to the floor. Gulping hard, I will my tongue to form the right words as I look at the blue-eyed man leaning on the table in front of me.

"What the hell are you doing here, Rory?"

Chapter Twenty-Nine

Rory reaches for the fallen folders without answering my question. He casually layers the papers inside like it's nothing at all. Like it's not a complete mindfuck to my entire system to see him. At DigitalDirection. In Boston.

Pulse flitting away rapidly, I find my voice and ask again, "I thought you were in jail."

He pauses, thinks, and then speaks. "I left Seattle."

"Jumped bail, I bet."

His non-answer is all the response I need.

"It's good to see you, Vanessa," he says with a slight lilt in his voice.

I take the offered stack of papers and cringe at his nearness. "It's *not* good to see you Rory. Or should I say Rodney."

He screws his face up, but smiles broadly. "So you know about my... troubles."

Reeling in the tumultuous flood waters of emotions I want to drown this guy in, I spit out, "Is that what you call abandoning your wife and child?"

He holds his hands up in front of him to deflect my words. "Look, I can explain. See, we got married because we had to. Then the kid came and I had to—"

I step around and set the folders on the table. "Not my problem, Rodney."

Rory steps forward and pulls my hands toward him, lacing his large fingers through mine. I fight him off until he won't let me pull away. "Stop being so adorable," he says.

I refuse to laugh.

"You're not welcome here," I say firmly.

I glare up into his face. The lines around his eyes aren't from laughter like I'd originally thought. They're from the harsh life he's been leading. The blue irises seem less vivid and his skin appears tired and sallow. I mentally berate myself for such mistaken judgment. I can't believe I ever saw anything in this man. He can't hold a candle to Kyle Nettles. Panic rises in my throat and renders me speechless realizing what conference room I'm in and knowing that Kyle will be here any minute. I have no idea how the hell will I explain Rory's presence here when everyone in our industry knows of his arrest. I've got to get rid of him. "I want you to go. Now."

He reaches for me. "Not until I explain."

I shake my head and pull my hands away, tucking them into the pockets of my jeans so he won't come looking for them again. If he does, I'll scream.

"Your explanation means nothing to me," I say with my chin hitched in the air. "I'm totally over you. I was after that first trip to San Francisco. I was going to break it off with you. That was until you didn't show. Instead, I find out you're married, have a kid, deserted your family in Indiana, and oh, and let's not forget that you were shacking up with the SalesTracker receptionist and her kid that's allegedly yours while cuddling with me. Does that about sum it up?" My heart is pounding ninety to nothing because my natural fight or flight mechanism kicks into overdrive. I've had this conversation—this confrontation—in my mind a dozen times. However, I never thought it would actually come to fruition. "Tell me *Rodney*, did you try to seduce me simply to get a demo disk?"

Bested by my tongue-lashing, he runs his hands through his long blond hair that desperately needs trimming. Guess life on the run doesn't exactly call for an appointment at the salon. Rory's eyes zero in on mine. "Look, it may have started out that way, but it changed. I feel something for you. I don't want to lose you, Vanessa."

I laugh sardonically. "You never *had* me."

"Sure I did."

"We made out three times. I'd hardly call that a relationship. My libido was out of control and I took advantage of being on the road. You paid attention to me, so I explored it. There's nothing else," I say firmly, unblinking.

Damn, that sounded good if I do say so myself. William and Griz would be proud of me. I mean it, though. Rodney Elmore is nothing.

He seems baffled. "I want you to come with me."

I scrunch up my face. "Come with you? Where?"

"I'm going to Mexico and I want you to come with me."

I start laughing so hard that I begin to cough. Rory moves to pat me on the back, but I stave him off. Getting a good breath, I say, "I'm not going anywhere with you. I have a job, friends, a life. And you're not part of it. Go back to your wife, Rodney."

He lunges at me and gathers me tightly in his arms. "I want you. There's something about you, Vanessa Virtue. You're a challenge I can't walk away from. Come on, take a chance on me. I've got a condo on the ocean in Acapulco. It'll be a *paradise bonita*. No corporate games, no real-life responsibilities. Just you, me, the sunshine, and enough cash to keep us happy for the rest of our lives."

I'm not tempted by this for even one nanosecond. Not in the least. This man is bat-shit insane. Off his rocker. In need of heavy sedation or further jail time to get him right. I want to make distance so I push away from his chest. He resists. I'm shaking profusely—not from fear or excitement—but from infuriation. I want him gone. Out of my life. Permanently.

"I'm going to call the Washington State Attorney General and tell them where you are—"

He smirks at me and moves his face closer. I can feel his breath. "You'll do no such thing."

His lips capture mine fiercely, stopping my protestation. For one millisecond, I relax, hoping to catch him off-guard, but he takes that as an opening and plunges his tongue into my mouth. I struggle to gain control from this onslaught. I don't want him. I don't want anything to do with him.

The taste of him is like bile in my mouth. All of the lies. All of the deceit. It's piled together in a heap of disgust that I want to spit out and run away from.

I'm about to deliver a hearty knee-jerk to Rory's privates when the door to the conference room opens and I hear, "I got a couple of Kit-Kats thinking we needed the energy and—"

Rory lets me go and we both turn to see Kyle standing there, mouth agape and eyes wide. His jaw tightens. "Vanessa?"

Holy Mother of God. "Kyle, I didn't know—I mean, I know this looks—"

"What do you think it looks like?" he asks.

My silence betrays me.

Kyle advances. "Okay, I'll tell you then. It looks like you're making out with the guy from SalesTracker in one of our company conference rooms."

I shove hard on Rory's chest, dislodging from his embrace. I've got to show Kyle I mean what I say. Without hesitation, I haul back and connect my clenched fist hard on Rory's cheek. He grunts loudly, doubles over, and covers his face that immediately turns crimson with my knuckle print.

Pain sears through my hand and I think I've broken something. "Dammit! That hurt."

Kyle's mouth hangs open.

I glare at Rory. "I told you twice to get the hell out of here, Rory. Do it. Now.

He chuckles sardonically. "I take it that means you're not coming to Mexico with me. Your loss."

Hands on hips, I say, "No loss at all, jerk."

Rory brushes past me and he never looks back. A floodgate of relief hurries out of my every pore. I shake my throbbing fist and think I handled that appropriately enough.

But Kyle looks ever so disappointed in me.

"What was that all about? I heard that guy was in jail."

"He jumped bail," I explain.

"And came here? Why?"

Embarrassed, I whisper, "For me."

Kyle's handsome face pales. "You and Ellery?"

"It was just a road fling. Nothing happened. Well, except the whole thing with the demo disk." I slap my hand to my mouth, not believing I let that tidbit of information escape.

Kyle's own mouth gapes open. "*You* gave SaleTracker your demo disk?"

"No! God, no! He stole it from me when he was in my hotel room." Shit! From the look on Kyle's face, that wasn't a much better thing to admit.

"He was in your—" He stops. Kyle flattens his lips and takes a step back. "You're not the person I thought you were, Vanessa."

"Really, it's not—"

My words collide in the back of my throat. The look of utter disappointment crossing Kyle's handsome face is almost enough to make me want to go fling myself out into the middle of traffic on Storrow Drive. He's right. I'm not who he thought I was.

"I just don't know what to say," he finally speaks up in the deafening silence between us.

Although Kyle and I aren't an item, the guilt is overwhelming. "I'm so sorry, Kyle."

He holds his hand up to stop my word. "You don't owe me an explanation."

"I want to explain."

Kyle shakes his head. "No. That's all right. I totally misjudged you. I thought you were different. I thought you were a nice girl."

Pleading, I advance on him and reach for his wrists. "I *am* a nice girl. The thing with Rory was completely stupid—"

His demeanor quickly shifts from disillusionment to rage like flipping on a light switch.

"Don't make excuses. Miss Go By the Company Handbook. I see, it's okay for you to sleep with the enemy, but not go out with me. If you didn't like me, you could have said so."

My ears ring and I sense I'm going to pass out from the fear of Kyle never speaking to me again. "You've got it all wrong, Kyle. I *never* slept with Rory."

"Semantics, Vanessa." He wrestles his wrists free like he's been burned by a hot pan. "I've been putting forth an effort when it comes to you—apparently under a false impression. Unwise of me. You're not who I thought you were. Good thing I found out before it was too late."

With that, Kyle turns and exits the conference room, leaving me shrouded in guilt, shame, and loneliness.

Hot tears burn around the edges of my eyes threatening to fall in steady streams down my cheeks. I bite my lip and buck up. It's all a terrible misunderstanding. I'll give it some time. Things will blow over and it will be all right. Kyle has to forgive me. He has to.

Of course, as if everything else in my world isn't already askew on its axis, Jack pops up from his cube and says, "Where have you been?"

"Dealing with my stupid life."

He stands tall. "Yeah, well the crap hit the fan. You know how Aislin took two extra weeks of maternity leave?"

"Yeah, so?"

"Well, Jiles and Nancy called her in to tell her that since she didn't return on time, they've eliminated her position."

I close my eyes and rub my face with my hands.

I don't know how this can get any worse.

CHAPTER THIRTY

A week later, I flop on the couch at home in sheer exhaustion and disgust. Everything sucks. Work is killing me with the twelve-hour days and no lunch. Kyle won't look at me—won't speak to me—so I've been on my own finalizing the Denver meeting. Jiles dumped most of Aislin's responsibilities on me with no additional pay. And to top it all off, I've lost my concentration so much that I almost forgot my upcoming birthday.

Twenty-six. My mom was twenty-six when she had me. That sounds so old. Not a kid anymore. Old enough not to be in this mess with Kyle, Rory, and the ugly truth of my tryst on company time. Old enough to right the wrongs.

The front door bangs open and I hear footsteps and laughter headed my way.

William holds up two large bottles of Pinot Grigio. "Just what the doctor ordered."

Griz slips in behind him with two boxes from the Greek place around the corner in her hand. "And I brought reinforcements."

Mia follows them with a large chocolate cake. "I'm actually giving up a night of studying for you, Vanessa."

"Thanks you guys. Just what I need. Carbs, grease, sugar, and alcohol."

We eat the greasy mess of mushrooms, pepperoni, and onions (who cares if I have bad breath) and pound back glasses of the chilled white wine. Mia got the cake at a Portuguese bakery and it tastes like it's fresh from some grandmother's kitchen. I'm starting to feel better already thanks to the prescription for friendship.

William licks sauce off his finger and then gasps. "I think we need to go out and celebrate your birthday for real tomorrow night."

"I couldn't agree more," Griz says.

"Count me out," Mia says as she picks up the empty pizza box. She bends down and kisses me on top of the head. "You know I love you, girl, but studying comes first."

I grab her hand and kiss it. Then I shrug. "Things have been awful lately, so I don't want to make a big deal out of it. Turning twenty-six isn't any kind of major milestone."

"You'll have to stop sleeping with a teddy bear," Griz says with a grin.

"No, that's when she hits thirty," William kids.

I throw a pizza crust at him.

Griz contemplates for a minute. "You know, it's your golden birthday."

"My what?"

"Your Golden Birthday. Haven't you ever heard of it?"

"No, never." I say, my mouth full of pizza.

"It's when you turn the same age as the day you were born. You're turning twenty-six on the twenty-sixth of the month. Get it?"

"That's pretty cool. Is this another preacher's daughter things?"

"No, it's another one of my fun things. We'll have to do something tomorrow night since you're leaving for the client party in Denver on Sunday. We'll have a golden time. We'll get you golden presents—"

"—Ooo, I like that." I'm starting to come back to life. Nothing like a party to lift a girl's spirits.

"We'll invite all the people from the office and go to dinner somewhere that has a gold reference—"

"I've got it," William interrupts. "How about McDonald's? It has golden arches."

"You are such a brat," Griz yells, launching herself to attack him. The two of them end up in a heap, tickling each other and laughing uproariously until Mr. Paulsen pounds on his floor.

"All right, all right," William shouts at the ceiling.

"Leave it to me. I'll set up everything," Griz says.

Hmm, a party. People from the office. I pick at a mushroom and wonder, "Do you think Kyle will come?"

Griz bites her lip, but then smiles. "I bet I can get Rick to talk him into it."

Popping the mushroom into my mouth, I say, "No, I don't want to force him to be around me, especially since he hates me so much." I cringe at the pang that crosses my chest.

"He doesn't hate you," she says. "It wasn't your fault Rory showed up in the office like that. Leave everything to me."

The next day, Griz makes reservations at the only place in the Boston metropolitan area with the phrase "golden" in the title. After work, we take the T out through Brookline to the Golden Temple restaurant. William meets us there, as well as a whole bunch of people from the office. Even Reagan, happily employed at a new company, shows up to wish me well.

But I'm still looking for that one person.

And he's not here.

Of course he's not. Kyle made it pretty clear what he thinks of my duplicitous behavior. He knows about the stupid demo disk farce and blames me for the extra man-hours at work that have led to everyone not having a personal life.

Then I shouldn't get to have one with him.

I don't deserve it. I don't deserve work friends. I don't deserve this party.

My heart nearly leaps to my throat, though, when I eyeball the last guest to arrive with Rick Churchman. Surprisingly enough, Kyle is carrying a small bundle of white roses. He approaches cautiously and holds out the flowers. It's killing him to be nice to me. I can tell by the forced smile, instead of his natural one.

"These are for you," he says quietly.

"Thanks, Kyle, they're really beautiful," I say in one breath. The flowers aren't nearly as lovely as the tingly sensation streaking from the ends of my fingers to the tips of my toes as our hands brush together. He has to feel it, too.

He breaks away from me and turns to talk to Reagan. Feeling my heart will surely crumble into pieces in front of everyone, I take my place in the appointed seat Griz has picked out for me. She's decorated our huge table with gold confetti and a bouquet of golden balloons for the back of my chair. She sits on my right and William on my left, but my attention is focused straight ahead across the table at Kyle. The fact that he's here means something.

Our group orders a ton of food and passes our plates around, sharing the barbecued ribs, Chilean sea bass, Chardonnay chicken, ginger scallion lobster, and plenty of wine.

Kyle and I play eye tag throughout the meal, acting like we're not really looking at each other. My heart trips along, yo-yoing back and forth every time there's a connection. I pray that he's forgiven me. The whole incident with Rory/ Rodney has made me finally come to my senses and I realize that no handbook, rules, or regulations can thwart my feelings for Kyle. Now, I just have to convince him that he still wants me. I'll do my best to win him over. I don't see how my life continue along on its natural course without Kyle Nettles being a big part of it.

At one point during dinner, I lick barbecue sauce off my fingers and I see Kyle watching me, intently. I nervously wipe the remainder off with my napkin. He looks away and picks up another fork full of the sea bass. My entire body melts in a mellifluous manner at the thought of a second chance with him. Whether he admits it or not, I can tell the he's still into me.

Course, maybe he's simply appalled at what I'm wearing. Griz dug an eight-year-old black and gold sweater—*is that lamé?*—out of her closet and insisted I wear it. There's enough shoulder padding to fill out a New England Patriots lineman's uniform. I look like a reject from the Dynasty Reunion show, but I play along since it means so much to her.

William breaks out the "Velvet Underground" dark chocolate cake from Rosie's Bakery in Cambridge and dishes out ample helpings to everyone. Everyone—including the restaurant's staff—sings happy "golden" birthday to me. Then, Griz presents me with a beautiful ivory Chinese vase with gold leaves nestled in colorful wrapping paper. It's very grown up.

"There's more," she says excitedly. "Pick it up and dump out what's inside."

Sure enough, there's something rattling in there.

"Don't shake it, dump it," she fusses.

"Here, Vanessa, I'll do it." William spreads the rainbow wrapping paper on the table and pours out the jingling material.

Out pours a mound of golden dollar coins—the ones with Sacagawea on them. The ones you get from the Post Office stamp machines but never know what to do with them. Well, Griz found a use for the shiny change.

"This can't all be for me," I say, fingering through the shimmering coins. There's got to be over a hundred bucks here.

"Everyone pitched in. A lot of other people at work anted up, too, because of all the great things you do for the company. I wrote them all down. Isn't it the coolest gift?"

"You guys, I don't know what to say. You're amazing." I look around at the fortune before me. Not just the money, but the good friends who took the time to share in my special day. As I look at the pot of gold in front of me, I can't help but see the face that sits beyond, just over the rainbow-colored wrapping paper. Kyle Nettles.

Despite the way I know he feels toward me, he smiles crookedly, causing my heart to do quite the flippity-flop. Almost painful. Is this what it's like to desperately want someone you can't have? I've never felt anything like this before in my life and I find it hard to take in air.

To get a grip, I lean over and squeeze Griz, turn to kiss William on the cheek and announce, "Midnight martinis are on me."

After dinner, the group heads to Lansdowne Street to go dancing at Avalon. Everyone buys me drinks and I can't be more content. It may not be the smartest thing, but I think I'm anesthetized enough to put a move on Kyle. He wouldn't be rude enough to turn down a dance with the birthday girl.

Kyle's standing with Rick and Griz (who are all over each other) sipping a beer. His eyes look me up and down and I swear I see a hint of a sparkle. It's probably something to do with the overhead strobes, but a girl can hope.

I reach for his hand. "Aren't you going to dance with me?"

He smiles weakly and resists. "Do I have a choice?"

"Nope. Guest of Honor demands it."

Begrudgingly, he follows me out onto the crowded dance floor. Students from Boston College and Boston University groove to the music, not holding their alcohol very well. I was one of those girls not too long ago. I'd like to tell them what's in store for their real future. Struggle, hard work, debt, corporate bullshit, mind games, heartache, and disappointment. But no. They'll have to discover it for themselves, just like I have. It's nothing that can be taught in a college classroom, even by the most degreed professor.

Linking my fingers through Kyle's, I pull him with me to a clearing on the floor. We dance to a fast-paced song by Milky, followed by DJ Sammy's "Sunshine." The lights coat me in a cloak of happiness, contentment, safety. I almost get the impression that Kyle is forgiving me, forgetting what he saw in the conference room. Disregarding the whole senseless situation. I don't want Rory. I want Kyle. I need for him to know what transpired and that I didn't know Rory was coming to Boston.

I would think that my rabbit punch to Rory's face spoke volumes.

Still, after each song ends, Kyle makes his distance, standing back and observing me cautiously. Not quite dissecting my actions, yet staring at me in a way that tells me he's experiencing some inner turmoil.

A while later, having given up my attempts to win Kyle over on the dance floor, I'm sipping a drink Jack bought me when a hand hesitantly skims my waist. I realize it's Kyle, so I suck in. In my exhaustion from the evening, I lean into his chest, feeling his hardened muscles against my back.

"I'm heading out in a little bit. I've got to pack for Denver," he says over the music.

I turn in his arms and move in close to make sure he hears me. "You can't leave. One more dance." My chest brushes up against his, causing my nipples to react on their own and stand at attention.

A Dirty Vegas song pumps out and Kyle takes the lead this time to tug me out to the crowded dance floor. I hold on to his muscular arms as we sway to the song. Because of the crowded space, I'm forced to loop my arms over his shoulder; hands behind his neck. It takes every bit of willpower not to plunge my fingers through his thick hair. He tenses at first, then relaxes. I feel his sigh in my hair. Then Kyle places his hands on my hips, steering my gyration in his direction. A slow, rhythmic, sexy motion. I struggle to breathe as his body brushes mine. Touching sensually in the darkened, jam-packed room.

He leans his forehead near and says something.

"What?"

I see his lips move again, but the music is way too loud to understand. So, I nod and smile. I hope it's the right reaction.

When the song is over and the lights stop flickering, he begins to move away. Thinking fast, I cover his hand with mine and instinctively our fingers entwine. It feels so good, so right, so natural.

"I really have to go, Vanessa," he says against my ear, the whisper of his breath touching my skin.

"I know." Still, I don't let go, gripping him tightly when another slow song kicks in overhead. "One more?" I whisper. "Please." It's not a question, rather a request from my heart.

He takes a deep breath and then gathers me close as we move to the sensual, slow beat. My head fits snuggly under his chin and I nuzzle against the open collar of his shirt, taking in his appetizing scent. I'm not sure, but I think his lips brush my hair. I tip my head up, looking deep into his eyes. Nothing should feel this good, this comforting, this safe. I praise the person who invented slow dancing, dark clubs, and cold winter nights meant to share with a warm body of the opposite sex.

When the song ends, he steps away like he's been scalded with hot water. My body screams out and the coolness of the club covers me, chilling the warm imprint left by his body. The brief look of pleasure on his face is replaced with a tense scowl. He scrubs at his cheeks, as if to get his senses back. "Look, I can't do this Vanessa. It's not right."

"Yes, it is," I say a bit pathetically.

He won't meet my eyes, so I know he's struggling with his emotions. I was getting to him, wasn't I? "I've got to go. I hope you had a great birthday."

"You helped make it great, Kyle." I stand on my tiptoes and boldly kiss him on the cheek. Embarrassed, I step off and let Kyle go. No use begging. Not tonight.

Feeling tears might overcome me, I press toward my roommate who hands me a bottle of water. "You two look hot together," William says.

Taking a deep breath to steady the rhythm of my heart, I admit, "Wills, I'm way past having a crush on this guy."

From this point forward, I'm determined to get him.

CHAPTER THIRTY-ONE

I should never drink that heavily before getting on an airplane. As if my fear of flying isn't enough, now I've got this killer hangover pelting my brain. At least it deadens the thought of Kyle easily walking away from me last night.

On the flight across country, comforted by my trusty Atavan and several pillows, I think about how to turn things around with him. We were so close. Then I got stupid. I put work regulations ahead of real adult feelings. The first I've ever really experienced. This isn't a few dates with a frat guy or a college set up. This could be forever and ever.

I have to right this.

I arrive at The Brown Palace Hotel and get to work on the details for tonight's party. At eight p.m., the clients arrive in the Onyx Room. I run through my mental checklists making sure there's plenty of wine, cheese, bread, and fruit to keep everyone happy.

"You clean up nice," Jack teases as he helps with set up the nametags on the check-in table.

My earlier nap and shower paid off and I feel quite confident in how the evening will turn go. I'm decked out in a blue short-sleeved Liz Claiborne dress I got on sale. It comes to my knees and shows off my legs.

Kyle steps into the room and I sense his presence even before I see him. It's like an alarm going off inside my head. *Hot man at twelve o'clock.* My chest tightens in delight while I take in his appearance. He's wearing a black double-breasted suit with a crisp white shirt and a smartly designed silver striped tie.

He approaches me cautiously, while I experience that lovely stomach dip when he smiles at me. It's nice to see that look replacing the pained one from last night.

"You look amazing, Vanessa," he says.

I sniff the air, memorizing every bit of him. He smells like Dial deodorant soap and Calvin Klein's Eternity. "Thanks, Kyle. So do you." We're so polite to each other, as if we don't know what to say.

Jack moves around Kyle and reaches for his nametag. "Nice suit, Nettles. Hugo Boss?" Kyle nods. "I already said this," Jack continues, "but Vanessa, you're the real belle of the ball."

"She certainly is," Kyle says.

"Thanks, you guys." I blush from head to toe. I've got to get back into event coordinator mode and get a grip on my raging hormones. "I should go check on the... err... cheese."

As the customers filter in, I play the perfect hostess. Our employees—all magnificently attired—are working it with the clients who dot the room. I make eye contact with Jiles who gives me the thumbs up. I resist flipping him off.

I'm making my usual every few minutes sweep of the room in search of Kyle when Ted, who has been on his best behavior since the holiday party probation, pulls me over to a group of clients.

"These guys are from Dyno Technologies here in Denver. They're our biggest and most important client," Ted explains. "This is Vanessa. She planned this party tonight."

"I've heard so many good things about your company," I say in the most professional manner. It's a total conversational lie. All I've heard is bitching and moaning about them.

Ted does the intros. "This is Bill Lambert, sales rep, Steve Sullivan, CIO and this"—he pauses dramatically—"is Larry Manilow, *the* most important guy because he pays the bills."

Everyone laughs and I join in only to have the opportunity to cackle at this guy's name. Larry Manilow. Seriously.

Larry's wicked cute—almost pretty—and, boy, does he know it. Bleck, I hate guys like that. His slicked back, jet-black hair matches his suit and his clear eyes are the same color as the room's cobalt ceiling.

I must be polite though. "Are you having a good time?"

Larry's lips hitch into a smirk. "I will be if you join me."

I set my wine down at the table and make small talk. I remember Jiles telling us to do "what's necessary" to make the attendees happy. I want to hang out with Kyle, but he's schmoozing clients, too. Besides, LBJ made it clear that employees are to mix with customers, not each other. So, I sit demurely across from Mr. Important who drones on about the weather and sports and snow skiing.

"Are you a ski buff?" he asks.

"I wouldn't say a buff, per se, but I like watching it." I have skied once in my life and made a fool of myself by somersaulting accidentally off of the end of the chair lift into a snow drift.

"Come on, you live in New England and you don't take advantage of the powder?"

"The only powder I take advantage of covers my face."

He thinks this is the funniest thing he's ever heard. Our laughter draws judgmental attention. Kyle stares at me from across the room. His gaze zeros in on me and a frown crosses his face. I wave timidly and return my attention to Larry.

I sip my wine, trying to feign interest in Larry's droning.

But his name... I can't get past it.

Maybe if I concentrate on the first name, I'll be okay.

His name is Larry.

Oh no, now I can't stop singing in my head. I'm doomed.

As the party winds down and everyone disperses to their respective rooms, I watch from the atrium at Kyle down in the lobby deep in conversation with Larry. He's perfect—and I mean Kyle. I may have misjudged the situation with Rory, but this time it's for real. I'm ready to take a chance again. Ready to put my love on the line.

"Dear God, help me. That's a Barry Manilow song."

The final round of schmoozing and boozing the next day is a total success. All except for my new stalker.

"Larry's been looking for you," Ted says, handing me a buffalo meatball at the closing reception.

"Eww, no thanks."

"To which? Larry or the food?"

"Both."

However, Larry is on the prowl and I can't avoid him. "There you are, Vanessa. Can I get you a glass of wine?"

I'm about to blow Larry off when Jiles' eyes tell me as if to say that I need to keep doing what I'm doing. So I sit with the mind-numbing accountant and pretend to be interested in his story about visiting a goat cheese factory in Provence last summer. I flinch and nearly scream when Larry feels up my knee under the table. I know LBJ wants us to be friendly; however, this crosses the line. I move my chair and Larry scoots with me. I try to keep up professional appearances until Larry completely throws me off course.

"Why don't you stay in Denver and I'll show you around?"

"Umm, no thanks. I have to get back to Boston," I say. "Besides, I'm already checked out of the hotel."

"You could stay with me." He pops his head to the right to watch my reaction as his hand finds my knee again.

I wiggle my leg until his roving hand falls away. "That's nice, but I have to get home. We've got this big thing at work tomorrow." There is no such big thing. I totally pulled that out of my ass. I've had enough of him. I don't care how important he is. He's too much to deal with and I'm too tired to try. I'm not in the mood for arm wrestling an octopus.

I'm about to excuse myself when I hear Kyle clear his throat. "Vanessa, can I talk to you for a second?"

"Sure thing," I say, way too excitedly.

He walks me a few paces away and then he returns to Larry. The accountant seems shocked, holds up his hands, and says, "Sorry, man."

When Kyle returns to me, I say, "Thanks for rescuing me." I see Larry slink off into the crowd. "What was that all about?"

"I told him you were my girlfriend."

I gasp and try not to smile so hard. "Thanks, Kyle. I'd had enough of his roaming hands."

"Sure you weren't enjoying it?" He's so teasing me. I can see if in his eyes. A little twinkle. My heart expands when I realize the old Kyle is back.

I muster up some intestinal fortitude and say, "Larry's not my type. He's way too oily."

Jake waves at me and points to an over-active sterno can raging underneath the pasta primavera. I nod at him, but Kyle stops me before I walk off. Leaning in, he smiles slyly and asks, "What *is* your type, Vanessa?"

Confidence surges through me.

The timing is right.

Get the ball rolling, so to speak.

I lift my eyes to sync with his. "I'll let you try to figure that out, Kyle."

CHAPTER THIRTY-TWO

Kyle, Ted, Jack, and I are on the same red-eye United flight home. Jiles, the Willies and several other Compass folks are on another flight. LBJ had insisted we all make it back to work tomorrow. You'd think he would have given us some time off instead of making us fly across the country in the middle of the night and then report to work the next morning.

I don't care right now. The meeting is over, the clients are happy, and I need all the energy I can get now to corner Kyle and *really* talk to him. He's a captive audience on the plane, so I know he can't walk away from me this time. Hopefully the 5-Hour Energy drink I downed will help boost my metabolism to get through this conversation.

He *will* hear me out.

I head to the back of the aircraft to my seat. Kyle weaves down the aisle behind me, stows his bag overhead, and plops down on the end of my row. (I planned it this way when I booked the flights home.) I sit in the window seat and yank off my knee-high boots. "Fancy meeting you here," I say teasingly.

Kyle pulls the armrest up from the first seat and slides to the middle so we now share the one on my chair. The warmth of his arm touching mine sends shivers down my spine.

"You mind?" Kyle asks.

"Not at all."

"It's easier to talk this way than shouting across the seats."

The plane jostles and adjusts toward the runway, but I don't recoil over the preparatory noises.

"No medicine tonight?" he asks.

I chuckle. "No, you were right. I've gotten used to flying." Actually, Kyle's the magical elixir I need. I'm calm, at ease, and not worried about what's going on in the cockpit.

"That's my girl."

His girl. I like the sound of that.

Silence looms between us while the flight crew explains the safety features of the airbus and precautionary tales of air travel. The quiet continues until we taxi onto the runway for takeoff. And, it ends when the pilot extinguishes the seat belt sign up around thirty-five thousand feet.

"Man, this trip was exhausting," Kyle says. "I'm glad it's over. I can have my life back now." He runs his fingers through his hair, causing it to stand on end.

"I'm sure our hard work will pay off."

"Yeah, the clients were blown away. You did a great job, Vanessa. None of this would have been possible without you."

"That's sweet, Kyle. Thing is, I enjoy what I do. Sure, it's frustrating to have to deal with someone like Little Baby Je—" I clamp my hand over my mouth.

"What did you call Jiles?" he asks with a laugh.

"Nothing. I didn't say anything," I mumble behind my hand.

"Come on, Vanessa." He pulls on my wrist. "'Fess up."

"All right. But you can't tell anyone." When I explain Jack's term of endearment, Kyle cracks up laughing. Someone a few rows up shushes us.

"Well, I'll hand it to you marketing people. You sure are creative," he says in a hushed tone.

"Don't ever repeat what I said. I'd totally get fired."

"They can't fire you. You're the heart and soul of the company. Everyone knows it."

My face feels fiery at the amazing compliment. "Thanks. It's nice to be appreciated."

This is it. The time is right. I have to do this now. Now or never. Okay, well, I have five hours for this conversation, but there's no time like the present. I have to let Kyle know how I feel. I have to know if we still have a chance despite all the personal and professional roadblocks.

"Kyle?"

"Yeah?

I gulp down my trepidation. "Can I talk to you? I mean, *really* talk to you?" I need to cleanse my soul. A mile-high confession.

His eyes darken into an ever-so-serious look. "You can tell me anything you want, Vanessa."

"And you'll listen. And not judge?"

He twists in his seat and runs his fingers down my left arm, leaving a trail of heat on my skin in its path. My arm tingles in a delicious way. Then he says, "I promise."

"You might not like what I have to say—at first—but I think you'll enjoy the ending," I say with a smile. I'm stoked by his encouragement. I can do this. Everything will be okay.

He slides his sturdy hand down my arm and entwines his fingers with mine. My insides ache and my heart sings out in relief. What a sweet gesture. One that melts my fears.

"This is nice," I say.

"Yeah, it is. I've wanted to do this since I first met you, regardless of the stupid company rules."

"I thought you were a stickler for the rules."

He shrugs, but his eyes speak volumes. "A job's a job, but no one should tell you how you can feel."

I let my head fall to his shoulder. "I wish it hadn't taken me so long to figure things out. I'm an idiot." I think of all the time I wasted on Rory when Kyle was right in front of me. On so many trips. Complimenting me. Supporting me. Saving me.

He leans toward me. "No, you're not. You're amazing."

I look up and meet his gaze. This sensation in my chest, this sweet, sweet pain, is astounding. I've never experienced anything like this before. I don't want it to ever stop.

I open my mouth to speak. Kyle stops me. "I'm sorry I've been such a jerk these last few days. I saw you with Ellery and it ate me up inside that you'd go for someone like him."

"That's what I want to explain."

"You don't have to—"

"—I want to," I say, squeezing his hand tighter. "I need to tell you everything about my lapse of virtue." He looks so disappointed in me already, yet I have to press on. "I had a small thing with Rory. First in Atlantic City, I distracted him so you could get to his client. Then, we hung out in Miami and then in San Francisco. It was a challenge and he made me feel good about myself. I knew you were off limits and he pursued me." I expect Kyle to pull away, rather he grips my hand. "There were no rules or handbooks telling me I couldn't explore a relationship with Rory, although my better judgment should have kicked in."

Kyle doesn't say anything as he listens patiently.

"Rory was in my room in San Francisco, but nothing happened," I say with emphasis. "When I couldn't find my demo disk, I assumed he took it. Whether he did or not, I realized I couldn't be in a relationship with anyone I didn't trust. That's the foundation of any bond and it was never there."

I gaze into his eyes, dilated from the dimly lit cabin.

I want you to trust me, Kyle.

"That guy was no good for you, Vanessa," he says softly.

"Yeah, I know that now. I got carried away being on the road and having someone pay attention to me."

A smile hitches on the corner of Kyle's mouth. "I've paid you plenty of attention, Vanessa."

"I know. Apparently I'm deaf, dumb, and blind." I want to finish while I still have the nerve. "It's all my fault that everything happened at work. That SalesTracker got our code and that—"

"Shhh... Don't. We don't know that. Besides, they could have gotten it from an angry customer. You're not responsible for someone else being dishonest or deceitful."

My pulse echoes through my fingertips and I know Kyle can sense the tremor running through me. I'm washed in relief, though, finally coming clean on the demo mess. And he's not judging me or pushing me away this time. Instead, he pulls me closer. "I wish I could've stopped the hurt you went through."

"I'm really okay. I'm tough. I had to get over it and stop hating myself for bad judgment. Now I'm back to doing what's best for Vanessa Virtue." Kyle's what's best for me. I want to change the subject and not bring the mood down.

"Yeah, I can tell. You and Barry Manilow really hit it off," he says.

I fall forward laughing. "His name was *Larry* Manilow. And he was a complete and total jackass. I never want to be in a situation like that again. Thank you for rescuing me. Why was that?"

"I saw him grope you under the table."

"And?"

"And I didn't like it." His eyes narrow, then he smiles. "It wasn't professional."

"I saw him staring at you today during the meeting," Kyle says. He's so close I can make out tiny flecks of gold in his hazel eyes. His pupils are enlarged in an ever-so-dreamy look.

I venture out courageously. "No more than when you stare at me during the sales, marketing, and client services meeting."

"It's a mutual stare," he says with great confidence. He leans his seat back as far as it will go and stretches out his legs.

"Kyle, I'm sorry for everything. For putting the company first, for not noticing all you had to offer, for screwing up with the competition, and for thinking HR regulations could keep me from the one person I wanted." I swallow hard and hope the words came out right. "You're the one I want. Maybe we can go out on a date and see if we've got potential?"

There. I did it. Cards on the table.

"Break company rules?" he asks with a grin.

The hell with the rules. "Well, yeah."

He tightens his grip. "I think we're already on a date."

I sigh and will my heart to calm down. "Then you forgive me?"

"Don't be so hard on yourself. We all screw up. God knows I have. It's how we handle things moving forward that counts."

For a few moments we don't speak. In the stillness of the plane, all I can hear is the hammering of my heart. The silence is coupled with an intense moment of our eyes syncing up. I let go of his hand long enough to lift the armrest that lies between us. Our bodies meet at several points: shoulders, elbows, forearms, hips, and knees. Delicious and sensual. My heart skips a beat when he drapes his forearm over mine, placing it on my thigh and resting his hand lazily on the inside of my left knee. A warmth covers me and settles in a long-ago familiar ache in my womb. The happiness inside me threatens to burst forth and sing like a Broadway musical.

I look over and see Kyle's eyes begin to close. Poor thing. He's been on the go so much he's ready to crash. (I shouldn't use "crash" when referring to someone on an airplane.)

"Kyle," I whisper. "You can't fall asleep during our date."

He rubs his hand up and down my arm in a soft, circular manner. "If we were at home nearing the end of our date, I'd ask you in to watch TV. We'd curl up on the couch and fall asleep, just like we did on the way home from Vegas."

I remember that fondly. "Sounds cozy," I say, pressing closer to him.

His head lops to the side and he whispers in a sexy voice, "I loved falling asleep—and waking up—with you."

I can't hold back any longer because I feel like I'm going to burst. "I'm crazy about you, Kyle," I whisper.

A broad smile crosses his face. "I'm nuts about you, too."

CHAPTER THIRTY-THREE

Kyle pulls me across the seat until I land on his chest. His arm serpentines around my shoulder and his fist holds my hand to his chest. I can feel the rhythmic beating of his heart that matches my own chaotic pulse.

The plane is dark except for the scattered overhead lights illuminating a few hard-working business people. The hue is like candlelight and the reflection dances in Kyle's eyes. His black lashes lower and his face moves closer.

Finally. The moment I've been waiting for.

"Can I get a goodnight kiss?" he asks, hovering above my lips.

"Is our date over?"

"Maybe..."

"What if I'm not ready for you to take me home yet?"

"What did you have in mind?"

I close my eyes. "A kiss, for starters."

Lightning surely strikes the plane and renders its passengers motionless because once Kyle's lips touch mine everything else ceases to exist. His mouth is warm, soft, and moist. I give in fully to the passion, melting toward him. His hand curves to cup the side of my face, stroking and tracing my neck as he deepens the kiss. I willingly participate in the delicious festivities, moving my hand up his chest, nearly searing my fingers on the warm flesh at the collar of his shirt. He shifts me, setting me over his lap, and angles his head to allow his tongue to probe deeper.

His lips are firm, but confident as they level over my mouth. His tongue brushes along mine, coupling, exploring, claiming it as his own. The kiss is a serious and sweeping union of our mouths. I can't remember ever being kissed this thoroughly in my life. I let out a moan of gratification as my mouth meets the light demand of his tongue.

I can't resist the urge I've had since the first day I saw him. My hand slips into his short, spiky hair, which is unexpectedly soft and satiny. I laugh against his lips at the silly thought entering my brain.

He pulls back a tad. "What?"

"I was wondering if that's your natural hair color?"

He holds my chin up with his forefinger and gives me a mock evil grin. "That's what you're thinking about while I'm kissing you? You want to know what color my hair is?"

"Well, my hands *are* in your hair."

"What you see is what you get." Before recapturing my lips, he says, "now be quiet."

The air sizzles around us as we touch and explore the texture of clothes, skin, and hair. I hear a guttural groan churn from deep within Kyle and I feel the manly physical reaction caused by our voracious appetites. These are adult kisses. A sensual ravishment. I want more. And I sense he does, too. We've waited a long time for this. But we're on an airplane. Hanging high in the night sky.

His hands move to my back, pulling me closer to him as his fingers splay down my sides. His fingertips brush the curve of my breasts and I gasp. Every hair on my body stands on end and I wait for what will happen next.

"Touch me, Vanessa." He sighs into my mouth.

I am touching him. My hands are spread over his chest. His lips, wet and cooling, venture their way down the side of my neck, stopping to engulf my earlobe before moving further down the open collar of my blouse. His nose nudges the soft red material aside as he bends down further, his breath whispers against the swell of my breasts. Tentatively, my hand slides down his firm and taut stomach. I tug at his shirttail that's tucked into his jeans.

Kyle sucks in a deep breath when my hand moves to the obvious bulge in his pants. I hold still for a moment, adjusting to the sensation of what's below. His desire is quite apparent and I want to stroke further although I'm apprehensive about our surroundings. I don't question his feelings or what I want to do. He's not using me. He's been up front with his feelings. He accepts me just as I am. He said he's nuts about me. There's nothing hidden beneath the surface. Well, there's *something* hidden that's making its presence known.

Suddenly, he stops my hand. His eyes scorch into mine and he sets me aside, moving away. He leans over and whispers so faintly I almost don't believe he's there, "come with me, you." He has a wicked evil grin on his face as he gently tugs me from my seat.

Hand in hand, we slip down the few remaining aisles to the back where a flight attendant is busy reading a novel, totally unaware of us at this late hour. Kyle opens the lavatory and pulls me in behind him, locking the door.

We're nose to nose, pressed together in the small space. "I'm being presumptuous," he says.

"I don't think so," I say, my heart pounding out a tribal rhythm he must surely hear.

"Are you sure?"

"Well, *this* is something I've never done."

"Me either." His laugh is warm against me; his hands running up and down my arms. "First time for everything."

For some reason I'm not nervous and I'm not concerned about what he's thinking or where this is going. I'm letting destiny guide me.

Kyle moves his face toward mine and his expression draws ever so serious. "Vanessa, I want you so much"

I gasp at his forthright admission. "I want you, too."

There's this intense thrill from him needing me and also over being in a public place where we might get caught. However, the sensation flowing through me is exhilarating. I don't think twice. In fact, I don't think at all. There's no need to.

This is about the two of us.

Alone.

Together.

Kyle holds me against the bathroom wall and presses his full length into me, slowly grinding his obvious passion into my thigh. I return his ardor by kissing him with all the strength in my tired body. My tongue traces the inner cavern of his sumptuous mouth. When I draw back to see his reaction, he's breathing heavily. I can feel the locomotion of his heart under my palms.

His eyes are smoky with desire as he takes my face in his hands and continues kissing me like I'm a precious commodity. This isn't just hooking up. I'm being worshipped, pampered, and I'm about to receive the most delectable treat ever.

My hands return to his half-tugged shirt bottom and I boldly draw it out of his waistband. I don't stop there. I haul the fabric over his head and drop it on the bathroom floor, under our feet. I run my fingernails over his lean flesh, feeling the heat from his body. He nearly tears the buttons of my blouse to reach my skin. Thank heavens I'm wearing my brand new lacy pale pink bra. I suck in, hoping no fatty rolls show, but he's not concerned with judging me...only loving me. He bends his head and kisses me through the fabric, bringing my nipples to attention. His nimble fingers unhook the clasp and my breasts fill his hands.

I push him back momentarily to gaze upon his amazing physique. Strong shoulders, a magnificent chest, and abs like a xylophone, sprinkled with a few dark hairs that taper down his middle into a dreamy stream to his manhood. My eyes consume him like a gourmet feast, his trim waist, his taut leg muscles, and his stunning erection that's meant only for me.

"God, you're beautiful," I say, unable to stop the words from escaping my mouth. His face breaks out in a deep-hued blush. I tug him toward me for another breathtaking kiss, kneading my hands into his powerful back as his nimble fingers move over my shoulders, down my sides and up under my breasts.

Then his fingers slide up and comb through my hair. He looks at me with those clear eyes. "So are you, Vanessa."

I bend and kiss my way across his expansive chest. When my lips bump into his nipple, I raise my eyes to meet his. Seconds turn into minutes that turn into eons. I slide my tongue over him with delicate licks and nips. I'm in complete control of this manly beast that stands before me, moaning with pleasure.

Before recapturing my lips, he says. "I can't take much more."

"Me either."

Fingers fumble with buttons, zippers, cloth, and elastic. Flesh couples with flesh and fingers entwine as we grind against each other in this infinitely small space.

Kyle directs me up onto the miniature counter. His hands skim down my hips and his thumbs hook in the waistband of my panties. I mimic his action, sliding his boxer briefs to the floor with his jeans. He wraps my legs around his waist and angles my body so his penetration will be perfect. When he enters me, I realize he has on a rubber. I mentally question where he got it, and then nothing sane enters my mind. All I know is I want him, need him, and I'm having him.

He apparently needs me as much because his hunger shows in his face. We're both consumed in the passion play and heat of the moment. Our motion is as dynamic as violent turbulence. There's that same nervous falling feeling, together with a gasping for air and a stronghold on something solid. Kyle's muscles provide that.

His movement inside me is forceful and strong, yet magnetic in its effects on me. With each thrust, I'm drawn around him more and more. His groan is beautiful to my ears as he speeds up to the climax. My legs drape around his back while I pound against the bathroom mirror. I bite my bottom lip to keep from crying out in sheer ecstasy. The faucet slams into my rear, but the pain mixes with the vast pleasures of this mile-high lovemaking.

I pull his forehead to mine and we hold each other while the stormy pinnacle shakes us both. His flesh throbs warm inside me and we both pant and sway and catch our breath, laughing with delight. He reaches up and traces his fingers along my chin and jaw. Then he gently kisses me as he slowly withdraws. I long for a bed so we can hold each other and never let go. Ever.

My heart races and I experience something I've never felt during sex. Deep emotions, strong feelings, and a true connection. It isn't just a physical act, but the melding of our souls. We're one in every sense of the word.

Is this what love feels like?

I want to cry.

"Holy shit," he says as he catches his breath. "You're amazing."

I laugh because I'm thinking the exact same thing. "You too. That was phenomenal."

He kisses me softly, nipping at my bottom lip. "You were worth the wait, Vanessa."

I don't want to tell him how long it's been since I've had sex, mainly because for the first time in my life, I've just made love.

"Thanks for not giving up on me," I say.

"Thanks for giving me a chance."

He refastens the front hook of my bra and I zip and button his jeans. We laugh and bump into each other in the small confines, checking to see if all of our clothes are back on before leaving the room.

"Think anyone needed to use the bathroom?" I ask.

"They were in for quite a wait." He stretches toward me for another sexy, languorous kiss. "We have to stop, or else we'll never leave this room and they'll have to call the TSA."

He's so damn hot that I can't help myself and I pull him back to me. "You don't happen to have another condom, do you?"

His evil snicker against my skin tells me all I need to know.

A long while later, we exit the bathroom unseen and ease back to our seats. He stretches out and pats next to him, motioning for me to lie down. I wrap my arms around his middle and snuggle on his chest. This gives a whole new meaning to "Fly United."

"I wasn't supposed to have sex with you until our third date," I joke, my voice muffled in his upper body.

"Mmm-hmm and I was supposed to wait three days before calling," he says, kissing my forehead. "I hate the stupid games. Let's not play them."

Thank God. This is more than a one-plane-stand. I have a future with Kyle. I've never felt so right, so warm, so treasured.

Kyle falls into a deep, contented sleep, warm in my embrace. Right before I drift off, I realize, I owe Griz a hundred bucks.

Oh well, it's totally well worth it.

CHAPTER THIRTY-FOUR

In the wee hours of the morning, Kyle and I deplane and follow the rest of the late night passengers down to baggage claim, never leaving each other's side. His large hand encompasses mine as he leads me through the terminal. That electric zap I felt when our eyes met his very first day at work sizzles right now through my entire body, warm from his and our mile-high loving.

As we wait for the luggage, he cups his hands around my face and gazes intently into my eyes. I dare not blink for fear of ruining the moment or waking from this delicious dream.

But no dream has ever kissed me so thoroughly. We angle our heads in opposite directions as his tongue crosses over my lips and into my mouth. I match his fervor with my own and wrap my arms around his muscular shoulders, not caring where we are or who may be looking at us. Airports are all about hellos and goodbyes. Kyle's erotic, wet kiss definitely speaks of more to come for us.

Eventually, we're the only ones left standing at the carousel as the two remaining black bags—ours—continue to loop around in the hopes that we'll retrieve them. My shoulders sag and my chest pings at the thought of this night or morning or whatever ending.

Kyle piles our bags onto a cart and pushes it with one hand toward the exit, while continuing to hold steadfastly to me with his other.

The whoosh of morning air does little to knock me back to reality. I don't want to go there. Not yet. Not ever. I want to drown in the memories of making love with Kyle until we can be together again.

"I'm not going to get much work done today," he says with an evil grin as we stand in line for a cab.

Tingles run up and down my arms, a sensation that shimmers over me from his mere tone of his words. "You wanna come home with me?"

He stops and thinks about it, tucking my hair behind my ear. "I should get to my place. Grab some sleep. Shave. Shower."

This time, I don't try to squash the vivid image of him naked and wet. It's something to look forward to seeing very soon in this relationship.

A cab pulls up to the taxi line. "Here," Kyle says. "You take the first one."

Can't we share? Course, I have no idea where he lives or if it's even in the same direction, so it's probably best to each go our own way.

He leans down and captures my lips again in a hunger, a need, a regret that we're parting. Finally, he releases my hand and I get into the cab and close the door, putting the most distance between us in about six hours. Kyle waves and watches until the red taillights of my cab are completely out of sight. Trembling fingers trip over my lips, remembering the many kisses we shared. I sigh when I realize we didn't make any follow-up plans. Ah well, we'll figure it out later today.

Once home, I float up the stairs in a lover's hangover. The faintest whiff of Kyle's cologne is still on my clothes. I should be dead tired, but I'm not.

I have to talk to someone.

"Wills?" I crack open the door and then crawl into his bed, trying to rouse him. "Wake up, hombre."

He pulls the pillow over his face. "What time is it?"

"Early. I couldn't wait to tell you my news."

William flips over, rubs his eyes, and gives me his attention. I spill everything, down to the delicious admission of my initiation into the mile-high club.

"I'm so happy for you. No one deserves this more than you."

I beam. "Thanks for putting up with me through all of my stupidity. I really think I've found the one." The pounding of my heart sounds out through my body, rattling me in a good way.

I nap briefly, jump in the shower, dress, and walk on air as I bound out to the Porter Square T station. Nothing bothers me. Not even the messy man on the train who's licking spilled coffee off his pants. I don't care about the mega-ton lady taking up two seats. I don't give a rip about the hygienically challenged man next to me or the guy with a hat that reads, "If Heaven ain't a lot like Dixie, I don't want to go." When I exit the Red Line, I even have a smile for the irritating man who shoves free newspapers in my face. The world is brand new and bright.

I'm in love.

Everything is perfect.

Until I get to the office.

My door code doesn't work, so I knock. Janine, our receptionist, buzzes me in and then checks my name off a list.

"What's this all about?" I ask.

"Just doing what I was told."

What did I miss by coming into work an hour late? The air is heavy with anticipation and it's deathly quiet. You can slash the silence with a carving knife. I wonder if someone on the plane last night saw Kyle and me folded up like a couple of bean burritos. I hope we haven't been ratted to any of the higher ups.

I stop and smile at the thought, realizing that I don't give a shit.

I do, however, wipe my sweaty palms on my black jeans as I exhale deeply in my cube. Settling into my chair, I boot up the computer and log into e-mail. There's a message from Jiles, flagged with that annoying red exclamation mark addressed to "All Staff."

I stare in disbelief.

DigitalDirection's Board of Directors is reorganizing. Layoffs will commence at noon today. Employees are to continue with assigned projects and await notification.

My fingers hover over the mouse and my mouth drops open. Let me get this straight. I may or may not have a job by the end of the day, yet I'm supposed to sit here and work. This is a joke. Some sort of April Fool's. Nope. It's still March.

They can't fire me. I'm one of the hardest working, most dedicated employees they have. I've got the stupid "Chef of the Year" spatula to prove it. They can't do without me.

I need Kyle.

I run down the hall to his cube. There's an open soda on his desk, telling me he's here. He's probably with the Willies.

I need Griz. She's not in her cube, either. I'm caught between euphoria and panic. I have to tell her about what happened on the plane because it's not something I want to elucidate in e-mail. And now I can't share good news because of the impending corporate doom.

Back at my desk, the hateful e-mail stares balefully at me from the screen. *Layoffs.* D-Day. Is my professional nuclear holocaust about to commence? Is it Nagasaki? Or Not-Gonna-Sack-Me?

I don't want to think about it. I want to think about Kyle. I dial his extension and it goes straight to voice mail. Just hearing his message calms me a bit. "Kyle, call me," I say, not leaving my name.

A warm relief washes over me momentarily as I think back to our playfulness on the plane. Never has anything felt so right, so perfect, or so in sync. I want that feeling again and again. Right now I've got to deal with my career, my future, my security.

Dammit, I felt so good a few minutes ago. What a complete buzz killer. Leave it to Jiles to screw with my life again. I understand these are trying times, but why can't we cut back on Xerox paper and not the number of employees? *We* should matter.

We don't, though. It's all about the bottom line.

They'll hire temps. They'll outsource to India. It's what everyone does these days.

I need to take a deep breath, relax, and wait until noon.

I think about looking for Kyle again, but I don't want to bring our liaison into the office. Besides, he's probably in a closed-door meeting about the layoffs. Did he know this was coming? No, I can't think like that. He would have told me.

I can't find Jack either. He's probably out running errands, going to the gym, or at the mall. Then I spot him.

I shout at him. "Where have you been?"

"Getting a hair cut. Did you know they've got a new code at the front door? Janine checked my name off a list."

"I know. Haven't you seen the e-mail from Jiles about the layoffs?"

"What layoffs?" He sets his Dunkin' Donuts coffee on the desk next to an old one from earlier this morning.

"Read your e-mail!"

"Okay, okay, hold on." He turns to the computer.

"I'm going back to my cube. E-mail me."

At my desk, I sit and fidget, rearranging the pens in my cup, moving my 8-ball around the desk and stacking files that are in place to begin with. My phone rings and I jerk my head to read the display, hoping—praying—that it's Kyle. Nope. Isabella.

I snatch the receiver. "Griz, where've you been?"

"They pulled us in with the engineers first thing to give a report on the graphics we've been working on. Everyone looks like they just came from a funeral."

In a short while, our fate will be sealed. "I don't know what's going to happen. Call me at home tonight."

"Good luck to both of us," she says.

Outlook dings and I see an e-mail from Nancy Mendelssohn, HR director: *Please report to the Larry Bird conference room.*

The shot clock is ticking down. I start shunting and feel like I will surely have a heart attack. When the readout on my clock shows 11:53, I grab a notepad and a pen and stop by Jack's cube. "Come on, Larry Bird room."

His brows furrow. "No, Bobby Orr."

"What?"

"Yeah, that's what my e-mail says."

I lean over his shoulder as my heart pounds away viciously and read his announcement. This is *not* a good sign. One of us is on our way out. We stare at each other; the silence hangs in the air like dirty laundry.

"Let's go," he says, patting me on the back.

I gulp hard knowing there's nothing I can do about any of this.

CHAPTER THIRTY-FIVE

Jack turns into the Bobby Orr room and I see Griz. I motion to her with the universal "call me" sign as I continue down the hallway to the Larry Bird room. I keep my eyes peeled for Kyle, but I still haven't seen hide nor hair of him.

In the designated room, Ted waves me over. I sit down and look around. There are a handful of programmers and a couple of people from accounting. Two client services managers are on their cell phones and one of the HR gals is up at the front. About forty people. These aren't slackers, either. Ted's our sales manager. They can't lay him off. Especially since he made two sales last night.

Last night... it now seems like last year.

The glass door creaks and Jiles marches in like a storm trooper. He sits down, staring ahead with his hands folded, looking like he's about to say grace.

A twisted, maniacal grace.

He turns to the HR lady. "Is everyone here?"

She does a silent head count and nods.

Jiles clears his throat and I feel like my heart is going to burst through my chest. Without making eye contact with anyone in the room, he announces, "Effective immediately, your position has been eliminated. DigitalDirection will no longer be in need of your services. You have fifteen minutes to pack your personal belongings and leave the premises."

With that, Little Baby Jesus—who has suddenly morphed into Lucifer himself—stands and marches toward the door.

I look down to see if blood is pouring from my body cavity since I've obviously been involved in a drive-by shooting.

The room is tomblike. The meaning of his words seeps into my system like deadly poison. Everyone mumbles and murmurs as form letters are passed out.

Ted shakes his head and laughs. "Slam dunked in the Larry Bird room." Leave it to a guy to make a sports analogy at a time like this.

This is unforgivable. This, this gangbang! They didn't even have the decency to bring us in one at a time and explain what's happening. Suddenly, my heart palpitations kick into overdrive. I'm not taking this sitting down. Jiles almost makes it out the door when I bolt from my seat and yank him by his arm.

"This is some kind of joke, right?" I peer into his beady little eyes, but only for a second. He won't make eye contact with me. "I worked my ass off for you, doing Aislin's job, organizing these client events, and this is the thanks I get. My position's not necessary? Are you fucking kidding me?"

"You should get down on your knees and thank me for all I've done for you, Vanessa," he says flatly.

"Oh, you're right, Jiles. Thank you for unemploying me after you worked me to death."

He continues to stare at my feet as he scratches his beard. His skin is almost green. I have the urge to reach underneath his chin to see if his face will peel off, revealing underneath that he's really a reptile sent here to destroy us.

I try to think of something appropriate, something meaningful. Words fail me.

This is it. It doesn't matter that I worked long hours and did everything that was asked of me. Vanessa Virtue doesn't matter. Only the Almighty Dollar is what's important to the company's bottom line.

Without saying a word, Jiles steps through the door and closes it in my face. I begin to shake fiercely, struggling to get a deep breath. I'm great with confrontation while it happens, then I fall apart. Ted pulls me to him for a friendly hug. I wish it were Kyle. I need Kyle.

The generic "here's why you're getting laid off" letter explains the company's financial problems, the need to cut back the workforce, yadda, yadda, yadda, blah, blah, blah. It's all bullshit.

Nancy clears her throat. "You have fifteen minutes to pack your personal belongings and exit the building. Please proceed to your cubes in an orderly fashion."

Orderly fashion. This isn't a fire drill.

I bolt down the hallway, only to stop and look into the Bobby Orr room at the "other" meeting. Everyone's sitting around looking confused. Griz and Rick have their heads bent together. I see Jack and several others I know, but no Kyle.

Where is he?

"You only have a few minutes, Vanessa."—Nancy's standing behind me—"I wouldn't waste any time."

"Or else what?"

"You're no longer employed here and don't belong on the premises. Now, please..."

Back at my desk, there's a cardboard box in my chair. Boy, they planned this out. I stretch my arm and sweep all of my toys and marketing chotchke into the box, not caring how it lands. I remove my personal files from the desk drawer. Then I pick up my phone to leave a message for

Kyle, but they've already disconnected it. I wonder if my e-mail still works. Yep. They haven't shut it off yet.

I open up a new message in Outlook and select "All Contacts" in the "To" field. My message is simple, telling of my demise, and that the company has laid off a third of its staff. I give my personal e-mail address in case anyone wants to keep in touch. Without anally proofreading the message, I hit "Send."

As I print out my contact info, I get a response to my "I'm Out of Here" e-mail from rory_ellery@salestracker.com.

"What the hell?" He's supposed to be hiding out in Mexico and not back at SalesTracker. I start to shake as I reach for the mouse and click on the message.

Nervously, I scan.

Wait a sec, it's from Gene Cappucci. He's been monitoring Rory's e-mail and thought he should respond.

I can't believe I sent this message to our competition. Stop. Reverse. Not *our* competition: *their* competition. I'm not on the team anymore. Booted off the island. Eliminated by the judges. Voted off by the viewers. Fine, whatever. Serves them right for canning me.

I read Gene's message: *Vanessa, Sorry to hear what happened. I hope it had nothing to do with the demo disk Rory got from you. He said you gave it to him. I never believed that. I destroyed your disk because we already had one that a customer got from your president, Jiles, and I didn't want it traced back to you. You didn't deserve that. I'm sorry things didn't work out with Rory, but you're better off. I wish you all the best. Gene*

Despite the current circumstances, relief cascades over me. The whole demo disk fiasco was *not* my fault! If I weren't so angry, I'd be jumping for joy. Stupid fucking Jiles. It was Little Baby Jesus' slipup all along, not mine. He's still here and I'm being thrown out into the streets.

I'm about to forward the e-mail to LBJ—with some edits, of course—when my Outlook craps out. Actually, my whole computer goes blank. I've been killed off the network. Oh sure, *now* those computer network guys work fast.

Nancy comes around with several people in tow, telling me it's time to leave. I join the end of the pathetic line and walk to the reception area. She holds the door open for us and asks for each employee's identification card. Then, I follow the procession down the stairs with the rest of the corporate rejects. Ted whistles "Pomp and Circumstance" while we descend the four flights. I'm back where I was two years ago when I graduated from American University— probably still single, jobless, and no idea what to do with my future.

"You need a ride home, Vanessa?" Ted asks when we round the last corner.

Stunned, I say, "Yeah, I hadn't thought about it. Thanks."

"Tell you what," he says, twirling his car keys around his finger. "Why don't we go get drunk instead?" He's certainly taking this well. Guys are a lot tougher, for sure. "Wait out front and I'll bring my car around."

We filter out of the building and say our goodbyes. People swap e-mails and cell phone numbers like kids who've spent summer camp together. I wave as folks make their way to the parking lot and toward the T.

Then, I'm all alone.

Shell shock turns to anger, which subsides to tears. And I dare anyone to judge me as being a weak female for crying. I just lost my fucking job. I put my box on the ground and sit on the lid, careful not to cave it in with my body weight.

This is not fair.

However, Jack isn't out here with his packed box to tell me life isn't fair and to buck up. I wonder if he still works here. And Griz. And Rick. There's no telling what went on in those other conference rooms.

Most of all, I think of Kyle and the many questions zigzagging through my mind: What happened with him? Why haven't I seen him? Why hasn't he sought me out throughout this? Did he know beforehand what would happen? Wouldn't he have told me I was losing my job? Or had he used me to plan those meetings?

I swat at the air as if batting away the mental queries. No. I won't believe something like that could've happened to me twice. I don't want to believe that. I won't believe it. I try to rein in my tumultuous emotions with deep, cleansing breaths.

My chest aches as I think of Kyle. He wasn't involved. I know that. I trust him. What stinks is I have no idea how to contact him outside of the office, other than his work cell phone. I can't exactly call work on Monday and ask for his home phone number. I don't know where he lives, either. My heart lurches at the thought of never seeing him again. In addition to losing my job, I'm losing my sense of cool and now I stand to lose Kyle. I drop my head to my knees in defeat.

A car horn knocks me out of my funk. I suppose it's Ted. I don't want him to see me like this, so I hide behind my hair and wipe my face. I hope my mascara isn't cascading down my cheeks.

"Vanessa! There you are. I've been looking for you everywhere," he calls out.

When I lift up, there are those hazel eyes that I truly do love.

"Oh, Kyle..." I say, more relieved than anything in the world.

He picks up my stuff and crams it into the back seat of his black Infinity. Then, he pulls me by the hand and draws me to him for a comforting hug. I squeeze my eyes shut and wrap my arms around his neck.

He rocks me gently and whispers, "Everything's going to be okay."

Ted pulls his car up behind Kyle's and beeps. "You, too, Nettles?" he asks.

"Sort of..."

I look up at Kyle curiously. What does he mean?

Ted smiles. "I don't guess you're coming with me 'Nessa."

I rotate in Kyle's arms. "No, I'm all set here, but thanks, Ted. Keep in touch."

"Sure thing. Take care of her Nettles. She's a jewel." He waves, gets back in his car, and peels off.

"I'll agree with that," he says, holding me tightly.

It feels amazing to be in Kyle's arms again. He's the only thing I'm sure about right now. How could I have doubted him? "Oh Kyle..."

He adjusts his head for another kiss, deeper this time, more emotional. I can tell he's hurting, too. "You okay?" he asks when he pulls back. He strokes my hair for reassurance.

"Just in shock. I know I should be stronger, but I've never had anything like this happen before."

"You are strong, Vanessa. I heard you told Jiles where he could go. I bet you were the only one smart enough to do that."

"Or stupid enough," I say with a snicker. "But I figured, what did it matter at that point?"

"Well, it's natural to feel hurt and confused."

"Used, more like it."

He rocks me in his arms. It's okay to lean on this knight in shining armor—well, in a shiny car, at least. I'm drawing strength from him and it feels pretty damn good.

When we break apart, I ask, "What did you mean when you told Ted 'sort of?' Did you get fired, too?"

He rests against the trunk of the car and wraps his hands around my waist, tucking his fingers into the back pockets of my jeans. Lifting his eyes to mine, he says, "Jiles called me in with the Willies and told me the Board gave him the ultimatum. Seems the books were a lot worse than anyone imagined. All due to his mismanagement. We're—they're—$3.2 million in the hole. Profitability isn't going to happen, so the Board said to cut a third of the personnel. Every position eliminated was Jiles' decision. When I found out you were on the list, dammit, Vanessa, I fought for you and you know what Jiles asked?"

My heart trills nervously again. "Do I want to hear this?"

"He says to me, 'why are you fighting so hard for her, Nettles? You fucking her?'" .

Horror fills my lungs. "Oh my God!"

"I swear, I almost leveled him, but I kept a cool head. I told him that was inappropriate and unprofessional. I said you were instrumental in saving the company's reputation with these meetings. I reminded him how you'd stepped into your boss' shoes. He said it wasn't about thanks or the work you'd done—that yes, you had excelled more than he expected—this was about the bottom line and marketing was too much of an expense."

I blink hard. "Jack got to stay, didn't he?"

"Yeah, he did. They think he can help with the PR fallout. There's going to be another round of layoffs in a few months if Jiles remains at the helm. Jack's not safe. No one is."

"So, do you still work there?"

Kyle fiddles with my belt loop and cocks his head sideways. "Actually, no. I quit."

"You quit? Over me?" My heart is going to burst wide open with what I feel for him.

305

"That was a big part of it. I'll admit I didn't like Jiles' management style or how he views customers. They're a means to an end for him and he doesn't understand that a little effort goes a long way to making a long-term relationship succeed. People want to be treated with respect and know they mean more than what you can get out of them. I couldn't stay knowing he didn't care about customers."

I can't help but equate what Kyle says to that of a mature adult relationship. He respects me and doesn't want anything from me—unlike someone else who shall remain nameless, but whose initials are Rodney Elmore.

With Kyle, I'm not a means to an end.

I hold his arms for support. "So what happened?"

He continues. "Well, I got pulled into the third conference room—"

"The third one? What were the other two?"

"You were in the 'getting canned' room, Jack, Isabella, and Rick were in the 'keeping your job' room and I got sifted into the 'stay for four more weeks to help clean up the mess' room."

"They actually had a group like that? How humiliating."

"I thought so, too. So, I told Jiles to forget it."

"You walked out?" He did that for me.

"Yep. I can't work here anymore. We spend more time at work than we do with those we care about, so what's the point if it's all for nothing?" He tugs me back to his chest. "Besides, without you there, I don't have a reason to go into the office."

I let my head fall forward and my hand snakes up to the back of his neck. "I was worried I'd never see you again once they escorted me out of there."

"Not a chance."

"You don't even have my phone number."

"I would've found you, Vanessa."

Ah, man, there's a heart clench moment.

"I don't know what I'll do now. I'm going to miss seeing you every day and working with you."

His lips turn up in an impish grin. "Well, you may not have to miss me. We're going to be okay. Trust me."

We? He said "we," right? This is a good sign.

I gaze into his eyes. "How so?"

"After I got wind of what was going down, I called my buddy, Todd Mattingly, who owns BioDynamics here in Cambridge."

I've heard of them and seen their massive, all-glass new construction. "They're right around the corner—huge with all of the biomedical technology."

"Right. Todd and I went to business school together and he owes me a favor."

"Oh, he does?" I tease.

"I introduced him to his wife, okay?" Kyle says with his dimple showing.

"Aren't you sweet?"

He smiles and looks embarrassed. "He's got a job for me," he continues. "Head of their client services. Todd's been bugging me to come work for him, so I took him up on the offer. I'm taking a few weeks off and then I'll start April first."

"Kyle, that's great."

"There's more," he says.

I don't know if I can take anymore. I tighten my hold on him and ask, "What's that?"

"He may have something for you."

"Really?"

"Really," he mimics with a laugh. "They're ramping up their marketing and just brought in a woman to head up the department. They need someone to coordinate events, so I told him about you. He said for you to send your resume over to him."

"Just like that," I say in surprise.

"Well, you still have to go in there for an interview and wow them with your knowledge and experience, but you can do it."

"Damn right, I can," I exclaim. And then I look into those amazing eyes again. "Kyle, what a great lead. I can't believe you did that. I don't know what to say. Thank you!"

"No thanks, necessary. Your experience and expertise speaks for itself. Oh, and there isn't any stupid office dating policy. I didn't even have to use my 'we're a package deal' line on Todd," he jokes, which makes me laugh.

I raise my eyebrow at him and smile. "Are you trying to get me to fall in love with you, Kyle Nettles?"

He touches his forehead to mine. "What if I am?"

"Then I'd say you're on the right track."

We seal the deal with a soulful kiss, right there at the front door of DigitalLostItsDirection. Kyle sets me back and says, "What do you say we get out of here?"

"Amen to that."

He opens the passenger side door and closes it behind me. Such a gentleman. He comes around, slides into the driver's side and pulls the car out onto the busy street.

I fumble with my keys and gasp when something catches my eye. "Oh no, I forgot to give this to Nancy." I wrench it off my key chain.

"What is it?" he asks.

"It's the key to that stupid tradeshow booth. My albatross."

Kyle brings the car to a halt at the red light—the one that holds forever—and looks at the tiny piece of metal in my hand.

"Hold on, I'll be right back. Don't leave me."

"Vanessa... wait..."

I unlock my seat belt and jump out of the car. Scrambling across two lanes of traffic, I cross the grassy bank to the railing of the Charles River. With every ounce of strength I can muster, I toss the silver key as far as I can; watching the water plunk as the key hits the surface. I brush my hands together. My virtue may be a little rusty, but I still have my pride. And my sense of humor. They'll never take that away from me.

I jog back to the car just as the light turns green.

Kyle smiles from ear to ear and says, "You're completely adorable."

I capture his chin between my thumb and forefinger, plant a big wet kiss on his lips, and say, "No, you are."

"No one can ever tell us 'can't touch this,' ever again," he says.

"Absolutely not."

Steering down Memorial Drive, he looks over at me with an evil grin. "So, your place or mine?"

"Mine's pretty close."

"Do you have a *really* tiny bathroom we can take advantage of?" he teases.

I lift my eyebrow at him, sure I'm beaming happiness like I never have before. "Even better, I have a king sized bed."

There's a wicked gleam in Kyle's eyes. He reaches over, takes my hand, and brings it to his lips. "That sounds absolutely perfect to me."

Yes, it does.

ACKNOWLEDGEMENTS

Thanks to everyone who read any version of my Vanessa Virtue's tale through my writing years and helped in her maturity, humor, and longevity. Now I send her out into the world to be judged... and hopefully loved. Special thanks to Jessica Andersen, Pamela Claughton, Charlene Glatkowski, Jennifer Keller, Megan Bremer, and Cathy Yardley.

Thanks to my wonderful agent, Deidre Knight, for who she is and all she does. Everyone should be so lucky as to have someone like her in their corner. Thanks to the kickbutt staff at The Knight Agency for helping make this book happen.

Thanks to my hero, Patrick Burns, for his love and support. I'm richer for having you in my life.

ABOUT THE AUTHOR

Marley Gibson is a young adult, contemporary romance, and non-fiction author best known for her wildly popular GHOST HUNTRESS series. Gibson appeared on the premiere episode of Biography's "My Ghost Story," as well as being on episodes of the Travel Channel's "Paranormal Challenge," and "Ghost Adventures." A certified SCUBA diver, a closet gourmet chef, and an avid traveler, Marley lives in the Florida Keys with her husband, Patrick Burns from TruTV's "Haunting Evidence," and their two rescue kitties, Madison and Boo. When she's not crafting novels, she makes hand-crafted zombie baby dolls called DagNabIt Dolls that are all the rage! She can be found online at www.marleygibson.com, Facebook at marley.h.gibson, and Twitter @MarleyGibson. DagNabIt Dolls can be found on Facebook at www.facebook.com/DagNabItDolls/ or at www. dagnabitdolls.com.

www.ingramcontent.com/pod-product-compliance
Lightning Source LLC
Chambersburg PA
CBHW030420180626
46812CB00005B/2096